CW0051728Z

Crucible of Shadows

Dawn of Assassins, Volume 3

Jon Cronshaw

Published by Wyvern Books, Ltd, 2023.

CRUCIBLE OF SHADOWS

First edition. February 1, 2023.

Written by Jon Cronshaw.

For Isaac.

Prologue.

"This cannot stand." The guild master cast his gaze across the pages again, taking in the report's implications. He leant back in his seat, the chair's crimson leather creaking beneath his slender frame. If the information was correct, the guild could not sit back and do nothing about this. "Have you confirmed the report is accurate?"

The journeyman shifted in his seat. "We have it from a reliable source, sir."

The master tapped on the pages and sighed. "Do you know what this means?"

The journeyman shrugged. "That Soren's dead."

"No. No. I don't mean that." The master pursed his lips and jabbed a finger down on the page. "The implications, man. The implications."

"Erm." The journeyman gave the master an unsure look. "That someone's killed one of ours?"

"It implies more than that." He leant forward, his voice dropping to little more than a whisper. "Someone has taken over."

"Oh." The journeyman nodded, his eyes widening. "Oh."

"Exactly. It would seem Nordturm has a new assassin."

"Is it one of ours?"

He shook his head and ran a hand down his thin beard. "The order for his death hasn't come from me. Hmm. Soren's work over the past decade has been exemplary. He was one of our finest masters."

"Was there not tension between Soren and Arfo?"

"That was five years ago. And once we drew up the proper boundaries between Nordturm and Nebel Hafen, that issue was solved."

"Fair point."

"And there's this." He pulled a sheet from the pile and pushed it over to the journeyman.

The pair sat in silence as the journeyman angled the shaded emerald lamp and read the words under his breath.

After a short time, he looked up from the page. "And this was done through the usual channels?"

"According to our friends up north."

The journeyman sent the page back towards the master and frowned. "So they just paid this Patrov off? Paid him to leave?" The journeyman's right hand clawed into a fist. "This goes against—"

"Everything." The master raised a calming hand and gazed across at the guild charter, its fine script embroidered on stretched human skin. "I think it might be the same person."

"What do we know of Dienerin?"

"She's still taking contracts on behalf of the guild, which would suggest she still has a master."

"Wait." The crease on the journeyman's brow deepened. "Wasn't he seeking an apprentice? I'm sure I remember hearing that."

"Soren?"

The journeyman nodded.

The master rose to his feet and stepped over to a filing cabinet. He rifled through papers and pulled out a letter. "Interesting." He slipped the letter back and returned to his seat. "It would seem you are correct."

"What did it say?"

"It was a letter of intent to take on an apprentice."

"The usual two?"

The master gave a slight nod. "Hmm. I wonder." He leant on his elbows and steepled his fingers. "Perhaps...perhaps, that's who we're looking for."

"One or two?"

"I would presume one."

"That would make sense."

"But it could be two..." The master sighed. "This is not good. Not at all. Blackmail? Conning?" His lip curled. "What kind of training did Soren provide?"

"It's a disgrace." The journeyman gritted his teeth. "What about our code? What about our values?" He slammed his fist down on the table. "Actions like this damage our reputation. What is the point in having a guild if people go around undermining our business?"

"My thoughts exactly."

"You should send someone to Nordturm. This needs dealing with. We cannot let this stand."

The master smiled. "My thoughts exactly."

The journeyman raised his hands. "Wait. I have—"

"You have your new assignment. Find out who killed Soren and if they are involved in this...this aberration." He gestured to the paper. "You know what to do. We need to know if these issues are related."

The journeyman took a breath and bowed his head. "As you wish, master. When should I leave?"

The master cocked an eyebrow.

"Yes, sir. I'll pack my things."

I. Plez

Greasy sweat coated Fedor's back and neck as he stared half-focused at the Rusty Sail's back room wall. Peeling gloss revealed bare pine beneath, the wood's knots and whorls shifting and expanding in time with his heartbeat.

His eyelids drooped again and the top of his head pressed against the wall behind him as a wave of pleasure washed up from the base of his spine, triggering sparks inside his skull, bliss mushrooming in his mind.

He breathed in another mouthful of smoke, its metallic tang setting his teeth on edge and unmooring his thoughts.

His muscles softened.

Burning flooded his lungs, the heat melting him to wax.

The pipe slipped from his fingers and his head flopped down onto the cushion, his eyes flickering shut, his breaths shuddering.

Something like liquid hands enclosed him, soft and warm and comforting and endless. The edges of memory caressed him—his mother holding him close to her chest, her cheek resting on the top of his head as she rocked him to sleep.

He floated in a pool of yellow light for a long time as colours danced around him, splashing him with love and beauty, every wish fulfilled, every problem, every worry, every anxiety no more than a distant contained dot, no more than an ant trapped under a jar.

The images subsided, melting into yellow warmth, dislocated from time...from everything.

His limbs disappeared, allowing him to drift—a formless self in the endless yellow nothing.

He became aware of another sensation, a sensation beyond his body, beyond the yellow.

A hand, a real hand, two hands. It gripped his shoulder, both shoulders, and shook him away from that place.

His eyes snapped open.

He focused on a familiar face for a second, tried to form a curse, and closed his eyes again.

Words struck his ears as if heard through deep water.

A slap to the face shifted his awareness.

Pain. Stinging. Heat.

He opened his eyes slowly, his hand drifting up to his throbbing cheek, and he met Lev's glare with one of his own.

"Mate, what the fuck? How many times?" Lev's features came in and out of focus. "Get up."

Fedor's head wobbled to the side and he mumbled something half-formed in his mouth. He just wanted to drift, to return to that place of bliss. If he closed his eyes for long enough, it would all go away—the memories, the pain—all of it would seep into nothing, become one with the endless yellow.

The shakes came again, this time harder.

He looked around the room at the other men and women staring at him and he met Lev's gaze.

Lev reached down and hoisted him to his feet.

For a moment, he feared he might continue up through the ceiling, and float off through the lower city and into the clouds, joining the balloons and wyverns and seagulls as they glided on the breeze.

"Mate. Look at me. Mate."

His attention latched onto Lev.

"No. Keep bloody focused on me."

Fedor closed his eyes and sank back to the cushion.

Another slap came to his face.

He found himself standing again and tried to wriggle out of Lev's tight grip. But his arms did not move in the way he wanted. "Leave me alone," he slurred. "Leave me here."

"No. You're coming with me." Lev cupped Fedor's face in his hands and held his gaze steady, those dark pupils burrowing into him. "You can't stay here."

Fedor stared at nothing.

The slap came again and his focus shifted back to Lev and his breath, tinged with whisky.

"Look at me, you fucking dickhead."

"Huh?"

"I said, look at me. You need to focus." Lev gestured to the door, his words slow and clear. "I am taking you home. Do you understand?"

Fedor gazed longingly at the cushion, his focus catching the play of light down the length of the pipe.

Lev jerked him in a twist and marched him from the back room and into the main bar.

A thin man in a robe blocked Lev's path and offered him a chequerboard smile. "Brother, your friend shouldn't be taken like this."

Lev drew his club and held it out with one hand, his hold on Fedor remaining firm. "You going to fucking stop me, mate? You want me to knock a few more of those teeth out for you?"

The man stepped forward, reaching for Fedor.

Lev shoved him back against the bar.

"Thirty-three, mate. This is a fucking thirty-three."

"Wha—"

"I'm taking you home."

Unable to protest, Fedor gave a weak nod, and allowed Lev to lead him away.

Lev staggered into the common room and struggled to keep Fedor from falling again. Three times this week he'd dragged him from the Rusty Sail, and three times his actions were met with resistance and insults. At least this time, Fedor had kept his mouth shut.

He shoved Fedor onto the sofa next to him and arranged his head against the back. For a moment, Fedor remained still, his mouth hanging open, his eyes glassy. With a faint groan, he tipped to his side, his head bouncing off the sofa's arm.

Sitting on the opposite sofa with Vern to her left, Onwyth rolled her eyes and gestured to Fedor. "That's the second time this week. We can't keep doing this."

"Actually, it's the third. You were off with Vern last time I brought him back. Still got the scratches on my hand to prove it."

"Prick," Onwyth said, her nose wrinkling.

Lev took a seat between Onwyth and Vern and let out a sigh. "What can we do, though? He's a mate." He stared at the scar on his left palm and let out another sigh. "We swore to have his back."

"But he needs to get back to work. He can't keep going out getting messed up on whatever he's getting messed up on like this and expect us to be there every time."

Lev nodded and removed his cap. "I'm trying to keep him away from there. But the sneaky fuck keeps slipping out."

Onwyth inclined her head. "Have you thought about getting some stocks? Maybe we could get a wyvern cage, or some rope. We could lock him in a room, slip him some food and drink until he's sweated that stuff out."

"We're not tying anyone up."

"We could beat him too if he acts up. We could do that thing where you get an apple in a sock and keep hitting him until the apple stops working."

Lev frowned. "How does an apple stop working?"

"When it's mush." Onwyth shrugged and looked down at her fingernails. "I don't know. I'm the only one coming up with solutions here."

"You could use a lemon too," Vern said.

"Right." Lev stared at Fedor. "We'll sort him out. I'm keeping an eye on him as much as I can. Twice he's done one when I've been on the privy. Might have to have you helping out when I'm occupied."

"I'm not going to do that."

"Why?"

"Because I'll know what you're doing and I'll be able to picture it."

Lev groaned. "You don't have to picture me doing anything."

"I know I don't have to, but the mind wanders." She tapped the side of her head. "You can't help what you think about. That's science. And what if you're on there for a bit longer than is absolutely necessary?"

"For fuck's sake, Onwyth. I'm here trying to come up with answers and you're shitting all over them."

"See. You can't help it. Now you're thinking about taking a shit."

Vern's laughter stopped when Lev glared at him.

"I'm not thinking about anyone taking a shit. All I'm saying is I'm stuck around here, keeping an eye on him, but I can't do it all the time."

Onwyth nodded. "So he's causing double the problem."

"How do you weigh that up?"

"Because you need to get back to work as well." She raised a finger. "He's keeping two people back from jobs. That could be millions of krones left on the table."

Lev smirked. "Millions?"

"You never know. You could be really lucky and hit big. But you can't hit big if neither of you are out earning."

"I know. I know." Lev rested his elbows on his knees and sank his head into his hands. "It's just until he's clean."

"And when will that be? If he keeps sneaking out to the Sail, he's not going to get any better. I say we go with the cage idea."

"We're not putting anyone in a cage."

"Your loss."

Lev nodded. "I guess that's a hit I'll have to live with. Anyway, I've not seen you two out earning either. What's your excuse?"

Onwyth pushed out her chin. "We're still in the planning phases."

Lev sniffed. "Planning phases, right. So what's that translate to, a big fat pile of fuck-all with a healthy side of nothing?"

"We'll get some," Vern cut in. "We're just trying to find a source."

"Get what?"

"The ravenglass." Vern gave Onwyth a look. "Erm, we're just in the planning phases."

"Exactly," Onwyth said. "Maybe if you weren't so worried about our messed-up friend here, we'd be out getting all the ravenglass we need. But no, Fedor has to get smashed up on plez."

"Don't blame me," Fedor said, his voice slurring. "You do..." His words trailed off into mumbling.

"I do blame you," Onwyth said. "I blame you very much. And if I'm being honest, Melita blames you too."

"Whatever." Fedor rolled over and faced the back of the sofa.

"Let's go down the list, shall we? I blame you. Melita blames you. Vern blames you. And Lev should be blaming you, but he's being too easy on you."

Lev narrowed his eyes. "You don't know shit, mate."

"In fact, I think he secretly does blame you and thinks you're being an insufferable dick at the moment."

Fedor swung his head up and his eyes fluttered open. He looked around the room, his gaze landing on Onwyth. "What's your problem?"

"See?" She glowered at him. "You're not even listening to a word I've said. I'm not repeating myself. You need to sort yourself out. Otherwise, we're going to be having words. Serious words."

Fedor rocked back and closed his eyes. "Whatever."

Onwyth exchanged a look with Vern and pursed her lips. "I don't know how much longer I can put up with this fucking twat." She sat back and folded her arms. "We're trying to run a business here."

Lev shrugged. "You're right. So why are you still sitting here?" He gestured to the door. "You two should get out there, find that ravenglass, or whatever you're doing. I'll stay here and look after my mate."

"What about you?" Onwyth asked. "You've not done anything since everything went down with all that merchant crap."

Lev gestured to Fedor. "I've been trying to keep this one from self-destructing, for a start." He raised his chin. "And for your information. I've got a good lead on another assassin con."

"You can't keep paying people off, expecting them to leave."

"Shows what you bloody know." Lev grinned. "This is what I'm talking about. It's one from the list."

"The list?" Onwyth frowned. "What list?"

"The list. Soren's list."

Her frowned deepened. "What are you on about?"

"It's how the bloody Jedrick thing got started in the first place. And I've got a new potential lead."

"Anyone we know?"

"Doubt it. Far as I can tell, it's some captain who hired Soren to have a rival bumped off."

"Aren't you worried it's going to go the same way as Jedrick?"

Lev raised his hands over his head and cracked his knuckles. "I thought we did quite well from that, everything considered."

Onwyth snorted. "You really think that went well? The Jedrick job? The one that nearly got us killed. The one that—"

"We made cash. That's the bottom line." He rubbed his stubble. "Think of it as testing the process, ironing out the kinks. It was our first attempt at a job like that, so you can't expect things to go perfect."

"Perfect?" Onwyth sniffed. "I'd be happy with semi-competent."

"We just need to figure things out and adjust. This is why these things need a genius to pull them off. And say what you want, Onwyth, we did pull it off."

"But we know where the real money is. That's what we should be focused on."

Lev shrugged. "If that's what you want to do, don't let me stop you. I've got my own shit to deal with. If you and Vern want to get into that, you're more than welcome. It's no skin off my arse. But if you think I'm going to be sneaking in the shadows to stab up some unsuspecting victim, you got another thing coming."

"They're not victims, they're contracts."

"Call them what you want, but I'm not doing it."

"Onwyth's right," Vern said.

"No," Fedor mumbled. "No more..."

"Nobody asked you," Vern spat.

Lev glared at him. "Watch how you speak to him. He might be in a bad way, but he's got more seniority than you."

"All I'm saying is he ain't helping any of us at the minute." Vern glared across at Fedor. "How we supposed to trust someone like that? Look at him. It's pathetic."

"He's just having a bad time," Lev said. "I'll sort him out. I swear it."

Vern nodded. "Make sure you do."

"Yeah?" Lev got to his feet and loomed over Vern. "You throwing orders now?"

Vern shrugged. "Meant nothing by it. I just don't know how he can have our backs when he's like that." He turned to Onwyth. "What was it you said about? Deri-something."

"Dereliction of duty," Onwyth said.

"Yeah. That was it. It ain't fair on the rest of us. He's a liability."

"Let me worry about that," Lev said. "You can focus on getting that ravenglass, or whatever. You just keep that gob of yours shut and we won't have issues."

Vern raised his hands. "Alright. Alright. I meant nothing by it."

Lev patted his club. "What you waiting for then?" He pointed to the door. "Get to work."

Vern exchanged a look with Onwyth who gave a nod. The pair got up and left, leaving Lev alone with Fedor.

Lev closed the door behind them and watched Fedor as he lay with his head back, his purple-rimmed eyes squeezed shut. "They're right, you know."

"Huh?" Fedor opened his eyes.

"This is serious, mate. Melita's not going to like this."

Fedor waved a hand and closed his eyes. "Whatever."

Lev shot across the room, grabbed Fedor's collar, and yanked him to his feet. "Don't fucking test me. I'm helping because you're a mate, but if you keep taking the piss, we're done. You understand?" He shoved Fedor back onto the sofa and stared down at him, his nostrils flaring as heat rose up his neck.

Fedor stared up at him with pleading eyes. "I'm sorry." He looked down at his grubby palms. "I know I'm a mess. I fucked up. I'm a dickhead. I know...I just—"

"No excuses, mate. This is serious."

"I know. I'm sorry. I'll sort it."

Lev prodded Fedor's chest with his club. "Make sure you fucking do. Because I'm done with your shit. It's time to decide what's more important. Your mates or those fucking drugs?"

II. Blackmail

Onwyth drummed on the library desk and slumped forward, her head resting in her hands. "This is so stupid. I don't think this is going to work."

"We'll figure something," Vern said. "Ain't nothing out there that can't be solved."

"You think?"

"Yeah. Why not? There's got to be something we can do."

Onwyth looked at him with one eye open. "Like what?"

Vern rubbed the back of his head and shrugged. "I don't know."

"And neither do I. You don't know where there's any. I don't know where there's any. And no one else wants to help us." She slapped a hand down on the table. "This is shit."

"Erm..." Vern looked down at his hands. "I think I might know where we can get some."

She sat up and folded her arms, her eyes fixing on Vern. "You know where we can get some?"

"I think so."

"And you're telling me this now?"

"I just remembered it then. Didn't think of it before."

"So we've been wasting all this time and you suddenly know where to get some."

"I'm sorry. I didn't think."

"Where?"

"The priests. Back when I—"

"No." She raised a hand. "Absolutely not."

"But—"

"I said no."

Vern let out a sigh. "Fine. It ain't like you've come up with anything."

"I don't know about you, but I like to keep as much distance as possible between me and those bastards."

"But they've got statues made of the stuff. I used to sneak out and look at them. And it was all weird. It was like you couldn't really look at it properly."

Onwyth shook her head. "No. We need to think of something else."

"Why?"

"You seriously asking me why?"

Vern nodded.

"You ever get beaten when you were there?"

"A few times. Only if I didn't make enough, or I sinned, or whatever."

"Do you know what the priests do to those who steal from their temples?"

"No."

"Neither do I, but I can't see it being pleasant."

"You've dealt with worse, ain't you?"

Onwyth shrugged. "Who knows? Maybe. Maybe not. They might have magic, or have secret fighting skills, or something."

"The priests?"

"Why not?"

"When I was there, Father Heinrich had a stick—a normal stick."

"Still hurt, though, didn't it?"

Vern frowned. "You're just afraid because you were a kid. Priests ain't shit. I bet you'd be able to take them on dead easy."

"I don't know." Onwyth shuddered. "Let's think of something else. There's got to be other places."

"Alright, where did Melita get hers?"

"It was Soren's." She sucked in her bottom lip. "Though, I don't think she'd be too happy if we nicked her blade. But I bet if we melted it down, she wouldn't know it was hers." She considered the idea for a moment and shook her head. "No. Bad idea."

"What about Fedor? Soren didn't have two daggers, did he?" He grinned. "Imagine having two ravenglass blades."

"Fedor got the stuff from a weathervane."

A crease set on Vern's brow. "What's a weathervane?"

"You ever seen those things on buildings that tell you which way the wind's blowing?"

"Are they like chickens and stuff?"

"Sometimes. I think his was from a wyvern."

"Someone made a weathervane out of ravenglass?"

"No. I think it was just the eyes."

Vern frowned for a moment and raised a finger. "I think I've seen it. Mercer's Company, across there, right?"

Onwyth shrugged. "Dunno. Maybe."

Vern's face brightened. "That's what we'll do, then."

"What is?"

"We look at all the weathervanes around the city. Collect the eyes and get the weapons made. Simple. Might take a bit of time, but it's not like we've got anything better going."

"We could..." Onwyth rubbed her chin. "Hmm...I don't know. I think Melita might have heard about it from a contact. I don't think it's a regular thing."

"Oh." Vern's shoulders sagged. "But—"

Onwyth grinned.

"What is it?"

Her grin widened and she got to her feet. "That's it."

"What is?"

"Come on." She ran to the door. "This way. Follow me."

Lev placed Soren's ledger on the desk in front of Fedor. Its leather binding crackled as he lifted the cover open. Sunlight poured in through the window, setting the library in a hazy glow. He flipped through the pages to the one he'd marked and ran his finger down the list of entries. "This is the bloke I was telling you about."

Fedor stared vaguely ahead, his eyes watery and rimmed with the hint of purple.

"You listening, mate?"

Fedor blinked and nodded. "Yes. That's the bloke you told me about...right."

"So what's his name?"

Fedor frowned at him. "What?"

"The name."

"I don't know. I didn't read it."

"For fuck's sake. The bloke's name is Captain Roubert."

"I've heard that name."

"Probably because he's a dodgy fuck. Or more likely because I've already mentioned him a couple of times."

"Dodgy covers a lot of ground."

"From what I know about old Captain Roubert, he's got his grubby fingers in a lot of grubby pies, and it looks like he had one of his own business partners knocked off a year or so back."

Fedor shook his head. "I don't know what to think about dealing with these unsavoury characters."

Lev smirked. "Unsavoury characters? Shit me, mate. And I thought you'd been hanging around with a bunch of junkies at the Sail. I had no idea you'd be hanging around with the priests."

"You know what I mean."

Lev prodded the ledger and held Fedor's gaze. "All these people hired an assassin. All these people are, as you so beautifully put, unsavoury bloody characters." He rubbed his hands together and smiled. "And these unsavoury fuckers are also potential goldmines."

"A goldmine that's probably going to get us killed."

Lev rolled his eyes. "Mate, you really need to start thinking about these things logically."

"I am being logical. It's just—"

"What is it I always say about risk?"

"And what is it I always say about not wanting to die?"

Lev glared at him. "You've got a funny way of showing it, mate."

"What's that supposed to mean?"

Lev snorted. "Please tell me that's not a real question."

Fedor remained silent.

"Look at you." He eyed Fedor up and down, his lip curling. "You talk about not wanting to die, but you're the one out there putting that shit in your body."

"Maybe if I didn't have to deal with all the crap I've got to deal with, I wouldn't feel the need."

"You talk about not wanting risk, but you're this close to bloody killing yourself."

"I can handle it. I just...I just need to forget."

Lev shook his head. "I don't know what to say, mate. We've got a good job going here." He gestured to the ledger. "This is easy money. And it's good money."

"Easy? How's any of this easy?"

"Mate, mate, mate. I did all the research. All we need to do is pay the mark a visit and get the cash. You just need to be there."

Fedor sniffed. "You did research?"

"Yeah. So?"

"I wouldn't exactly call going through Soren's old papers research."

Lev tapped his nose. "Shows what you bloody know then, doesn't it? Trust me, I know who this bloke is, what he looks like, and that he's got a ship coming in today."

"Today?"

"Yes, today. Remember me saying he's a captain? One of his many pies is a little smuggling operation between here and Molotok."

"Smuggling what?"

Lev shrugged a shoulder. "Let's just say he brings things in he'd like to keep away from certain tax officials and certain Magistrates."

"Like booze and stuff?"

"And stuff, yeah."

"Right...and you've got it all researched?"

Lev nodded. "Yeah."

"How are we going to work it?"

"Piece of piss, really. We board the ship, tell him what the deal is, and we get paid. It's that simple."

Fedor shook his head and sighed. "But it never is though, is it?" He pushed the ledger away. "I don't know. We need to think about this."

"Trust me, mate. I've done all the thinking we need. You just need to turn up, play your part, and I'll play mine. We just need to time it right so we get him alone. Honestly, there's nothing to worry about."

"Isn't that what you said about Jedrick?"

Lev groaned. "Not this again." He sank onto a seat across from Fedor. "As I keep explaining, the only reason the Jedrick thing didn't work smoothly is because we didn't go with him to get the money. This time we stick to our mark until we get the payout. That way, there's no messing about. We get paid and we do one. End of story."

"And what if he refuses?"

"What if he does? Use your imagination. Shove him in that shadow place if you have to."

Fedor glowered. "No."

"Not for long. Just enough to shit him up a bit. If he knows you can do magic and stuff—"

"I'm not doing it."

"You've changed your tune."

"No, I haven't."

"I seem to recall you trying to get me into that place."

"Until I knew..." His voice trailed off.

"Fine, fine. But we should try to come up with a few different plans in case things go sideways."

"In case things go sideways? If I've learnt anything from doing jobs with you, Lev, it's that things going sideways is par for the course."

"We've done loads of jobs that have gone fine. You just don't think about them because they were easy."

"Yeah, easy. You know, you're not the genius con artist you think you are."

"Oh, yeah? What kind of con artist do I think I am?"

"You think you're better than you are. What can I say? We've been lucky so far, but luck won't keep us safe forever."

Lev let out a bitter laugh. "Lucky? It's more than bloody luck, mate."

Fedor shrugged. "It's only by luck the Jedrick stuff went the way it did. That could have been us getting our throats cut."

"Nah, you make your own luck."

"Luck only takes us so far."

"That's why we've got to plan. That's why you need to know what we're doing instead of pissing off to the Rusty Sail every other day to get fucked up on plez. And I'm not the only one saying this. It needs to stop."

Fedor nodded and looked down at his hands. "It's so hard. It keeps pulling me back."

"You seen some of the addicts around the docks? The ones who've been on it for years?"

"Yeah. What's that got to do with anything?"

"That'll be you, that will, mate." Lev pointed to the door. "The others are beyond pissed off with you. You need to stop. You need to promise me you're done with that shit. It's putting us all at risk."

"I can't—"

"No arguments."

Fedor sucked in his bottom lip and gave a slight nod. "I'll try."

Lev rolled his eyes and growled. "Mate. This is serious. Do you know how serious this is?"

"I don't know. Very serious?"

"Beyond serious. There's talk about kicking you out. We've all got your back, and maybe I've got your back more than others, but you're taking the piss, and it needs to stop. Just...fucking clean yourself up."

"I will. I will. I just—"

"I'm done with your excuses. We all are." He took in a deep breath and gestured to Soren's ledger. "Let's just focus on this job. Keep your mind busy, alright?"

"Yeah. I can do that."

"Good. Because old Captain Roubert isn't going to blackmail himself, is he?"

Onwyth banged on Melita's office door and entered before giving her the opportunity to turn her away again.

Melita looked up from her papers, a crease etching her brow. "What's wrong?" She glanced at the door. "Has something happened?"

"What's that fence called?"

"I'm sorry, you'll have to be more specific. I know quite a few fences around here."

"You know. The fence. The fence fence."

Melita's frown deepened. "As in a fence who deals in stolen fences?"

"No. The fence. What's his name. The ravenglass one."

"Oh, do you mean Garrett?"

"No, no, no. Isn't he supposed to be dead or something?"

"Yeah."

"So the other one."

Melita shook her head. "What other one?"

"The ravenglass one." Melita may have been the boss, but she could be so dense. "The ravenglass one. You tried selling to him from that weathervane job, remember?"

"I remember."

"I seem to recall them being a bit pissed off with you for pitting them against each other."

"Oh, you mean Walter."

"That's the one." Onwyth slapped her forehead. "I'm always so crap with names. Walter. Walter. I remember it now. Where is he?"

"What, right now?"

Onwyth rolled her eyes. "You know, sometimes, you can be really unhelpful."

"What? Do you expect me to know where every fence is in the city at any given moment?"

Onwyth pursed her lips and placed a hand on her hips. Sometimes it wasn't worth arguing with a fool. "I need to see him."

"About what?"

"About getting some ravenglass, for fuck's sake. Just tell me where I can find him."

"I didn't sell him the ravenglass."

It took all of Onwyth's will not to leap over the desk and smack Melita's face. "He was in the market to buy ravenglass." She spoke in a slow deliberate voice, as though addressing a stupid kid. "Maybe he's still in the market to buy ravenglass. I have some ravenglass I would like to sell. Do you understand?"

Melita held a sickly-sweet smile. "Leave it with me. I'll arrange a meeting."

"Good." Onwyth turned to the door, hesitated for a moment, and looked back, forcing a smile. "Thank you."

Lev strolled along the docks with Fedor at his side, skirting past mooring posts and scanning the names of ships. If he kept Fedor busy, if he kept him close and his attention on the job, maybe he could keep him away from the plez.

"I'm pretty sure it's one of these." He gestured vaguely to the ships nearest the open sea gate leading to the Braun Sea beyond.

"What's it called again?"

"For fuck's sake, mate. At least try to keep focused while we're on this. It's the Golden Blade. Got that?"

"The Golden Blade, right. Got it."

"You sure? Because that's three times I've had to remind you."

"I've got it. I Just need to keep focused. We're looking for the Golden Blade. Do you know what kind of ship it is?"

"It's a ship. I don't bloody know, mate. Just look out for the names."

Fedor inclined his head and pointed to a three-masted ship. "I think that's the one."

Lev sighed. "That's the Seablade."

"Exactly."

"No. We're looking for the Golden Blade."

"Oh." Fedor shook his head. "I'm sure you said..."

Lev waited for Fedor to finish, but he stood staring at the ship. "What you saying?"

"Doesn't matter."

"Mate, just look for the Golden Blade. That's all you need to do. The Golden Blade. Come on, I know you can do this."

"Too many blades. It's confusing."

"Wouldn't be confusing if you weren't coming off plez."

"We should split up," Fedor said.

"No. There's absolutely no fucking way I'm letting you out of my sight. You're staying with me. I'm not having you pissing off again. We've got a job to do."

"What kind of ship is it?"

Lev groaned. "Seriously? We've been through this. It's a bloody ship. I don't know what ships are called. It's the bloody Seablade."

"I thought it was the Golden Blade?"

"That's what I said."

"No, you said it's called the Seablade."

Lev stopped and frowned. "You're confusing me now. We're looking for the Golden Blade."

"Right." He signalled further along the docks. "Maybe it's over there where they're unloading."

"Let's take a look, shall we?" Lev shifted past lobster pots and fishing nets and wrinkled his nose at a group of sailors cutting up a whale. He gazed up at a figurehead showing a mermaid with red pouting lips. He never understood the appeal of mermaids. Maybe it was too much time at sea, but what were you supposed to do with one once you got a mermaid home? He inclined his head and squinted at the name. "The Siren's Wake. Nope."

He carried on, his focus skipping between the names. "Kraken's Bane. Lovely Claire. Dietmar's Hope." He squinted at a five-masted ship, its name daubed in faded yellow. "Can you read that one, mate?" He looked around and saw no sign of Fedor. "For fuck's sake."

He adjusted his cap and glanced back over his shoulder, scanning between sailors and dockers, searching through the movement for signs of Fedor.

He dodged past a swinging crane and scrambled onto an upturned crate to get a better view.

A grey-bearded man barked something at him in a tongue he did not recognise. "Whatever, mate." He hopped down to the ground and cursed under his breath. Where was he?

Lev raced from the docks and into the lower city's commercial district, barrelling past shops and cafés, running at full speed until he reached the Rusty Sail.

He rushed inside, almost knocking over a man at the bar, and barged past a couple waiting outside the back room. Through the smoke and dim light, he saw human forms stretched out on cushions. "Where is he?" He grabbed a man's shoulders and shook him. "Where's Fedor?"

"Huh?" The gaunt man looked up at him with a frown and curled back into a ball.

"Shit."

Lev turned on his heels and went back outside. He stopped and caught his breath before jogging back towards the docks. Where was he?

He skirted along the water's edge, checking the surface for signs of his friend. If Fedor had fallen in, was he in any fit state to swim?

He started and spun when someone grabbed his shoulder. He drew his club without thinking and readied himself to fight.

"I think I found it," Fedor said. "Whoa! Careful with that." He raised his hands and stepped backwards.

"There you are." Lev lowered his club. "Where the fuck have you been?"

Fedor frowned. "Looking for the ship...The Golden Blade. Like you asked."

"Good." Lev slipped his club back onto his belt and let out a relieved sigh. "Any luck?"

"I found it." He pointed to a ship moored near the sea gate.

Lev gave a nod and squeezed Fedor's shoulder. "Good work, mate. Let's go speak to old Captain Arsehole."

"Captain Arsehole? That can't be his real name, can it?"

"Honestly, mate." Lev shook his head and grinned. "You need to sort yourself out. Of course he's not called Captain Arsehole. That was a joke."

"Oh."

"He's called Captain Nob Cheese."

"No, he's not."

"Alright. You got me. It's actually Captain Dick Nose."

"Now I know you're messing with me."

"Good. It's about bloody time." He held Fedor's gaze and dropped his smile. "Now, are you sure you can do this?"

"Yeah."

"Swear?"

"I swear."

Lev studied him for several seconds, wondering whether this was a good idea.

"Do you need me to make a promise to Creation?"

"Nah. I just need to be sure you're on board."

Fedor licked his lips. "You know I am."

Lev couldn't help sniffing. "Just let me do the talking. And don't bloody do your disappearing act again. I was worried you'd fucked off to the Sail."

"Why would I do that?"

Lev rolled his eyes and shook his head. "Let's just speak to this bloke and get this shit done."

"You know you curse a lot more than you used to?"

"Can you fucking blame me, mate? After all the shit we've been through. Either come the fuck on, or fuck the fuck off. Your choice."

Fedor let out a sigh. "Fine. Lead the way."

Fedor stopped and stared down into the black waters, its surface reflecting the white alchemical light shining down from the dock's cavernous ceiling. The water appealed to him. He could slip beneath its surface and never come up—no longer a burden, no longer haunted by guilt.

"Mate?" Lev tapped his shoulder. "You coming?"

Fedor nodded and trailed Lev up the gangplank, ducking his head as he entered the Golden Blade. Stepping onto the deck, he allowed his eyes to adjust to the ship's gloom, his nose wrinkling at the stench of stale sweat, vomit, and tar.

He crept along the dim passageway, keeping a few paces behind Lev in case either of them had to call a thirty-three and needed space to run. "Do you know where we're going?"

"Shh. It's this way, mate."

Fedor glanced back over his shoulder at the passageway stretching behind him. "We should have checked it out first. What if he's not here?"

"We're checking it now, aren't we? And, trust me, I know he's here. I saw light from his quarters from the docks."

Fedor continued forward, his ears pricking as the boat creaked around him. "How do you know? That light could be anything."

Lev stopped and glared at him. "It's the biggest room on here. That's where the captain will be. Stands to reason, mate." He shook his head and sighed. "We doing this or what?"

"What if he's not?"

"Then he's not." Lev shrugged a shoulder. "We'll just have to wait until he turns up."

"But what if the ship leaves?"

"For fuck's sake. You really do need to let me do the thinking." Lev turned to him and looked him up and down. "You're really not doing a great job of it at the moment."

Fedor frowned. It was Lev's lack of planning that had got them into trouble with some of their previous jobs. "I'm just asking."

"Yeah? Well, maybe just think about it for one bloody second, before you go opening your mouth. They're not going to sail off until they've unloaded, are they?"

"Probably not, no."

"Well, there you go, then. Keep the thinking in check."

"Whatever." Fedor looked back over his shoulder, worried they'd not checked how many sailors were on the ship. "I don't like this."

"And I don't appreciate you poking holes in the plan when you don't even know what the plan is, but here we are."

"I'm not poking holes, I just think—"

Lev stopped and raised a hand.

"What is it?"

"It's my attempt to get you to shut the fuck up so I can think." He gestured to the door ahead of them. "That's where we're headed. I'll do all the talking. You just do the brooding menace stuff, if that's not too much to ask."

Fedor held in a sigh. "Fine."

"And pull your bloody hood up. You're meant to look all mean and mysterious, remember? I don't think Captain Nob Head's going to flinch at some sweaty-looking plez-head, do you?"

Fedor came to a stop behind Lev and pulled up his hood. He checked his blade and flexed his fingers as Lev pulled out his club and knocked at the door three times.

The door opened and a man with a thick grey beard stared out at them, his head swaying from side to side, his breath reeking of rum. "What?" His gaze shifted between Lev and Fedor. "Who're you?"

"We've just come to have a little chat," Lev said, barging past.

"A chat?" The bearded man frowned. "Who you with? You the tax people?"

Lev shrugged. "In a way."

"You should speak to—"

Lev shoved the man back against the nearest wall and pushed his club against his throat. "Are we going to have a problem here? Because I'm done with fuckers like you fucking me around."

The man waved his hands. "What you doing here? This is my ship and you're...you're on my ship."

"Your ship?" Lev pushed out his bottom lip. "I guess that makes you Captain Roubert then?"

The man nodded. "Yeah, so?"

"So you're the bloke we're here to see."

Fedor slipped into the room and remained silent. Black and white tiles stretched across the floor, their surfaces polished to a deep shine. A mahogany table surrounded by chairs stood beneath a crystal chandelier, the table and chair legs bolted to the floor.

Lev gestured with his club. "Now, I suggest you take a seat, mate. And don't try anything stupid because I'm not in the bloody mood."

Fedor clicked the door shut and eyed the man.

"I never liked you tax people." The man gave a slight nod and staggered to a seat. "Payments are up to date. We declared—"

"Mate, mate, mate." Lev shook his head and sighed. "Let's not do this, please."

Roubert looked between them and dragged a sleeve across his brow. "What do you want then?"

"See? This is how you conduct a discussion."

"Huh?"

"You don't go throwing assumptions around. You ask good questions and you get good answers."

Roubert grabbed a handful of his beard. "You're not making sense. You said you're here for tax."

Lev grinned. "I said, in a way. And in a way it is. But if you think I'm here with the customs house, or any of that crap, let's just say you've got the wrong end of the stick."

Roubert glared at Lev and then at Fedor. "So who are you? What you after?"

"I want to take you back to something that happened two years ago."

"A lot happened two years ago."

"Didn't you have a little deal with a wyvern...a little deal involving a certain business partner?"

The captain's eyes widened. "What is this?"

"This is what you call a shakedown, mate. We know who you had killed. We know when he died and how much you paid. We also know there are a number of interested parties who are offering a lot of money to know who did it."

Roubert grunted. "Should have killed the little shit-bag myself."

"But you didn't, and now we're here."

"You can't prove anything."

Lev grinned. "We can prove it all, mate. And if I'm being brutally honest, you lie like a cheap rug."

Roubert glowered at him.

"But that doesn't matter now. What's done is done. The past is the past. But secrets have a funny way of popping up if you don't deal with them properly."

Roubert narrowed his eyes. "What are you saying?"

"What I'm saying is that the secret's out. We know what you did. And I'm sure you'd agree this is the type of thing to keep away from, let's say, people like Magistrates and other interested parties."

"Hmm."

Lev leant close to Roubert. "But, let's be honest. We don't want trouble. You don't want trouble." He tapped his club on the table. "And I think we have a way to work this all out."

Roubert squeezed the bridge of his nose and let out a breath. "So it's blackmail then? This is your play?" His jaw tightened. "And you really think you can waltz onto my ship and expect me to pay you to keep a secret?"

"Damn right we do."

Roubert yawned and got up. "How much?"

Lev began to pace. "Ten grand should cover you."

"Ten grand?"

"Ten grand."

"And if I don't pay?"

Fedor stepped forward and revealed his dagger.

Roubert stared at the blade for several seconds before shifting his attention back to Lev. "So you have a club and a dagger?" He drew a pistol and grinned. "I think I'll take my chances."

Lev waved him away. "I really wouldn't do that if I were you. We've got friends outside poised to deliver the evidence to the Magistrates and a bunch of other people who I'm sure you wouldn't like to know about this." He moved towards the captain and pushed the pistol down. "And if I'm being perfectly honest, the last thing I want is to see my friend have to use that blade of his again."

"Show me the evidence."

Lev smirked. "I don't have the evidence on me, obviously. It's all ready for the Magistrates. And if we don't return very soon with our cash..." He checked his pocket watch and cocked an eyebrow. "Well, time's running out."

"Ten grand, you say?" Roubert slipped his pistol back into its holster and raked a hand through his beard. "I take it you'd like to be paid Wieter krones?"

"You'd take it right, mate."

Roubert raised his chin and held Lev's gaze. "And you give me your word this will all go away?"

"Like we never existed."

"And the evidence?"

"Gone. We might be blackmailers, but our word is stone."

Roubert studied Lev for a long time before nodding. "Price of doing business, I suppose." He breathed a heavy sigh and reached into his coat and pulled out a leather purse. He rolled out a pile of notes and held them out to Lev. "Ten thousand Wieter krones." He waved the cash. "Take them. Now. Before I change my mind."

Lev snatched the money, counted it with frantic fingers, and stuffed it into a pocket. "We were never here, mate." He tapped the side of his nose. "And as far as we're concerned, you hiring an assassin never happened."

Roubert smiled. "Good to know. And just so we're clear, if I ever see you or your friend on my ship again, I'll have you shot on sight."

"Understood. But we're all done here. We've got what we wanted. You've got what you wanted. It's a win–win as far as I'm concerned." He stepped to the door. "Don't worry, mate. We won't be back here again."

"Make sure you're not. Because no one pulls one over on Captain Roubert and gets away with it."

"Whatever you say, mate." Lev stopped by the doorway and raised a finger. "Maybe we'll keep hold of that evidence for our own protection. So if anything does happen to us, I'll have our friends do what we said and take it to the Magistrates. How's that sound?"

Roubert's nostrils flared. "Go. Get off my ship. We're done here."

Lev dipped his head in a mocking bow and gestured for Fedor to leave. "A pleasure doing business with you, mate. Just remember what I said."

Fedor returned to Kathryn Square and stepped into the shop behind Lev. He locked the door and closed the shutters, checking through the windows to make sure Captain Roubert hadn't followed them.

Melita came down the stairs, gripping her dagger, then slipping it back into its sheath. "How did it go?"

Lev shrugged a shoulder and grinned. "As expected."

Melita sat behind the counter and sighed. "What happened? Did Fedor call a thirty-three?"

Lev chuckled and dipped a hand into his pocket. "How about ten grand?" He tossed the roll of cash across the counter. "All there. All good."

Melita flattened out the cash and looked up at Lev. "How?"

"Blackmail."

"I know it was blackmail. What I mean is how did you make it work...you know, after last time."

"What can I say? Bloody genius, me."

"So you actually made it work? No issues? He just heard what you had to say and paid up?"

Lev turned to Fedor. "You hearing this, mate? Can't believe she's doubting us like this."

Fedor joined his side. "It's true."

Melita shook her head and smiled. "I can't believe you actually made it work."

Lev snatched up a thousand krones and returned them to his pocket. "What have I said about doubting the blackmail? We just needed to work it right...and we worked it right."

"This is great." She gestured to the cash. "Who was it?"

"Bloke called Captain Roubert."

Melita frowned. "I think I know that name."

"He's a smuggler, apparently," Fedor said.

"Maybe," Melita said. "I think he works with some of the fences, shipping stuff overseas."

"Who bloody cares?" Lev said. "We had him bang to rights."

"And he just handed the cash over?"

"Yep."

"Just like that?"

Lev shifted his weight. "I mean, bloke did pull a pistol on us, but I talked him round."

"You?"

"Yeah. Why?"

Melita shrugged. "No reason. So there was just you two and he had a pistol, and he handed over the cash like that?"

Lev tapped his temple and turned to Fedor. "You see? This is what I'm talking about."

Fedor exchanged a confused look with Melita.

"It's about layers. It's about taking a step back and looking at the bigger picture. It's easy enough to go in there making demands, but you need another layer."

Melita frowned at Fedor. "Do you know what he's on about?"

"Erm..."

"Don't ask him. He can hardly string a bloody sentence together these days. No. It's all about incentives."

"What is?"

"Blackmail."

"Right."

"He had the incentive to pay up because he knew if he didn't, we'd blab to the Magistrates about him having someone knocked off."

"You'd hand him to the Magistrates?" Melita asked.

"Of course I wouldn't. The less I have to do with those masked fuckers, the better." He raised a finger. "But old Captain Nob Cheese doesn't need to know that."

A crease set on Melita's brow. "Who's Captain Nob Cheese?"

"It's the mark," Fedor said. "Captain Roubert."

"Right. I see. So that still doesn't explain why he didn't shoot you there and then."

"This is the genius part. I told him that if anything happened to us, we've got friends who'll deliver everything to the Magistrates."

Melita pushed out her bottom lip. "That's actually pretty smart."

"Pretty smart? It's bloody genius." Lev sighed. "Honestly, how many times do I have to tell you? No, let's start that again. How many times do I have to show you that I'm on this before you start having a little faith?"

Melita gestured to the door. "Were you followed?"

Lev shook his head. "We were careful."

Fedor nodded. "We did a few loops around the lower city and went through the back way. We definitely weren't followed."

"Good."

Fedor licked his lips and reached for his share of the cash.

Melita slammed her hand down, stopping him from picking it up. "I don't think so."

"What?"

"You can have your share when you're clean."

Heat rose up Fedor's neck. "But...but that's my share."

"She's right, mate." Lev clapped a hand on Fedor's shoulder. "You'll just spend it on that crap."

Fedor's mouth dropped open. "But it's my share."

"And you'll have it when you're clean," Melita said firmly.

"So what?" He pulled away from Lev. "You just get to keep back my share now?"

Melita shook her head. "No. You can spend it how you want to. Just not until you're clean and not on that stuff."

"This isn't fair." Fedor began to pace, his heart racing, his hands trembling. "You can't do this."

"Mate, this is the best way," Lev said. "We've got your back. We made an oath, remember?"

"Lev's right," Melita said. "We're just looking out for you. That's all it is."

Fedor looked between them and sucked his teeth. "Bastards."

III. Patrov

Lev patted the cash in his pocket and smiled to himself as he sauntered across the lower city's market square. He nodded a greeting at one of the Clam's bouncers and slipped him ten krones before entering the brothel.

His eyes adjusted to the low light, while the scents of perfume and incense mingled with the faint hint of opium drifting from somewhere in the back.

Sidling up to the bar, he ordered a cider and eyed one of the women walking past in a tight silk dress. He scanned the booths across from the bar, his gaze lingering over the soft curves just visible in the shadows.

"Lev."

He turned and offered Velvet a smile. She slid onto a stool next to him and tossed her red hair back over her shoulders. "Drink?"

She cocked an eyebrow, the small hint of a smile curving her painted lips.

"You'll have the cash. Right." He fished out a ten-krone note and set it on the bar between them.

Her hand glided over the cash and it disappeared.

"I still think you'd make a great thief."

"What makes you so sure I'm not?"

Lev grinned. "How are the...erm...you know. How are things?"

"Things are fine. But let's not talk about things right now." She ran a finger down his biceps. "You looking for some fun?"

Lev took a sip of his cider. "You know what I'm here for."

She let out a sigh. "I know. I know. But you can't blame a girl for trying."

"Business alright, though? You being treated well?"

"Everything's fine, Lev. Everything's fine."

Lev glanced down at his glass and swirled the cider around. "Sorry for asking."

"Don't worry about it. I'm not here to make small talk about business and the weather."

"Right." He cleared his throat and shifted his weight on the stool. "So what do you like talking about?"

Velvet shrugged a bare shoulder and examined her manicured nails. "I prefer to do other things with my mouth. Maybe I could take you to one of the booths and show you? Tara might have the experience, but I can do things she could only dream of..." She looked him up and down. "And I'm sure that would be the same for you."

Lev smiled. "I wouldn't dream of underestimating your talents for a second. But..."

"But Tara, Tara, Tara. Yes, I know."

"What? It's nothing personal."

"What does she have that I don't?"

Lev shrugged. "You're a good-looking woman, what can I say? It's just...I don't know, Tara's different."

"You prefer older women, is that it?"

"I just know where I am with Tara. She knows what I need."

Velvet leant close to Lev, her lips brushing against his ear. "I can be whatever you want," she whispered. "Whatever you want."

Lev turned to her and met her gaze. She looked up at him and fluttered her eyelashes. "But you can't."

She pursed her lips and sat up straight. "Because I'm not her."

"As I say, it's nothing personal."

She sniffed and crossed her legs. "Nothing personal. Sure." She placed her hands in her lap and turned to him. "Ignore me. I'm sorry. You're here for a good time. But you can't blame me for trying."

"Don't worry about it. Already forgotten." He looked along the bar towards the door leading up the stairs. "Is she here?"

"She's speaking to someone. She shouldn't be too long."

"Talking to someone? Is that a euphemism?"

She shook her head, the movement of hair revealing a thumb-shaped bruise on her neck, just visible through powder.

"What's that?"

She adjusted her hair to cover the mark. "Let's just call it the cost of doing business."

"Did one of the blokes here do that to you?"

"Nothing like that."

"A boyfriend?"

She laughed and gestured to the door leading upstairs. "Tara is speaking to him right now."

"Bastard. Someone should sort that fucker out."

She nodded and gestured to the door. "She's coming down."

Lev followed her gaze as Tara entered the bar. He rose to greet her and stopped as a man entered the room behind her.

Lev's mouth dropped open at the sight of the man he knew.

"Shit." Lev pulled his cap peak down to hide his face. "What's he doing back?"

Tara and Patrov stopped near the entrance, while Lev kept his eyes on his cider and kept his ears open.

"Just let the rest of the girls know I'll be back every week to take my cut," Patrov said. "Whatever deal you lot have with the Crows isn't my concern."

"Between you two, that's seventy per cent," Tara said. "We can't—"

"If they give you hassle, you have our protection."

"What good is protect—"

"You will pay with coin, or you will pay with fingers. It makes no difference to me. Be seeing you."

The door slammed shut and the bar dropped silent.

Velvet got up from her stool and moved over to Tara.

The pair exchanged words in a low whisper.

Lev couldn't stay. He had to let the others know. He knocked back the rest of his cider and headed for the door.

"You not staying?" Velvet asked.

"Nah. Something's come up. You take care of yourselves."

Onwyth sat with her back against the panelled wall and gazed across the Rusty Sail's lounge, taking in the faces, most familiar, some not. She cursed herself for not having a watch with her, but she was certain Walter should be here by now.

"Is that him?" Vern sat up and gestured to a man entering through the door, a cloud of pipe smoke surrounding his head.

"No. That's Patrov." A line set on her brow. "I thought he'd left to go and live in Molotok or something." She shrugged to herself. "I don't know what he's doing here."

"What's Walter look like again?"

"I'll recognise him when I see him."

"Should I wait here with you?"

Onwyth sighed. "Just be cool. Here, take this." She waved a ten-krone note in front of Vern and gestured to the bar. "Get us both a drink."

"Cider? Rum? Ale?"

"Whatever. Just get what you want and I'll have the same. Anything to keep you from asking more questions."

She leant back and watched the door. By the time Vern had returned with the drinks, Walter had entered and removed his hat. He looked around, but did not seem to recognise her.

Onwyth waved to him and caught his attention.

He came over and smiled. "I don't think we've had the pleasure," he said, shaking Onwyth's hand.

"I'm Onwyth. This is Vern."

Walter pulled out a seat and placed his hat down on the table before sitting. "Your boss said you had a proposition for me. How can I help you?"

"I wouldn't call it a proposition exactly. It's more we're in the market for something that you might be able to help us with."

"Oh? And what sort of thing might that be?"

"We're looking to get our hands on some ravenglass. Melita said that's the type of thing you sometimes deal in."

"She is correct. But I'm afraid you're out of luck."

Onwyth frowned. "But I'm the luckiest person I know."

"You aren't today."

"So you don't have any."

He opened his palms and shook his head. "It doesn't tend to come along very often. And when it does, I can usually find several buyers at short notice."

"How often?"

"I come across a sizeable piece maybe once or twice a year."

"When did you last get some?"

"I'm not sure how that's relevant."

"Have you had some recently?"

"No. But—"

"So you might get some tomorrow?"

Walter frowned. "I mean, it's possible. It depends on what I get offered."

"He ain't got none," Vern said.

"I'm sorry I couldn't be more helpful."

"Do you know anyone else who might have some?" Onwyth asked.

Walter shook his head.

"So you can't help us?"

"I'm afraid not."

Onwyth knocked back her cider, downing it in one large swig, and got to her feet. "Then there's nothing more to talk about. Come on, Vern. Let's go. This bloke's no use." She marched out of the pub before Walter had a chance to respond.

When Vern caught up to her, she turned to him. "We'll have to go with your plan."

"What plan? I don't—"

"The priests. We'll go to the priests. And if I happen to see Father Heinrich, I might have to whack him with something."

"I thought you said it was a bad idea."

"It is. But it's the best we've got. Let's go."

"What, now?"

She yanked his coat sleeve. "Yes, now."

Melita glared at Fedor across the common room and drummed her fingers on the arm of the sofa. How much longer could she keep him around? Yes, they had made an oath to have each other's backs, but that oath worked both ways. If he kept getting screwed up on plez, he was letting the others down.

She eyed him as he lay curled up on his side, his knees against his chest, his breaths shallow. She was surprised he hadn't started sucking his thumb already. How long was he going to be like this? Maybe she needed to set out some stricter rules, some harsher punishments for anyone in the gang who got themselves into this state. It was selfish and was putting everyone else at risk.

Heat rose in her chest and she slapped her hand down. "Are you just going to lie there all night?"

Fedor's shoulders moved almost imperceptibly, his mouth letting out little more than a whispered grunt.

She gritted her teeth. "I asked you a question."

He remained still.

"Oi, dickhead. I'm talking to you. Are you planning on lying there all night? Because if you are, can I ask that you take whatever this is to your room so I can relax in peace?"

Fedor turned towards her and half-opened one eye, his face scrunched into a web of creases. "Leave me alone."

"No, Fedor. I won't leave you alone. If you're planning on lying around feeling sorry for yourself, at least do it where no one can see you."

Fedor sat up and scowled. "What's it to you? It's not like I've got any money to go anywhere."

Melita rolled her eyes. "Yeah? Well, maybe if you hadn't pissed it all away on that shit, you might have some cash in your pocket. But, oh no, Fedor can do what he wants and to the void with everyone else."

"I said I'll get clean." He dragged a hand back through his hair and met her gaze with watery, pleading eyes. "How many times do I have to say sorry?"

"I don't need your apologies. I need you sharp. If you're not earning, the rest of us have to take the slack. That's not fair. We're supposed to have each other's backs."

"I could say the same thing."

Rumbling footsteps approached along the stairs.

Melita shot to her feet and drew her dagger. "You expecting anyone?"

The door swung open and Lev rushed in. He staggered to a halt and raised his hands, his eyes switching back and forth between Fedor and Melita. "What's going on?"

With a shuddering breath, Melita slid her dagger back into its sheath and sat back on the sofa. "I thought you would be out until late."

"So did I."

"What's wrong? Couldn't perform?"

Lev shook his head. "Nothing like that. Didn't even get chance to—that doesn't matter. We've got a bit of a problem."

"There's always something." Melita folded her arms and sighed. "What is it now?"

"Patrov."

She frowned. "What about him?"

"He's back."

"Back? As in, back back?"

"As in, he's back in town. He's back in business. He's bloody back."

"Shit." Melita's jaw clenched and she began to pace. "We made a deal. I can't believe he's gone back on it...and so soon. I can't believe this. Fuck."

"This isn't good for us," Lev said.

"Of course it isn't good for us," Melita snapped. "Shit. You know what this means?"

"Dunno. Could mean a lot of things."

She stopped and turned to him. "It means we're back to where we were. He was supposed to leave. We saw him go. For fuck's sake. If he's back in business, who are we supposed to pay? The Crows? Patrov? Both?"

Lev nodded. "But it's not just that though, is it? If Patrov's around and we know, I'd say it's only a matter of time before Myker knows...that's if he's not already onto us."

Melita ran a hand back through her hair and sank back into the sofa. "Shit. He's going to want his money back, isn't he?"

"That's just for starters. We ripped him off. He's not going to like that."

"This is Patrov's fault. He's the one who didn't keep up his end of the deal."

Lev shrugged. "We should have seen it coming. It's bloody Pat the Rat we're talking about here."

"We should leave," Fedor said, slipping his legs from the sofa. "We can't stay here."

"Mate, mate, mate. Let's not be hasty. We need to think this through."

Fedor inclined his head, his brow knitted. "What's to think through? Pat's back. Myker's going to want a refund, maybe more. We can't stick around here. He's probably got his lads after us already."

Melita looked between Lev and Fedor and weighed up their options. "I have to agree with Lev. Let's not be hasty."

"See, mate. Lita knows I'm making sense."

"Whatever," Fedor said.

"As far as I can tell," Melita said, "we have two options here. We either need to deal with Patrov, or we need to deal with Myker. Either way, we need to get a good plan together."

"Or we can run," Fedor said. "Why are we even considering trying to negotiate with either of those two? It's a waste of time. Pat thinks we're after him. And from what I've heard of Myker..." He shook his head. "We can't stay here."

"So that's your big idea. We run?" Lev shook his head. "Where would we run to exactly? You got somewhere in mind? I don't know about you, but I quite like having a decent place to live. And if you think I'm starting again in another town, you got another thing coming. Nah, mate, we need to deal with this." He took in a long breath through his nostrils. "I hate to say this, but I think we should have just killed him when we got the job."

"Enough," Melita said. "We don't know what we're dealing with yet. Patrov could be visiting, or tying up some loose ends. Who knows?"

"I'm telling you," Lev said. "He was in the Clam. He's been shaking down girls, taking his usual cut. I even saw he'd been rough with one of them...and he could have been like that with some of the others."

"Maybe he was getting money owed."

Lev shook his head. "With all due respect, you can be so bloody naïve sometimes. He said he was coming back next week. Does that sound like someone who's just visiting, someone who's just here to collect back payments?"

"Shit." Melita stared at her palms. "Shit."

"You've got an in with the Crows," Fedor said. "Can't you speak to that boyfriend of yours? Get this smoothed out."

Melita tried to hold back a glare. "He refuses to talk about business with me. Can't say I blame him."

"But you need to try. It's not just about you, is it?"

"I'll see if he'll speak to me. I can't promise anything."

"I don't know about this," Lev said. "Things are going to get real awkward if his boss has put a price on our heads."

Melita nodded. "I think we need to accept we need to pay him back."

"Who, Myker?"

"Exactly. It's not ideal, but I think it's the best way out of this. We apologise for the mix-up and get him his thirty grand."

Lev shook his head and laughed. "And you really think that's going to be enough? Nah, he's going to want more from us. I can see it now."

"I'll talk to Brak. I'll tell him something got mixed up and that we're willing to refund and forget any of it ever happened."

"You think that'll work?"

"It's worth a try. You got anything better?"

"Think about it," Lev said. "Since we sent Pat off, Myker's expanded his business on the assumption Pat's no longer around. He's going to want blood. He's going to want revenge."

Fedor leant forward and raised a finger. "Wait. I've thought of something...I think we'll be alright."

"Really?" Lev folded his arms. "And how do you figure that?"

"The wyvern. It was all done through Dienerin. We can blame her. She's the one who took the job. She's the one who said what we were doing. We can throw her under the cart. She's the one to blame."

Lev removed his cap. "Mate, I don't know what's going on in that head of yours, but Myker knows who we are. Do you not remember? We were in his office. He saw our faces. We spoke to him about the job. We can't just blame it on some stinking wyvern and expect him to believe us."

"Oh." Fedor's head sank forward. "I forgot."

Melita shot across the room and shook Fedor by the collar. "Unless you've got anything valuable to add, I suggest you shut the fuck up, Fedor."

He shifted back and glared up at her. "I just forgot. For fuck's sake, my head is foggy and I'm just trying to help."

"And whose fault is that?" Melita curled her lip. "You really need to sort yourself out. I can't have you forgetting important stuff like that."

"I'm trying." He rubbed his head. "You don't know how hard it is."

"I don't care. I just need you sharp. This isn't the first time you've forgotten basic, basic stuff. You're a disgrace."

Fedor closed his eyes and placed his head in his hands.

"That's right," Melita said. "You just ignore it. Everything will be fine if you bury your head."

Lev rested a hand on Melita's arm. "Just give him a bit of space. It's going to take a bit of time."

"I know," she said. "But we need to figure this thing out."

"So what's the plan?"

Melita raised her chin. "I'll see if I can find anything out from Brak, put out some feelers, see how much he knows."

"That's good. Myker might still be in the dark about this, but it's only a matter of time before he knows."

"Maybe we can arrange a sit-down with him. See if we can work something out, nip it in the bud before it turns into a problem."

"Bad idea." Fedor looked up at her again. "I say we just keep our heads down. Maybe they'll go—"

Melita shot him a glare. "Didn't I tell you to shut the fuck up?"

"Hear him out," Lev said. "I think I know where he's going."

"Go on then," Melita said. "Before I change my mind."

"This was all about Myker taking over Patrov's business, right? It's about the Crows expanding, or whatever."

Melita frowned. "So?"

"So it might buy some time."

Melita turned to Lev. "Do you know what he's on about?"

"I think I do." Lev grinned. "And I think he's onto something. It's about letting them sort it out between themselves."

Fedor nodded.

"Myker's not going to be happy with Patrov knocking around, trying to re-establish himself."

"Exactly," Fedor said. "That's what I'm saying. Let them fight it out among themselves. We just keep out of it."

Melita tapped her chin. "That actually makes sense. Let them go to war. We could see the lie of the land when the dust settles."

"Could work," Lev said. "I've heard worse. But if Myker comes out on top, he'll probably be more pissed off with us than before."

"True," Melita said. "But it does buy us some time. We can raise some funds and have it ready to pay him off if we need to."

Lev nodded. "And if Myker dies..."

"Then we're in the clear." She considered this for several seconds and then nodded to herself. "Or, maybe, we just take care of Myker. Finish it before it becomes a problem for us."

Fedor shot to his feet, went to say something, then stormed off.

Melita watched the door swinging shut and sighed. "Keep a close eye on him. He is becoming a liability."

Lev nodded. "Don't worry, I'm already on it."

Onwyth came to a stop outside the church. It stood in the shadow of a cavern, carved from the stone itself. She took a breath. How long had it been since she'd last set her eyes on those walls?

"This is the place," Vern said.

"I know." She shook her head, her mouth turning dry. "I can't believe I used to live here."

"How long were you here?"

"A few years." She hugged herself. "I hated every day of it and I swore to Creation I'd never go back."

Vern placed a hand on her shoulder. "It ain't breaking a promise if you're just going in to nick something."

She smiled. "I suppose you're right, but I'm not sure how I feel about taking something from the church."

"Why? It ain't like they're using the stuff."

"What if all the Creation stuff is real? What if She comes down and smites us, or whatever?"

"I ain't saying the Creation stuff ain't real. But the church ain't shit. It's just some dusty old pervs using Creation to get kids to make cash for them."

"I think you're right. This isn't about Creation. This is about us getting what we need." She gestured to the gas lamp shining over the doorway. "It's just the one entrance, isn't it?"

"As far as I remember." He shrugged a shoulder. "Place is dug out of the rock, so I don't think there's a back way we can sneak in."

Onwyth glanced over his shoulder as foundry workers milled around, the heat from their forges prickling her skin. "We should go in before people start asking questions."

Vern turned to her, his eyes growing wide. "What, now? I thought we was just looking around to get a plan together."

"No. You're right. I was actually thinking we come back sometime next year. Maybe next winter."

Vern frowned at her. "We're doing it now, aren't we?"

"Yes. Now." She tugged his arm and walked towards the door, its oak surface dulled by time. She lifted her chin and put on a smile. "It's all about looking like we're meant to be here. Just act confident."

She turned the handle and the door creaked open. "See? Easy."

Stepping inside, she stopped and took in the old familiar scent of polish and incense, the lingering hints of ash and sulphur. Her memories flooded with images from her childhood—the beatings, the abuse, the nights lying awake in fear.

She placed a hand on the wall and took in several deep breaths.

"You alright?" Vern asked.

She shook her head. "It's this place. I'll be fine...it's been a long time."

Vern gestured behind them. "We can go. We ain't got to do anything."

"No. We're here. It's fine." She squeezed her eyes shut. "It's fine." She opened her eyes and took in a deep breath. "Where's this stuff then? The quicker we can get done in here, the better."

"It'll be in the main church bit."

Onwyth followed the corridor to the nave. The room opened out before her, its vaulted ceiling criss-crossed with white stone. She gazed up at the great carving of a chalice, the symbol of Creation's abundance, shaped from grey stone hanging down from the ceiling. Burnt offerings lay on the central altar.

She scanned past statues and checked along bookcases, her gaze landing on a ravenglass shield atop a high shelf. She froze for a moment, her breath caught in her chest, and gestured to the shield. She nodded to Vern.

"This way. You keep watch." She jogged over to the shelves and began to climb.

Halfway up, she wondered whether some of the higher shelves would hold her weight. Would she be able to climb back down with a shield in her hands? Could she survive a fall from such a height?

Her hand slipped and she slapped her forearm down on the shelf, her arms shaking as she regained her focus.

When she reached the top, she glanced back down and gave Vern a reassuring nod. She gripped the shelf with one hand and reached for the shield with the other.

She recoiled when she touched it, its icy bite sending a shock along her fingers.

"What's wrong?"

"Nothing. It's just cold. I'll throw this down to you."

Using her teeth, she dragged a sleeve up over her hand and grabbed the shield's edge. She pulled it, but the shield remained fixed to the wall. "Damn it."

"What's wrong?"

"Nothing. Stop asking."

"Is it stuck?"

"Yes, it's stuck. Just let me focus." She jerked the shield with all her strength, but it stayed fixed in place. "I've got an idea. Get ready to catch me."

"Catch you?"

She pulled her other sleeve down and grabbed the shield with both hands. She shook it, then leant back, letting the shield take her weight. With gritted teeth, she pushed her feet against the wall. "Come on."

The bracket shifted and she let her legs drop, her hand still keeping hold. The shield tipped.

"Get ready!"

She fell and landed on bended knees, Vern's catch doing little to take the fall. "You alright?"

Onwyth stumbled to her feet and raised the shield above her head. "Got it. Let's—"

Alchemical light shone across their faces. "What is the meaning of this?" A robed figure emerged from the doorway wielding a lamp and staff.

"Thirty-three." Onwyth charged at the priest, shield-first, knocking him onto his back.

"Come back here!" the priest called. "Stop! Thief!"

Onwyth toppled a bench behind her and Vern pushed over a statue.

She raced from the main door with Vern at her heels and ran into the tunnels, laughing.

Fedor lay in the dark on the library floor, staring unfocused at the ceiling, his eyes welling with tears. Why did Melita hate him so much? The plez had hooked him. He'd heard the warnings. He thought he could handle it. But every part of him cried out for more.

What would he do if his crew abandoned him, if he were forced to leave? No doubt he'd find himself back at the Rusty Sail, whiling away his days until his body finally gave out.

He didn't want any of that. His friends were important to him. They had made an oath in blood. But this drug had burrowed deep into his mind and captured his soul.

His only option was to get himself clean, to resist the pull, the temptation, the bliss that came from such a tiny thing.

But the alternative...the alternative frightened him just as much. How could he live with himself? How could he go around with so much death hanging over him? And not just death. If he believed Dienerin, death was a blessing compared to the eternity of non-death in the shadow realm.

She said those creatures fed on the minds of the lost. How far was he from such a fate? Was he already lost?

He covered his eyes when light filled the room, and he forced himself to sit up.

Onwyth and Vern placed something heavy on the table and spoke to each other through laughter.

He forced a smile at Onwyth. "Hey."

"Hey, yourself." She frowned at him and turned her attention back to the desk.

Vern took a seat next to her.

Fedor got to his feet and squinted at the ravenglass form. "What you got?"

"A shield," Vern said. "Got it from the church."

"You stole from the church?"

"Yeah, so? Church ain't shit to us."

"I know, but—"

"How did you get your dagger forged?" Onwyth asked.

Fedor rubbed his eyes. "Gottsisle."

"I asked how, not where. How did you do it?"

"We had to collect some of our own blood and tears in a vial and then the smith—"

"You're putting the cart before the horse." Onwyth waved a hand. "How did you arrange it?"

"I didn't. It was Soren."

"Of course." Onwyth looked around. "Maybe your slimy friend can help us?"

"I've not seen her."

"Can't you summon her? Don't you have a way you can snap your fingers and get her here?"

"I don't know. She just seems to turn up—"

Dienerin flew through the door and landed on the desk. "Are you ready to take on a new contract, Fedor, Fedor, master?"

Fedor rolled his eyes. "Can you arrange to have some new weapons forged like you did my dagger?"

"But you are the master. Your weapon is sufficient."

"I was thinking it would be good to have a few more of us with ravenglass weapons."

"Only those taken on as apprentices may have weapons."

"What if I took on Onwyth and Vern as my apprentices?"

"Then I can send a letter of intent to the guild and the rest can be arranged. Though I can't foresee them allowing you an apprentice until the investigation is completed."

Fedor blinked. "I'm sorry, I've no idea what you're talking about."

Dienerin inclined her head slightly but did not speak.

"What investigation?"

"There has been an allegation that one of your contracts was not completed as arranged. The guild is investigating."

"I'm so confused," Onwyth said.

"What's going on?" Fedor asked.

"It has been alleged that you did not complete a contract as arranged," Dienerin said. "And so the guild is investigating. It is that simple."

Fedor looked between Vern and Onwyth and shrugged, before turning back to the wyvern. "Who's investigating?"

"The guild."

"What guild?"

"The guild."

Fedor growled. "What guild?"

"The guild." Dienerin dipped her head and spread her wings. "Fedor, Fedor, master, please. I have answered your question. I can say nothing more."

"Fine...you just get the stuff arranged."

Dienerin raised her head. "What stuff?"

"We need those weapons forging. Do what you need to do to set it up."

"When the investigation is complete, you will be allowed to forge only one weapon."

Fedor frowned. "Why one?"

"It is how guild succession works. You should familiarise yourself with the charter."

Fedor rubbed his chin. "Can't we pay them or something?"

"You do need to pay them. The apprentice must offer their payment in blood and tears. And you must pay the smith in coin earned from your contracts to craft the blade."

"What kind of fee?"

"One hundred thousand krones."

"Wow." Fedor shook his head. "That's a lot of money...you could buy a small house with that."

Onwyth grabbed Fedor's shoulders and met his eyes. "I need this weapon."

"I know. I know." Fedor pulled away from her.

"I'll do whatever it takes."

"I know." He looked at the shield. "I'll see what I can do."

Men and women danced in a frenzy as the drums rose to a booming crescendo, while Melita sat in a booth away from the stage and stared into her cup. Cheers and laughter washed over her as she studied the play of light on the eddying surface of her spiced rum.

She glanced up at Brak and tried to smile.

"Are you sure I can't get you to dance?" he asked over the noise. "I think it'd do you good."

"I don't want to. I'm sorry."

"Right." The corners of his mouth twitched. "We can go, if you want."

She ran a finger around her cup. "I'm sorry. I'm miles away."

"I can tell." He got up, shifted around the table, and sat next to her, placing an arm around her shoulder. "You can talk to me, you know?" His words brushed against her ear.

"You brought me out to dance and I just keep thinking about Fedor."

Brak pulled his arm away and leant back in his seat. "What's he done now?"

She sighed. "I'm just worried about him. He's not been doing well. I just think he's heading down a bad path."

"Is it the drugs?"

She gave a slight nod and took a swig of her rum. "I keep feeling like I should have done something, like I could be doing more to help him, but instead"—she gestured to the stage—"I'm out getting drunk and dancing."

"You haven't danced," Brak said.

"You know what I mean. I'm letting my crew down. I should be there, but instead I'm leaving it all to Lev. That's not really fair, is it?"

"Don't talk like that. Fedor's his own man. If he can't deal with this life, that's his fault, not yours."

She turned to him. "But I'm his boss. I'm supposed to look out for my crew. We're supposed to have each other's backs. And instead..."

"You're not his keeper, Mel." Brak sipped his rum and wiped his mouth. "What he does in his own time is his own business." He drew a line with his finger on the table. "You have to keep things separate. Business. Personal."

"I don't think it's that simple."

"Only because you've let it not be. Do you really think Myker has any say in how I live my life outside the business? So long as what I do in my own time doesn't get in the way, it's not his concern. He's made that clear and I suggest you do the same with your crew." He gestured to each side of the imaginary line. "Personal. Business."

"But it's not that easy."

"It is that easy. You care too much...and I like that about you. But you're running a business, not a charity."

"You don't understand. We made an oath in blood." She met his bright blue eyes. "That means something."

Brak nodded and seemed to consider her words. "Sounds to me like he's a liability. If he was with the Crows, he'd be dead meat already. We don't tolerate that sort of shit."

"That's harsh."

"That's just the rules. And that's why we're taking over this city."

"Well, we never needed that rule."

"Maybe that's why he's doing what he's doing. He knows he can get away with it. He's got no real consequences if he fucks things up for you."

"So what am I supposed to do?"

"You need to cut him off. It's that simple. Cut him off and move on. He's an infection. And like an infection, you cut it out before it spreads."

"Or you can work to heal it."

Brak shook his head and got to his feet. "I've come here to dance." He gestured to the throngs of people. "Are you coming or not?"

Melita let out a sigh and stared into her cup. "No. You go ahead. I'll wait here. I need to think about a few things."

"Suit yourself. Your loss."

When Brak disappeared into the crowds, she got up and knocked back the rest of her drink and slammed it back down on the table. "Fuck this." She ran after him. "Wait."

Fedor drove his fist into the training room's punchbag, throwing punches and elbows in quick succession, all his anger, all his frustration focused on striking as hard as his limbs would allow.

A series of frantic kicks and knees turned into a barrage of curses. He screamed and charged at the bag shoulder-first. He bit into the bag's leather exterior, trying to rip it apart.

When the surge of energy dropped, he sank to the floor and clawed the sand, his breaths coming quick and heavy, his throat thick with spit.

His lungs burnt. His legs ached. Fine blood dripped from his torn knuckles.

He forced himself to stand and gazed around at the dummy and the weapons. His hand drifted to his ravenglass dagger and he drew it slowly from its sheath, his grip tightening around its icy handle as distant whispers filled his mind. The words were unclear and spoken in a language he did not recognise, but the meaning was all too clear—the blade wanted him to kill again.

He trembled and slid the blade back into its sheath, to whispers fading into his mind's usual chatter. Did the whispers come from the blade? From somewhere else? Perhaps another realm? Or, more likely, they were figments of his own imagination, signs of his burgeoning insanity.

Had the drugs poisoned his mind forever? Was he doomed to wander the streets—a lost husk, with his mind trapped in that other place?

"Fedor? Mate?"

Fedor blinked. Lev watched him from the doorway. "What?"

"Just checking in on you." He stepped into the training room and looked around, his gaze lingering on Fedor's knuckles. "You were just standing there."

"I'm fine." Fedor cleared his throat. "Just catching my breath."

"Good." Lev strode around the circular room and stopped in front of the weapon racks. "That's what I like to hear."

"Well, you can stop checking up on me. I'm just training."

Lev strode over to Fedor and patted him on the shoulder. "Mate, it's alright. No judgement here. I'm just looking out for a mate. You know this."

Fedor folded his arms and looked away. "Yeah, right. I bet Melita sent you down here to spy."

"To spy? On what? On you standing in the training room doing nothing?" Lev sighed. "We made an oath, remember? We've got your back. All of us—Me, Lita, Onwyth, Vern—we're all looking out for you. We've all got your back. Don't push us away."

"Got my back?" Fedor laughed. "Got my cash, more like. You tell me how Melita withholding what I earned is having my back in any way?" He pointed at his temple. "Don't think I don't know what's going on. I'm being pushed out. I'm being cut off. I'm sure you'd all love a bigger cut."

"Honestly, mate. You're just being paranoid. No one is cutting you off."

"Bullshit." He pointed to the door, his eyes growing wide. "She's taken my cash, kept it to herself, as if I wasn't the one out there risking my neck for it. That's a grand—a fucking grand. And she's keeping it to herself."

"No. You've got that all wrong. I'm with her on this—"

"So, what? You splitting it between you? Giving yourself an extra five hundred to waste on whores?"

Lev sneered. "Don't fucking start, mate. She's holding onto it until you're clean, that's all. It's fair enough and it's for your own good. And if I'm being honest, I'd be doing exactly the same if I was running this crew."

"How's that fair? It's not her decision to make. That's my cash she's holding."

"Trust me, she knows what she's doing. It's for the best." He squeezed Fedor's upper arm. "We're going to get through this. You just need to keep your head down and stay clean. We've all got your back."

"And since when does everyone else get to say what I can and can't do?"

"Oh, I'd say about the time we swore an oath in blood." Lev held up his hand, his white scar catching the light. "Those things mean something. Few people have that."

"So what am I supposed to do without funds?"

"You're not going hungry, if that's what you're worried about. You've got a good place to stay and a comfy bed. What more do you need?"

Fedor's nostrils flared and he glowered at Lev. He wanted to scream at him, to punch that smug face of his, but all he could do was breathe and listen to the pulse thumping inside his skull.

"See? You'll be fine, mate. Everything's good."

"Good?" Fedor laughed bitterly. "You don't know what it's like. You think you can just turn it off? You think you can just make it stop like a fucking tap or something?" He pointed to the door. "All I want to do is go back to the Sail."

"I know."

"I need to go back to the Sail to forget about this..." He swept his hands around. "Soren, Garrett, Xandru. All this shit piled on top of me...it's driving me mad. I keep hearing voices, Lev. I keep hearing whispers." He grabbed Lev's coat and shook it. "I can't deal with it."

"You can. And you will. We're here for you. But you've got to stop moaning about everything."

"Excuse me?"

"Someone needs to say something, and I'm sure you'd rather it came from me."

Fedor curled his lip. "Oh, so you've all been talking, have you? I see what's going on."

"Trust me, all you do at the minute is moan and I'm sick of it. Everyone else is sick of it too. We're done with your fucking woe-is-me act."

"Act? Do you know what I've been through?"

"Yeah. And we've all been through shit. But that's life. Deal with it."

Fedor narrowed his eyes. "So the others have been saying this as well?"

"No. They don't need to. It's obvious. You need to sort yourself out, or someone is going to smack you one."

"Is that a threat?"

"No, mate. It's not a threat at all." Lev held up his hands. "And I doubt it will come from me first. But who knows? I'm sure the others can see what a state you're in."

"But—"

"Don't. Just don't." Lev rubbed the back of his neck. "Listen, I need your help. That's why I came down here."

"Yeah, right."

"This might have slipped your mind, but we've got a job to do. And I'm not letting you out of my sight."

"A job? A job I won't get paid for, you mean?"

"Melita is holding your money." Lev rolled his eyes. "How many times? You'll get it back when you're clean."

"Fine." Fedor pursed his lips. "What is it?"

Lev grinned. "I've got another mark."

"For what?"

"Honestly, mate. What kind of mark do you think?"

"I don't know. Blackmail, maybe?"

"Exactly. Fuck me, these drugs are making you dense. It's like trying to get through to a stupid dog."

"How can you say that?"

"With my mouth. That's how it works. Keep up, mate. It's a bloke who lives north of the city. Owns a whole load of properties, apparently."

"Who is he?"

Lev tapped the side of his nose. "Doesn't matter. I need you to come along, so we can do our usual little chat. Best not worry about the details. Just bring that blade of yours and remember to look like someone you shouldn't mess with."

"Is it someone from Soren's list?"

"What do you think?"

"Just asking."

"Well, don't. You're not on the level. In fact, I'm thinking this might be a bad idea."

"I can do it." He rubbed his eyes. "I'll come with you."

"Come on, then. Let's go."

Lev pulled his coat around him and dipped his head against the chill wind blowing in from the Braun Sea. He trudged north along the Kusten Road, keeping half an eye on the path ahead, and half on Fedor. If he could keep Fedor busy, keep him focused, or at least distracted, maybe he'd be able to keep him away from the Rusty Sail.

He gestured ahead, pointing out a road leading towards rolling hills in the distance. "Just a bit more. I think it's one of the bigger houses up this way."

Fedor stopped and stared, his watery eyes rimmed with purple. "How far are we going?"

"Not too far, mate. Just keep with me. Keep moving."

Fedor remained still and glanced back over his shoulder.

"Come on. Don't want to be hanging round outside all day. I'm freezing my arse off out here." Lev patted Fedor's arm. "Let's take a look."

"I think we're being followed."

"Right." Lev scanned the road behind them, looking between carts and beyond to the balloon port. "I don't see anything."

"I'm sure of it."

"You don't think it's another wyvern, do you?"

"Not a wyvern. I keep catching a person. In the corner of my eye."

Lev cocked an eyebrow. "Yeah?"

"I was right about the wyvern." Fedor folded his arms and dipped his head. "You need to trust me. Someone's following us."

"So what do they look like? Short? Tall? Man? Woman?"

"I don't know." Fedor shook his head. "It's just...it's just a feeling I keep having, a feeling like we're being followed."

"Just a feeling...right."

Fedor glared at him. "I'm serious, Lev."

"I don't doubt you are, mate." Lev carried on walking. "But you know that plez stuff makes you paranoid, right? Have you considered the distinct possibility you might be seeing or hearing stuff that isn't there?"

"No. This isn't in my head."

Lev forced a smile. "Of course it's not. Don't worry. There's no one there now and we'll keep an eye out for any shifty characters lurking in the shadows."

"You don't believe me."

"You're right. But that's only because no one's after us."

"You sure about that?" Fedor pointed back towards the city. "What about the Crows?"

"What about them?"

"If Pat's back..."

"Mate, you ever seen the Crows sneaking around? That's not their style. If they're after us, we'd know about it."

"Like with Pat?"

"Fair point. But that was different."

"Different how?"

"Stands to reason, mate. Myker wanted no connection. I bet Pat's none the wiser."

"He guessed, remember. He worked out who paid us."

"Whatever, mate. All I'm saying is that if Myker wanted us gone, he'd have already sent his lads round to rough us up a bit."

"So what? He's keeping us alive?"

"I'd say we're probably worth more to him living than dead."

"Maybe."

"Think about it." Lev kicked a stone along the road ahead. "He's going to get a steady stream of cash from us once he gets his money back from the assassin job and—"

"You can't be serious." Fedor stopped. "You're planning on us paying him back?" His mouth dropped open. "That's thirty thousand krones. We can't afford that."

"We'll be fine. Trust me. It's all taken care of. We just need to do a few more of these blackmail jobs before he calls round. That way, we'll have the money ready and everything will be good."

"I guess."

Lev made a left off the Kusten Road and came to a stop outside a large house with boarded-up windows, covered in twisted ivy. "This is the place."

"It looks pretty abandoned."

Lev shook his head. "Could be the bloke who lives here wants us to think that. I say we try anyway."

"Why? There are weeds growing across the path. The place is empty."

Lev regarded the house for several seconds. "Ah, shit." He screwed up the name and address scrawled on a scrap of paper and tossed it into the puddle at his feet. "I hate to admit it, but you're bloody right. Doesn't look—"

"Wait." Fedor started and pointed past Lev. "There."

Before Lev had a chance to react, Fedor ran at full speed towards the crossroads and disappeared around the lefthand corner.

"For fuck's sake." Lev ran after him and raced south along a broad street, checking between houses, and scanning along rooftops. "Fedor? Mate? Where you at?"

He reached another intersection and watched the carts zipping past. He scanned for Fedor, but saw no signs of him.

After retracing his steps, he returned to the house covered in ivy and sighed.

Resigned, he walked back along the Kusten Road, his pace quickening as he drew closer to the lower city.

He headed straight to the Rusty Sail and checked the back room, but Fedor wasn't there.

Where had he gone?

Cursing to himself, he made his way back to Kathryn Square, into the den, and trudged upstairs. He entered the common room and stopped.

Fedor smiled at him from one of the sofas.

"What the fuck happened to you?"

"I told you we were being followed, didn't I?"

"Yeah, so?"

"I saw someone. They ran away and I couldn't catch them."

"Are you absolutely sure?"

Fedor nodded. "I'm not making it up."

"You should have said, mate. I checked the Sail for you. I thought...you know."

"No. I didn't want to lose them."

"What did they look like?"

"I don't know."

"What do they want?"

Fedor shrugged and gazed down at his hands. "I don't know."

"Where did they go?"

Fedor looked up with a defiant glare. "I don't know."

"You don't know much, do you?" Lev sat on the sofa across from him and sighed.

"What?"

"You." Lev pursed his lips. "I made a mistake. This is on me, mate."

Fedor furrowed his brow. "What do you mean?"

"Shouldn't have taken you out. You're not ready. You're not thinking straight."

"I know what I saw."

"Yeah?" Lev sniffed. "Well, apparently you don't."

Fedor looked up. "I swear to Creation I was being followed." He met Lev's gaze. "We were being followed. I promise you."

"So let me get this straight. We were being followed, but you don't know by who, what they wanted, or where they went?"

"No. But—"

"You see this puts me in an awkward position?"

Fedor bit down on his bottom lip. "Why won't you believe me?"

"I'll have to do these jobs myself, I think. You're becoming a liability, mate. I can't have you jumping at shadows. It's that shit you keep smoking. When I—"

"That's not fair."

Lev rose to his feet. "Let me tell you what's not fair, mate. It's not fair that I have to partner up with someone whose head's not in the game, someone who sees things, someone who, if they disappear for a second, I'm worried they've gone off to get mashed up in the Sail."

"But I haven't. That's you being paranoid, not me."

"It's about trust, mate. I need to trust you. And I can't at the minute." He squeezed the bridge of his nose, his voice turning soft. "I think you need to sit out until you're clean."

"I'm fine. I'm getting there."

"But you're not, are you?" Lev waved a hand towards him. "Look at you. You're sweating like it's the middle of summer."

"Because I've just been chasing after someone."

"Of course you did." Lev shook his head. "You just need to realise that shit's all in your head. The plez is fucking you up. You don't know what's real anymore. It's stopping you from seeing straight."

Fedor met his gaze. "What are you saying?"

"I'll help you out, mate. But until you're clean, I'm not doing jobs with you."

"Whatever."

Fedor rolled over in his bed again and kicked his sheets aside. He stared up into the darkness, his breaths and heartbeat racing.

Sleep had not come. Sleep would never come. At least not the type of sleep that helped him rest. No, the only sleep he found was haunted by those he had killed, or left in the shadow realm, sentenced to a state of lifeless non-death.

Sweat danced along his neck and back, stabbing him with shots of ice, cruel barbs that burrowed into his skin before melting and boiling around his muscles, sending involuntary spasms along his fingers and toes.

Lev's snores came like drills to his skull, the deep rumbling setting his bones on edge, and reverberating through his teeth, tightening the muscles in his jaw until the point he thought they might snap.

Tiny sparks fizzed along his arms and legs, like thousands of teeming insects crawling beneath his skin. The itching came in waves and he'd already scratched his forearms and shins until they bled.

He shot to his feet and took in a breath, his hand resting on the headboard as he tried to regain his centre, the world pitching around him.

He glanced across at Lev, his friend deep in sleep. A pang of jealousy gripped his chest. How could he sleep so easily? After everything they'd been through, why did he not wake up with nightmares and terrors? Perhaps it was because Lev hadn't killed. Lev hadn't done what he had.

Fedor ambled to the bathroom and stared at himself in the mirror, his cheeks gaunt, his eyes sunken, his lower lids like puffy bags, swollen and purple.

Turning away from himself, Fedor filled the washbasin with cold water and splashed his face, trying to shock himself more awake and to wash away some of the lingering sweat.

He scrubbed his face and neck and soon the water turned a murky grey.

He stared at himself again, wondering what had happened to the boy, what had happened to Fedor. Was he one of the lost Dienerin had mentioned, a slave to a creature in the shadow realm? If that did happen, would he even know?

After a while, he returned to his bedroom and dragged on his clothes from earlier that day, their armpits stinking of stale sweat. He crept out into the night.

The full moon shone down on him, the air cold and clear as he made his way through the upper city.

He moved without thought, the siren's call of the Rusty Sail whispering to him, tempting him to do what he knew he shouldn't. But he had to. He needed to sleep. He needed to stop his thoughts from running away into the pits of darkness.

His pulse quickened as he crossed the Kusten Road and followed the ramp down to the lower city's entrance.

He paused for a moment as a tall ship left the docks through the sea gate, its windows glowing with internal light. Perhaps it was the Golden Blade, returning to sea, set on a mission to recoup some of its losses from their blackmail. Cash he'd earned. Cash held back by Melita. Cash he would probably never get to see.

He cursed her. Who did she think she was? He earned that money doing a job. How dare she think she could keep back what he was owed? Like he was a child and she was a stern parent. No. This was betrayal. This was—the flicker of movement caught his eye.

He stopped, frozen mid-step.

He stared into the darkness, his ears pricking at the slightest sound. He scanned the shadows, searching for a shape, listening for movement.

But the night remained the same, the shadows still, the sea shifting in its endless tidal rhythm.

Perhaps Lev was right. Maybe plez had toyed with his mind, twisting his senses so the lines between dreams and reality blurred. It seemed the longer he stayed away from the drug, the worse it got, as though the rush of bliss kept his sanity from shattering into a thousand pieces.

Certain he was alone, he entered the lower city and passed through the tunnels. The arena stood empty, its lights dull, the air still thick with the stink of sweat and booze. A few drunkards lingered around the market square and a man lay slumped outside the Clam with his head in his hands.

Keeping close to the wall, Fedor drifted through the docks and stopped to watch the play of alchemical light reflecting off the sea gate as it closed.

He carried on through the commercial district, its shops closed, its streets and alleyways empty save for the occasional sailor staggering by in a strange loping gait.

Movement caught his eye again. A figure slipped into an alleyway.

Fedor ran.

He scrambled up onto a row of shops and scanned the streets behind him. He could just make out a broad-shouldered figure pressed against a wall, hooded, and dressed in patched grey.

Fedor took a zigzag route across the rooftops, leaping over an alleyway before slipping into a tunnel towards the warehouse district. He glanced behind him and confirmed his fears—he was being followed.

Fedor sprinted between storehouses, the silence punctuated by squawks of nearby chickens.

He staggered to a halt in front of a blocked-off door and drew his dagger. He spun and shifted into a ready stance. His fingers gripped the handle, the cold burning his palms.

He stood and waited, but no one came. He was certain he'd been followed...almost certain.

But what if Lev was right?

Arms shaking, he fumbled inside his coat and pulled out his vial of tears.

He splashed the blade's edge and drove the point into the door, tearing open a portal.

With a deep breath, he stepped through the rift, sealing it behind him.

Sounds and smells vanished and he allowed his body to adjust to the change.

He glanced back to see the warehouse district as little more than a net of white lines, the distances and forms difficult to sort in his mind.

He focused on a glowing mind lingering not too far away. It moved slowly, circling the area. This was no hallucination. He had been followed.

Fedor slipped his blade back into its sheath and wondered whether he could manipulate the mind from the shadow realm. Could he destroy it with his dagger?

But instead of finding out, he turned and ran, fearing not only his pursuer but the creatures Dienerin had hinted at.

He emerged from a fresh portal into the upper city and ran as fast as he could back to the den.

He charged inside, slamming the door behind him, and threw himself up the stairs.

Melita emerged from her room, holding her blade. Her shoulders relaxed and her relief turned to a frown. "What are you doing?"

"I was being followed."

She looked down the stairs. "What do you mean, followed?"

Fedor gestured behind him, his words struggling to come out through his panting. "I don't know..."

"You must have an idea?"

"Maybe it's the Crows." He leant against the wall to catch his breath, his thighs starting to burn. "Maybe it's one of Patrov's crew. I don't know." He hunched over and coughed. "It happened earlier. A few times. Someone's after me. I think it's an assassin."

Melita folded her arms and shook her head. "An assassin?"

"I think so. It looked like an assassin."

"And you're sure they were after you?"

Fedor nodded.

"And you led it back here?"

Fedor sucked in his bottom lip. "I managed to get away from him. I used the shadow realm. I wasn't followed."

"I thought you were done with that place?"

Fedor shrugged. "I needed...I needed to get away."

"But you're safe?"

"Yeah." He wiped sweat from his brow. "We're all good."

"That still doesn't explain what you're doing out at such a ridiculous time." She grabbed his cheeks with one hand and looked into his eyes. She turned his face this way and that, examining him. She pushed him back, her lip curling. "How could you?"

"I haven't done anything." He held out his hands. "You think if I got messed up, I'd be talking to you now?"

She looked him up and down. "But you were going to, weren't you?"

Fedor didn't move.

"You were on your way to the Sail and someone came after you."

Fedor looked down at his boots.

"I'm right, aren't I?"

Fedor remained silent.

"I asked you a question."

He shot her a glare. "I went for a walk. I couldn't sleep. I didn't do anything." He shoved past her and marched upstairs.

"This isn't finished, Fedor."

"I don't care. I'm going to bed. Just...just leave me alone."

Lev spent much of the next morning searching the den, returning to the library again and again, checking on shelves and behind books. He removed his cap and paced back and forth, his frustration growing. "This is ridiculous."

Hearing the others come in, he headed to the common room to meet them. He leant in the doorway and jabbed a thumb over his shoulder. "Anyone seen Soren's book?"

Onwyth and Vern exchanged a shrug, while Fedor sat on the sofa, staring at nothing.

"What book?" Melita asked.

"The book." He tugged his hair. "Soren's ledger. It's got a list of all his contracts—all the people he killed. It's gone."

"Gone? Gone where?"

Lev glared at her. "If I knew the answer, I wouldn't be bloody asking around, would I?" He turned his attention to Fedor. "You moved it?"

Fedor looked at him and blinked. "Huh?"

"The book. Soren's ledger. You moved it?"

"I haven't touched anything." Fedor held out his hands. "Where did you last have it?"

"Where it always is. I always put it back."

"Maybe it's fallen down the back of something."

"I've checked. I've checked everywhere. I'm not saying someone's taken it...but someone's taken it." He held Fedor's gaze. "You want to tell me something, mate?"

"I haven't moved the book."

Lev nodded. "Alright. Tell you what I'll do. I'll go out and grab some breakfast, and if the book happens to get returned, I'll say no more of it."

"Why are you looking at me like that?"

Lev rolled his eyes. "Mate, I'm trying to give you an out here."

Fedor shook his head. "I haven't moved the book."

"Maybe you forgot you moved it."

"I haven't moved it." Fedor folded his arms and huffed. "How many times?"

Lev held up his hands. "Alright, alright. Settle down, mate."

"I'll settle down when you stop accusing me of stuff."

"Mate, no one's accusing you of anything. If you claim you haven't moved the book, I believe you. All I know is that it's gone and I haven't moved it either."

"Where have you looked?" Onwyth asked.

Lev shrugged. "Where do you think? Where it's kept. Where it should be."

"But it's not there now?"

"No. For fuck's sake. It's not there. Someone's moved it." He eyed Fedor again. "I reckon it might be someone who's pissed off with us for holding back his cash."

Fedor scowled. "I haven't moved the fucking book."

"Maybe he didn't move it," Onwyth said. "You know with these things, whenever you lose anything, it's always in the last place you look."

Lev sighed. "I'm trying to find a book that's worth a lot of money to us and you're making bloody jokes?"

"What?" Onwyth threw her hands up. "It's true."

Vern chuckled.

Lev turned to him. "And you can wipe that fucking grin off your face. This affects us all."

Vern's smile dropped.

"Alright," Onwyth said. "Name one thing you've found that wasn't in the last place you checked?"

"Onwyth." Lev squeezed his eyes shut. "Do you ever think before you open that mouth of yours?"

She leant back in her seat and raised her chin, her mouth clamped shut.

Lev looked at the others. "So none of you have seen it? None of you have moved it? It's just disappeared into thin air?"

"No." Fedor sat up. "It can't have gone far. Do you want me to help you look?"

"Yeah, right, mate. Let me guess. My back's turned and suddenly, oh look, Fedor's found it. What a hero." Lev shook his head. "I gave you that chance and you blew me off." He loomed over Fedor. "I know you've moved it. It's sad really. What is it? The cash? Or is it the fact you're pissed off because we're trying to help you?"

Fedor leant forward and pointed at Lev. "If you think I've taken the book, you're wrong. You think you're so clever, that you know everything, Lev, but you don't. You've got an idea and you're just running with it. Well, you're wrong."

"Yeah? Where is it then? Because I haven't moved it."

"Neither have I." Fedor rubbed his head then looked up at Lev. "Wait. Maybe Dienerin has moved it for some reason."

"You should speak to her," Melita said. "Before Lev starts accusing everyone else."

"I will," Fedor said.

Lev gestured to the door. "Go on, then. What are you waiting for?"

Fedor got to his feet slowly and wobbled. "I don't actually know where she is."

"Well, maybe you need a system to summon her. Honestly, mate."

Fedor glared at him. "You can be a right prick sometimes."

"You starting? Or you going to find that stinking wyvern?"

"I'll see if I can find her."

"Good. And then you can bring that bloody book back."

When Fedor left, Melita turned to Lev. "You shouldn't speak to him like that. We're supposed to have each other's backs."

Lev smirked. "He needs to bring that book back."

"I don't think he took it."

"Then who took it? These things don't just disappear on their own. It's either him or the wyvern. Unless you've nabbed it for some reason."

"I haven't. If Fedor took it, I'm sure he would have said."

Lev looked back over his shoulder towards the door. "I don't know what to think of him anymore."

"He's your best friend. Be there for him."

"A best friend who's messing with my business." Lev flipped his cap back onto his head. "He needs to sort himself out. I need to trust him and he's jumping at shadows."

"What's that got to do with your book?" Onwyth asked.

"He's paranoid. He's not thinking right. That plez is messing with his head."

"And we'll help him get off it," Melita said.

"Yeah. I know." He sank onto the sofa and placed his head in his hands. "He slipped off yesterday, saying someone was following him."

"In the night?"

"Nah, during the day. He—"

"He came back in really late. I heard him come running in. He said someone was after him."

Lev looked up. "He went out? Was he—"

Melita shook her head. "I don't think so, but something definitely spooked him."

"This is what I'm talking about. He's jumping at shadows. Who knows what he's thinking?"

"I don't think he moved your book, though. Maybe take another look around. I'm sure it will turn up."

Lev's jaw set. "Yeah. I'm sure it will."

Fedor followed the stairs down to the antique shop on the den's ground floor. Thin strips of sunlight poked through the shutters, highlighting dust motes as they danced in the air. "Dienerin? You about?" He turned on the light and checked around for the ledger. "Where are you?"

He turned to the stairs and stopped at the sound of flapping wings.

Dienerin flew past him and landed on the counter. She bowed her head and spread her wings. "Yes, Fedor, Fedor, master?"

"Have you seen Soren's book?"

"Which book?"

"His ledger. The one where he noted his contracts."

"Is it not where it always is?"

"No."

"Then I do not know. Perhaps ask Lev. I often see him looking at the book. Perhaps he has moved it."

"No. He's the one looking for it."

"Then you should ask Melita. She might know where to find it. I often see her searching in different rooms for things."

"No. He's already asked the others."

"How about Onwyth?"

"Yes. She's one of the others I'm referring to."

"Vern?"

Fedor let out a long sigh. "So you've not seen it?"

"I have seen it."

"You have?"

"That is correct."

"Have you seen it in the past day or so?"

"I have not."

"Right, will you let me know if you do?"

"Yes, Fedor, Fedor, master."

Fedor moved back towards the stairs and stopped. "Have you seen any-one following me?"

"No. You have not asked me to come with you. Would you like me to come with you?"

"Maybe. I'm worried. I think I'm being followed."

"Is it another wyvern?"

"No. I think...I think it's an assassin."

"That would make sense."

Fedor blinked. "What do you mean?"

"I warned you. I warned you about the guild."

"What guild? You never told me about a guild."

"Yes, I did. I was very clear."

"If you were so clear, how come I'm asking you about it now?"

"Perhaps your mind is addled from your trips to that room in the Rusty Sail where you smoke drugs."

Fedor gritted his teeth and his fists grew tight. "What guild?"

"The guild."

"It must be a guild of something."

"It is the assassins' guild, Fedor, Fedor, master."

"Mate. Mate."

A pair of hands shook Fedor's shoulders, tearing him away from the first hints of true sleep he'd had in a long while. Bleary eyed, he gazed up at Lev. He mumbled something and rolled back onto his side, dragging his blanket around him.

"Mate. Wake up."

"Leave me alone."

"You need to get up. It's important."

"No."

Lev ripped the sheet away and tossed it to the floor. "Don't make me get water. I really can't be arsed arguing with you. You need to get up."

Fedor glared at him. "What do you want?"

"Lita's called a meeting downstairs."

"So?"

"We're waiting for you."

"What? So you can all tell me how crap I am and how I'm a burden and how I'm letting everyone down? Don't think I don't know what—"

"Enough." Lev raised a hand. "Honestly, mate. Just get your head out of your arse for a second. There's more going on than your shit."

Fedor licked his parched lips and nodded. "Right." He rose to his feet, his knees like jelly, and stomped across the hallway towards the privy.

"Where are you going?"

"For a piss," Fedor snapped. "If that's allowed. Or is Melita planning on taking that away from me too?"

"Do what you need to, mate. Just...just don't take all bloody day about it."

Fedor entered the bathroom, a sinking feeling settling in the pit of his stomach, and locked the door. He was sick of the others getting at him. What business was it of theirs what he did or didn't do in his own time? Melita had gone too far and she was starting to turn the others against him. He sank on-to the toilet and held his head in his hands. How could he find a way through this?

"Mate?" Lev knocked at the door. "You still in there?"

"Yes. For fuck's sake." Fedor looked up and sneered. "I'm taking a shit if that's alright with you?"

"Just checking up. The others are waiting."

"Yeah? Well, let them wait."

"Don't be a dick."

"I'm not being a dick. You're the one who's being a dick."

Lev's footsteps moved away from the door.

Fedor could just make out his mumbling.

When he finished, he splashed water on his face, and joined Lev in the hallway.

"You alright?"

"I'm fine."

"I'm not falling out with you, mate. I'm on your side, remember. I've got your back."

"You've got a funny way of showing it sometimes."

Lev shoved Fedor against the wall and pressed hard against his chest with a forearm. "Don't you ever doubt my loyalty. When I say I've got your back, I've got your back. You need to trust me."

"And you need to trust me. I didn't move your book."

Lev released Fedor and nodded. "Alright. I believe you. And I'm sorry I accused you. I just don't like it when important shit goes missing and I don't know where it's gone."

"Me neither. But you can't—"

"Mate. Just drop it, yeah. I said I believe you. Let's just see what this thing's about."

Fedor nodded. "I'm sorry."

Lev patted Fedor's shoulder. "Don't worry about it. Let's go see the others."

Fedor followed Lev down to the common room to find Melita waiting near the door. Onwyth and Vern sat on the nearest sofa.

"Sit," Melita said.

Fedor glanced awkwardly at everyone, before taking a seat next to Lev.

"It seems this Patrov issue has come back to bite us," Melita said with a heavy sigh. "I don't know what's happening yet. Brak is keeping quiet. But I think we are in trouble."

"Shit." Lev said.

Melita began to pace. "But I think we can nip this in the bud before it becomes too much of a problem for us."

Fedor threw his head back and laughed. "I said that whole Pat thing was a bad idea. I said it—"

"We need a plan," Melita snapped, cutting Fedor off. "If you've got nothing valuable to add, you know where the door is."

Fedor nodded. "Sorry."

"As far as I can tell, we've got two issues. Patrov is back, trying to reclaim his turf. Which in turn means Myker must know."

"You're forgetting about the third one," Fedor said.

Melita frowned. "What third one?"

"He's talking about the assassin following him," Lev said.

Melita waved a dismissive hand. "Oh, that."

Fedor shook his head. "What do you mean by that? An assassin was following me. It's only because I got into the shadow realm that I escaped. Dienerin thinks it's the guild coming after us, probably because of this Patrov stuff."

Melita and Lev exchanged looks.

"Dienerin told you that?" Melita asked.

"Yeah."

"Did you ask her about the ledger?" Lev asked.

"She hasn't seen it."

Melita glared at Lev. "We can deal with that later. What did she say about this guild?"

"She said we'd been reported to the guild. I don't know."

"Fuck."

"What is it?" Vern asked.

Melita turned to him. "If Fedor's saying what I think he's saying"—she shook her head—"we might be dealing with the Welttor Assassins' Guild."

"I've heard of them," Onwyth said. "Didn't think they were real, though. You sure it's right?" She met Fedor's gaze. "And now they're after you?"

He held out his hands. "I think he's after all of us. It wasn't just me who worked this thing out with Patrov, remember?"

Melita took in a breath and she rubbed her forehead. "So we have three problems to deal with."

Lev cleared his throat. "Actually, make that four."

Melita's frown deepened. "What is it?"

"Soren's book. It's gone. I can't find it. I've searched this place up and down. And the wyvern hasn't seen it either."

"I've already said we can deal with that another time. It's just a book."

"No. It's not just any old book. You don't understand."

"Then make me understand."

"That book's where I'm getting all my jobs. That's our revenue, that is. If we're not doing those blackmail jobs, we've got nothing coming in."

"Perhaps we could take on some real jobs," Onwyth said. "Make some real money."

"No." Fedor said. "We're not doing that. We're supposed to be thieves, not killers."

"You can't stop me," Onwyth said. "Maybe we'll take on our own jobs. We don't need you and we don't need that stinking wyvern stinking the place up."

"She doesn't stink," Fedor said.

"Yeah? Well, we don't need her. We've got it all planned out. Me and Vern have been training."

"Training?" Fedor shook his head. "Do you know what you'll have to do? You ever slid a blade into someone? You ever had to get rid of a body?" He pursed his lips. "We're not doing it."

"You don't get to tell me what to do, Mister Plez-Face. We're doing it and you don't get a say."

Melita raised a hand. "That's enough."

"So what are we going to do?" Lev asked.

"That's what I'm getting to. I'll keep trying with Brak, see what I can find out about the Crows. But in the meantime, I think you and me should pay Patrov a visit, find out what he's doing here. We can scare him if we need to."

Lev nodded.

"Onwyth, you take Vern and ask around about Pat's crew. See if you can find out whether Myker's put out a hit on any of us."

"Will do." She leant forward and raised a finger. "You know, a lot of this can go away if we just take Pat out."

"We're not killers," Fedor said.

Onwyth laughed. "Maybe you can push him into that shadow realm, or wherever. Either way, we need to deal with him."

"Let's just see what he wants first," Melita said. "Maybe if he realises we know he's back, we can apply the right pressure and maybe he'll leave."

"Yeah," Lev said. "And if you can get back the cash we gave him to do one, even better."

Melita nodded. "Right. Let's just prioritise what I said. Any questions?"

Fedor shifted in his seat. "What about me?"

"Just try not to get under our feet."

"But I want to help."

"The only way you can help is to keep out of our way."

"That's not fair."

Melita stepped towards him and pointed a finger at him. "Don't you fucking start. You're hanging by a thread as it is. Don't give me a reason." She patted her blade's handle. "Because I swear to Creation, I won't hesitate to use this."

Fedor swallowed.

IV. Myker

Fedor let out a trembling breath and stared up at the common room ceiling. He traced the route of a spider's web, no more than a thin shadow against the white paint. The pull of plez occupied his thoughts. And he couldn't help thinking of his mind like that web—threads stretching in all directions, taut and ready to snap at the slightest pressure—pressure from the drugs, pressure from his crew, and pressure from that uncanny whispering he associated with the blade.

He feared something had to give. And once it did, everything else would unravel. How was he going to get out of this?

Melita hated him. Lev was growing increasingly frustrated with him. And Onwyth sneered at him every time he caught her from the corner of his eye. He needed to regain their trust, but perhaps they would never see him in the same light again. He could never go back to how things were before. How could they? Everything was different now.

He didn't want to go back to the Sail, but what choice did he have? He should have listened to Lev, to Melita. But they didn't understand. They didn't know how the drugs helped with the other thoughts. The thoughts of Soren in his final moments, his flesh turning to ash. The thoughts of Garrett's skull smashing under the weight of the ravenglass orb. The thoughts of sentencing Xandru to an eternity of non-death.

They dragged him along a road of despair, pulling him deeper into guilt and helplessness. The worse he felt, the more he pushed those who cared about him away. And, yet, he couldn't stop.

His will was no longer his own and he hated the world for it—perhaps even more than he hated himself.

All he wanted was a quiet life, a life with friends and love, a life without murder, a life without drugs. But the world, it seemed, had other ideas.

A tear ran down his cheek and he wiped his eyes. He scrambled from the sofa and reached into his coat. He took out his vial of tears and allowed the drops to fall inside, bringing its contents back up to half-full.

He held the vial up to the light and curled his lip. Maybe he should enter the shadow realm and stay there. He should let one of those creatures take him. "Fuck."

"Shit me, mate." Lev entered and stood near the doorway, ready to leave in his cap and coat. "What's wrong now?"

Fedor wiped his eyes and looked across at him. "Nothing. I'm fine."

"We need to see Pat."

"Right. I guess I'll see you later, then." He squeezed his eyes shut and lay back down on the sofa. He opened one eye when Melita came in.

She eyed him and frowned. "I've changed my mind."

Fedor frowned at her. "About what?"

"About you staying here." She shook her head. "You're coming with us."

"What happened to me not being on jobs?"

"As I've said, I've changed my mind. You can come along. But you keep silent."

"Why?"

"Because I'm not having you staying here alone. Look at you. We left for a few minutes and you're already twitching."

Lev stood at her side. "She's right, mate. This is the best thing for you. We'll keep you busy. Keep you distracted. If your mind's on the job, it won't be on...well, you know."

"Oh, I get it." Fedor glared at them both. "You don't think I can be trusted."

"You can't," Melita said flatly. "We're all going to see Patrov and get this stuff sorted."

Fedor sniffed. "What happened to me being a liability?"

"You can still be useful if you stand there and try to look intimidating. Make sure you bring that blade of yours."

"I'm not using it."

"Just bring it," she snapped. "No arguments."

Fedor sighed and rose to his feet. "Fine." He dragged on his coat. "Lead the way."

Melita blocked the door with an arm and leant close to him. "And if you fuck this up, you're done. Stay focused. Do as your told. And don't even think about slipping off to the Sail."

Her words came like a punch to the gut. "I didn't. I won't."

She pursed her lips. "Good. Make sure you don't."

Fedor flipped up his hood and stepped out into the cold as Melita locked up the den behind them. A chill wind howled around Kathryn Square, sending fallen leaves in swirls. Was he no better than one of those leaves? A husk picked up by external forces with no will of his own.

He wanted to sleep. He needed to sleep. But Melita wanted him to join them, not to participate, but to stand there as little more than a tailor's dummy.

His gaze drifted to Melita and Lev speaking to each other in hushed tones, occasionally looking back at him and signalling for him to keep up.

He patted his blade, making sure it was in easy reach. They could gossip and conspire all they wanted. It made no difference. If they were plotting against him, he would know and he would act first, taking them by surprise before they had a chance to hurt him.

Keeping at least ten paces behind, he followed them along the street towards the Kusten Road, keeping his head dipped against the cold.

He stopped at the sight of a figure watching him from an alleyway.

Without thinking, he ran towards the figure and drew his dagger. He stopped at the alleyway's entrance, taking in the shadows and silence, primed for any hint of sound or movement.

"What's wrong with you?" Melita asked. "Come on. We've got a job to do, remember?"

"But we're being followed."

Lev rolled his eyes. "It's all in your head, mate."

A young man dressed in black dropped down from the rooftop and three more appeared from across the street and surrounded the trio.

"Not you lot again," Lev said. "We've already been through this with your boss."

The tallest lad gripped a pair of knives and a crow feather hung from his ear. "We know."

Lev rummaged in his pocket and pulled out Myker's feather token. "Does this mean anything to you lot? Aren't we supposed to be under your protection or something?"

"I doubt it." The taller lad edged forward, his eyes narrowing. "The boss wants to see you."

Lev stiffened. "As in Myker?"

"Who else?"

"I don't know how a gaggle of Crows organises things."

The taller lad grinned. "It's a murder of Crows. Maybe you'd like to find out what that means."

"Wait," Melita said. "When does he need to see us?"

The lad turned to her. "You in charge?"

"Yes."

He inclined his head. "I've seen you knocking about with Brak. You're his bird, ain't you?"

"I'm no one's bird, as you put it. When does he need to see us?"

"Yesterday. He said if you don't come, you're dead meat. Do you understand what I'm saying? Do you understand what that means?"

"I do."

Something jabbed against Fedor's back.

"And don't you try anything, you fucking junky."

Fedor spun, knocking the lad back, and drew his dagger. "Who's first?"

Melita placed a hand on Fedor's wrist and signalled for him to stop. "Let's not have any trouble."

Fedor glared at the lad he'd knocked over. "You call me a junky again and I'll cut off your tiny balls. How's that sound, you little fucker?"

"Who you calling a little fucker?" the taller lad asked, squaring up to Fedor.

"Enough," Melita said, shoving between them. "Let's not escalate this any more than we need to. We have a misunderstanding with Myker that obviously needs sorting."

The tall lad took a step back and nodded. "You'd better go see him, then."

"We will go and see your boss now," Melita said.

"You're damn fucking right you will."

Melita entered Myker's office first with Lev and Fedor trailing close behind. Myker's office was smaller than she expected, with no windows and a large desk filling much of the space. When she entered, she passed a pair of lads standing guard outside the door, and noticed another pair waiting inside.

Brak stood to Myker's right, staring into the distance. He did not meet Melita's eyes.

Myker looked up from his papers and slammed a fist on the desk. He cast his gaze slowly between Melita, Lev, and Fedor, letting the silence hang for several seconds before speaking. "You know why you're here, don't you?"

"We do." Melita fingered the coin around her neck. "And we were just on our way to intercept him when your lads brought us here."

Myker smirked. "Really?"

"It's true," Lev said. "Honest word. If your lads hadn't jumped us, we'd probably be there right now dealing with him."

"How convenient." Myker ran a hand down his beard and pointed to Melita. "Answer me this—how is a dead man still alive?"

"I don't know," Melita said. "I honestly thought he was."

"You thought he was, huh?"

Lev removed his cap and stepped forward. "Mate—"

"I'm not your fucking mate, you piece of shit." He jabbed a finger towards Lev and Fedor. "I hired you to do a job. I had assurances from a wyvern that the contract was complete." He leant back in his seat, his gaze burrowing into Lev. "You ripped me off."

"Honestly, it wasn't like that." Lev wrung his cap. "You see, we reached an agreement with Pat. We had our own deal going on, so he's the one who ripped us off. And, trust me, we're as pissed off as you are, but really, when you think about it, it's Pat you've got the problem with. He's the one—"

"I do have a problem with him, you little arsehole." Myker bared his teeth. "That's why I hired you."

Lev glanced down at the floor. "I know."

"And now I've got a problem with you lot, it seems." Myker leant back in his chair and studied the three of them, his teeth grinding. "Really, I should kill you now. I should gut all three of you and feed you to the fucking birds."

"We're here to make it right," Melita said.

Myker grinned. "You're here because I had my lads drag you here."

Melita raised her chin, all the while trying to catch Brak's eye. "We will do anything you need us to."

"Really?"

"Yes. Really."

"And you expect me to trust you when I paid you for a fucking job and you couldn't deliver?"

"I know. But we're here now."

"That's not to mention trying to rip me off." Myker's nose wrinkled and he whispered something to Brak.

"Would you like us to kill Patrov?"

"Would I like you to kill Patrov?" He drummed his fingers on the table. "Would I like you to kill Patrov? Hmm...let me think." He turned to Brak. "She wants to know if we want them to kill Patrov."

Brak did not respond, his gaze remaining fixed on a point in the middle-distance.

Myker turned back to Melita. "You're damn right I want you to kill Patrov." He slammed his hand down again. "That's what I fucking paid for in the first place."

"There must have been some misunderstanding. Some miscommunication—"

"Don't feed me shit. Your crew tried to pull a fast one and now you're going to pay."

"We'll get the job done, as promised."

"Good." Myker nodded and steepled his fingers. "That's a good start. But we've also got a little issue of handing over thirty thousand krones for a job than never got done."

"We can return the fee," Melita said.

Lev went to protest, but Melita shot him a glare.

"Returning the fee is a good start."

"I'll make sure we get it to you as soon as we can."

"And then there's a fee for me not killing you. Let's call that another ten thousand."

Lev whistled. "Fuck me, forty grand?"

Melita took in a breath. "We can do that."

Myker smiled. "I think you're misunderstanding me here." He pointed at each of them in turn. "I count three of you. That's ten grand each. Plus, the thirty you already owe me." His smile widened. "And because I'm a man of my word because, unlike you lot I stick to my agreements, I'm going to let off the fifteen you'd normally owe." He held out his hands. "Can't say fairer than that, can I?"

Melita ran through the numbers in her head. "We don't have—"

"I don't care what you do or don't have. You fucked me and I'm giving you the chance to make it right."

Melita lowered her gaze. "And we appreciate that. Thank you."

"Sixty grand and Pat dead."

"But—"

"You've got three days. Otherwise, you're all dead meat."

Melita stepped from the Crows' headquarters and marched into the lower city. She did not look back.

"That went well," Lev said.

Melita stopped and turned to Lev and Fedor, her heart racing, her hands trembling. "How the fuck are we going to find sixty grand in three days?"

Fedor shrugged a shoulder. "Erm...maybe we could up the price on the blackmail jobs."

Lev shook his head. "Mate, mate, mate. Soren's book. It's gone, remember?"

Fedor frowned. "So?"

"So until that book turns up, we've got no new leads, no new targets." He breathed a sigh and blinked up at the tunnel's ceiling. "Until that turns up, we're back to where we were."

"Shit."

Lev raised a finger. "You need to talk to that stinking wyvern of yours."

"For what? I've already asked her. She doesn't know where it is."

"Tell her you're open for contracts again. Tell her you'll take on as many as she can get."

Fedor shook his head. "No. I'm not doing that."

Melita grabbed Fedor's collar and pulled her dagger. "Ask her."

"Let go of me." He twisted away from her grip. "We're not doing any assassin jobs."

"You don't actually need to do it." She rolled her eyes. "We can run it as another con." She looked down at her blade. "I'll do it myself if that's what it takes."

"Let's try to calm down a bit. Let's think this through." Lev stood between them. "Lita's right. Think about it. We don't need to do the jobs. We just take the deposits."

"Rip more people off, you mean?"

"Yeah. Why not?"

"Why not? Why not?" Fedor pointed back towards the Crows' headquarters, his eyes widening. "This is why we're in this mess. We can't keep ripping people off like that and expect it not to come back and bite us. We've played our hand too many times and I'm sick of having to watch my back."

"I thought that's what we did, mate. We rip people off, people who deserve it, and we take home the cash. If that means watching our backs a bit more, so be it. I'm happy to rake in the coin."

Melita pointed her blade at Fedor and lowered her voice. "You need to speak to Dienerin. You need to get us some jobs."

"Fine." He raised a finger. "But I'm not killing anyone."

"See?" Melita sheathed her dagger. "That wasn't so difficult, was it?"

Fedor pouted. "It's not like you're giving me a choice."

"We've all got choices, Fedor." She took a step towards him. "I've chosen to keep you on our crew when you're the one causing us the most grief. Maybe if you just did the job as you were asked in the first place, we wouldn't be in this mess."

"I'm a thief, not—"

"Keep telling yourself that." She narrowed her eyes. "But we all know it's bullshit. You just need to embrace who you are. You need to accept what you've done. There's no going back. The line has been crossed."

Fedor grimaced. "You're not putting this on me."

"I'm not. It's on all of us. And we're going to deal with it." She carried on walking, the carved tunnels blurring by.

"What should we do about seeing Pat?" Lev asked, matching her pace.

"I'm too rattled to think about that right now."

"We need to figure something, boss."

"I know." She took in the smells of grain and animals as they passed the warehouse district. "I just need to figure a few things out."

"Who knows? We might be lucky for once."

She turned to him. "Lucky? Lucky, how?"

"Pat might do the work for us."

Melita frowned. "What do you mean?"

"Think about it. He knows it was Myker who hired us. Maybe he's got his own things in motion. If he takes out Myker, we're in the clear."

"Yeah," Fedor said. "We should keep our heads down until Patrov deals with it."

Melita shook her head. "No. If Pat takes out Myker, that's great. Maybe we will be lucky. But we can't rely on that." She shrugged a shoulder. "All I know is we need to find sixty grand in three days."

"What about the cash from the other jobs?" Fedor asked. "What's in the coffers?"

Melita considered this for several seconds. "We've got about ten grand as backup."

"That's a start," Lev said.

"But we still need another fifty."

"Fifty is better than sixty. See?" Lev grinned. "Our lucky streak's just beginning."

Melita laughed. "Real fucking lucky."

"Do you think things will ever get easier for us?" Fedor asked.

Lev patted Fedor's shoulder. "Where would the fun be in that?"

Fedor stopped and glared at him. "You think this is fun?"

"You've got to admit there's something a bit fun about it."

"Well, I'm not having fun. I haven't had fun for a long time."

"So what do you suggest?" Melita asked. "What's your great plan to get us out of this mess? At least Lev's trying to keep our spirits up. You're just dragging us down."

Fedor glanced behind him. "I think we should leave the city. We should run. We get set up somewhere else, somewhere far away, where Pat and Myker and talk of assassins is a distant memory."

Melita sniffed. "And you think it's that easy?"

"We've got ten grand. That's way more than we had in the past. We can go down south, maybe hide out in one of the smaller villages, or leave Wiete altogether. We can start something new, something legit."

"No," Melita said. "We've worked too hard to throw it all away now. We've got a good place and real money coming in for the first time ever. We can figure this out. We can get through this. We always do."

"And what if we don't?"

"That's not an option."

"Of course, it's an option. And if we're being honest with ourselves, it's the most likely option. We've—"

"No. We're going to get through this and you're going to do as I say. Ask Dienerin to get more jobs, while the rest of us work out another way through this."

"Fine."

"I don't know if this is the best thing," Lev said.

"And you're not the boss," Melita snapped.

"You're right." Lev raised his hands and made a right onto the docks. "But as far as I can tell, none of the options are good."

"Unless you've got something in mind, we're going with what I said."

"I don't know, boss. As far as I can tell, our best option in all of this is to take out Myker. He needs to go. Pat is Pat and we can deal with him as and when. But Myker's put us in a bit of an awkward position."

"That's an understatement," Melita said. "I'd say it's more than an awkward position."

"Alright. He's backed us into a corner and that can't stand." He shook his head. "As much as it pains me to say it, the fucker needs to go. We need to take him out."

"We're not killing Myker," Fedor said.

"You want to say that any louder, mate? There's probably a couple of ships past the sea gate that might not have heard."

Fedor looked at the ground. "Sorry."

"You're apologising a lot at the moment," Melita said, coming to a stop. She ran a hand through her hair and closed her eyes for several seconds. When she opened them, she found Lev and Fedor looking at her expectantly. "It's not just Myker we'll need to deal with, is it?"

Lev glared at her. "You mean because of your boyfriend?"

"I don't just mean him, I mean—"

"You should get him to put a word in for us."

"It's got nothing to do with Brak. He's got a big crew. We might be able to get in to do the job, if we're lucky. But getting out is another story."

Fedor sighed. "So I guess that just leaves us doing what he wants?"

Melita nodded and carried on towards the market. "Whatever happens, we need to work it as if that's what we're doing. And if something else comes up in the meantime..."

"But fifty grand," Lev said. "That's a lot of bloody money."

"We'll work it out."

"Maybe we could give him Fedor? That'd save us ten grand right there."

Fedor shoved him. "Fuck you."

"Mate, come on." Lev raised his hands and laughed. "It was a joke. Fuck me. Can't you take a joke anymore?"

"It didn't sound like a joke."

Lev groaned. "You need to lighten up, mate."

Melita went to say something but thought better of it—she had more important things to worry about.

Onwyth threw another knife. It spun through the air, its point landing in the centre of the dummy's chest.

Vern followed it up with a blow dart, its tip lodging into the dummy's neck.

Onwyth turned to him and grinned. "We're getting good at this." She gestured to the dart. "There's no way anyone would survive that." She moved towards the dummy, pulled out her knives, and plucked out Vern's dart.

"I bet we could take out a boar with these dead easy."

"I was thinking we should get the word out about what we do."

"What about Fedor and the wyvern? Ain't that gonna cause issues?"

"Screw that scaly bitch. And screw Fedor. We'll do our thing. They can do theirs." She handed the dart back to Vern. "I was thinking we start off small. Maybe charge ten grand at the beginning. We can get some jobs under our belt and get our names known. And then we can raise the price and really start bringing in the money."

"What about the others? What will they say?"

Onwyth shrugged. "They'll get a cut. But I'm sick of waiting around for Lev's blackmail jobs to come through, or some burglar job falling into our laps. We can do this."

Vern nodded. "Yeah. We can."

Fedor entered the den behind Lev and watched him go upstairs.

When they were alone, Melita turned to him. "You need to do what I said."

"About what?"

"About Dienerin. Get some jobs booked. We need cash."

"But—"

"No arguments. This needs doing." She moved towards him. Her eyes narrowed. "Are we going to have a problem here?"

"No...I'll sort it."

"Now."

"Now." He nodded. "I'll do it."

"Good." She pointed at him. "I don't know what's going on in that head of yours, but I need you sharp. Lev was messing with you back there. You know how he is."

"It didn't sound like he was messing."

"Well, he was, and you should know that."

"Yeah? Well, maybe if you all hadn't been ganging up on me, I wouldn't think like that."

"No one's ganging up on you. We just want you off that shit. We need to be able to rely on you."

"You can."

Melita raised her chin. "Good. In that case, speak to Dienerin."

"I will." He watched her leave, hating the way everyone spoke to him. Maybe Lev had been joking, or maybe he hadn't. Either way he was sick of being disrespected by his own crew.

He called out for Dienerin and wandered aimlessly around the shop, picking up a bowl, watching the play of light around its rim.

At the sound of wingbeats, he placed the bowl down.

Dienerin glided past him and landed on the counter. She spread her wings flat, bowing her head. "Yes, Fedor, Fedor, master."

"I want you to start accepting contracts again. As many as you can."

The wyvern looked up at him and tilted her head slightly. "No."

Fedor blinked. "I thought you were supposed to follow orders."

"There will be no contracts."

"Why not?"

"I'm sorry, Fedor, Fedor, master. Until the guild has completed their investigation, there will be no contracts."

"I don't understand. Just do your job. We need those contracts."

"When you agree to a contract, the charter states you must complete said contract. That is the code. And it is believed you have broken the code."

"What code? No one told me about a code."

"The guild is investigating. It is believed you have broken the code."

"Honestly, I haven't. It's all a misunderstanding."

"When the investigation is complete and the guild finds no wrongdoing has occurred, I will be able to agree to contracts on your behalf."

"Right. And until then?"

"There is nothing I can do to help you, Fedor, Fedor, master."

Fedor trudged up the stairs to the common room and slumped on the sofa across from Onwyth and Vern.

"What's that face for?" Onwyth asked.

"Nothing," Fedor said. "I'm fine."

"You don't look fine. If anything, you look the opposite of fine."

"I said, I'm fine. Why does everyone keep getting at me?"

Onwyth smirked. "You sound like a stroppy ten-year-old. What happened?"

"Nothing happened. And I'm not being stroppy."

"I bet something did happen." She turned to Vern. "What do you reckon?"

"I dunno. He's always moaning."

Fedor glared at them both. "That's not true."

"He's sometimes defensive too," Onwyth said. She studied Fedor and grinned.

"What?" Fedor asked.

"Nothing."

"No, what? Spit it out."

"I think I know why you keep going round with that face."

Fedor stared at her.

"I think you've smelt your own farts."

"Piss off, Onwyth."

Vern laughed. "Yeah. I bet he keeps farting and it goes right up his nose." He reached up to his throat pretending to gag.

Onwyth joined in the laughter. "Yeah. It goes right up his nose and stinks so bad. He says he's been on plez, but it's just farts. That's what's making his face funny and eyes all purple." She pointed at Fedor, tears streaming down her cheeks. "You keep sniffing them and you've got addicted. You're a fart addict, admit it."

"Fart addict!" Vern cried out with laughter. "Do you think we can heal him? Maybe we could send him to the doctors and they can pump all the farts out of him."

Fedor pouted. "Vern, has anyone told you to piss off recently?"

"Maybe. Can't hear through all the farts."

Onwyth roared and slapped Vern's back. "Yeah. I bet when he has a piss, he does more farts."

"Pathetic," Fedor muttered. "So fucking childish."

"What's so funny?" Melita asked, entering the common room with Lev.

Onwyth waved her away. "It's just Fedor's too funny."

"Really?" She folded her arms and glared down at him. "While you're here telling jokes, we're trying to think of a way out of this Myker mess."

Fedor sat up. "What did I do?" He pointed to Onwyth. "She's the one—"

"Do I look like I care?" She fixed his gaze. "Did you speak to Dienerin?"

"Yes."

"Good. Let's—"

"No. It's not good. She's not getting any more contracts for us."

Melita frowned. "Why not?"

"She said we broke some code. The assassins' guild is investigating."

"I don't like the sound of that," Lev said. "Maybe we should do what Fedor said, and do one."

"Or, maybe we just complete the original job as agreed," Melita said. "If the contract is complete, there's nothing to investigate."

Lev shifted his weight. "You think they know about the blackmail? I bet that's not going to sit well with them."

"How could they?" Melita shook her head. "I think all this is Myker's doing. He's the one who reported us."

"You reckon?" Lev asked.

"It's the only thing that makes sense."

"I don't know," Fedor said. "It could have been Patrov. Maybe he let them know so he could get back here without us giving him trouble."

Melita nodded. "It doesn't really matter who it was. What matters is we need to work out the best way through this."

"What does that mean for us?" Onwyth asked.

"I don't know. If the assassins' guild is onto us, there's a good chance that it won't matter whether we complete the job or not."

"Sounds to me like we're being set up," Lev said.

"Possibly. Myker gets everything. Pat's dead. Plus, he gets sixty grand. And then we're out of the picture too."

"Shit," Fedor said.

"Shit. Indeed, mate. I think we should do one. We've had a good run here, but we can't stick around with this hanging over us."

"I still think we can work it out," Melita said.

"You really think we can outrun the assassins' guild?" Lev shook his head. "Nah. We're screwed whichever way this goes. Even if everything does work out, I can't see us raising sixty grand in three days."

"Fifty," Melita said.

Onwyth cleared her throat. "Actually, we might be able to help."

Melita inclined her head. "Oh?"

"I might have put the word out that we're doing assassin jobs."

"When you say we, who do you mean?"

"Me and Vern."

Melita gave a slow nod. "And, when were you planning to tell me about this?"

"We wanted to make sure it worked first," Vern said.

"Fine. Do you think you can get two jobs in the next few days?"

"Why two?"

"So we can get sixty grand."

Onwyth exchanged a look with Vern. "But we're only charging ten."

"But our price is thirty."

"No. That's guild prices for a master." Onwyth shrugged. "We figured we'd build our reputation a bit. Do a few jobs and then we can raise prices once word gets around."

Melita sighed. "If that's what you want to do, I'm not going to stand in your way, but that still doesn't help us."

"So what's our next step, boss?" Lev asked.

"I need to speak to someone." She turned to the door. "Leave it with me."

"Where you going?"

Melita did not answer.

Melita waited outside of the Crow's headquarters for almost an hour before Brak emerged. She checked her blade and approached him from behind. "Thanks for speaking up in there."

Brak turned to her and smiled. "Mel—"

"Why didn't you say anything?"

"Remember what I said about mixing business and pleasure? If you can't keep those things separate—"

"I can't believe you just stood there. You pretended as if you didn't even know me. What the fuck, Brak?"

"You can think what you want. But you shouldn't go assuming things when you don't know what I did for you."

"And what did you do for me?"

"Put it like this." His voice dropped to little more than a whisper. "The only reason you and your little gang are still alive is because I spoke up for you."

"When?"

"Before he sent some lads out after you."

"Oh. I didn't know."

Brak nodded. "And that's my point. Do you have any idea what he was going to do?"

Melita shook her head.

"He was going to put a hit out on you. Not just you, but everyone in your gang. And not just that, he was going to have some of the lads torch your building."

"Oh."

"And I might have convinced him that if your lads did what they originally agreed and paid back the cash, no harm was done." He shrugged a shoulder. "Granted, he added the extra ten grand each, but I'd say you got off lightly."

"I didn't realise."

"I know you didn't. So don't come running to me saying I did nothing. But, whatever. This thing needs sorting. Pat's already moving back into our territory and it's causing confusion with our clients. Myker's not going to let that stand."

"Is there nothing else you can do?"

"I've already done enough." He held his palms open. "I don't know what else to say."

"Well, thank you, I guess." She kissed him on the cheek and he pulled away.

"You fancy going out later?"

Melita shook her head. "Let's just see how the next few days play out, shall we?"

Brak sighed. "Have it your way. Just make sure you get this done."

V. The Message

Melita entered the Rusty Sail with Fedor and Lev close behind. She checked her dagger's handle and signalled to Patrov who sat at the far end of the bar.

A pair of men stood near him, both holding crossbows under their arms. A cloud of white smoke surrounded Patrov's head. He looked up at Melita's approach and sighed.

Melita slapped her hand on the table and leant towards him, her eyes burrowing into his. "You're back then?"

"Ah, little missy. It's a pleasure to see you again. And right on time too. If it's one thing I like, it's punctuality." He looked past her and grinned. "And you've got your little friends with you as backup."

Melita gritted her teeth. "What are you doing here?"

"What's it to you?" Patrov made a show of looking around. "As far as I can tell, this is a public bar. The bouncers seem fine with us being here. The landlord's not kicked up a fuss." He took a puff from his pipe and breathed the smoke in a stream towards Melita.

"We let you live." Melita tried to not let the smoke bother her, to not let the tickle in her throat make her cough. "We paid you to go." She pointed to the door. "You said you were going to Molotok."

"And I did." Patrov smiled. "The pictures really don't do it justice."

"Why are you back?"

Patrov leant forward, his voice dropping to a whisper. "Let's just say the food didn't agree with me." He sat back and waved a hand. "Whatever works. I don't have to explain shit to you."

"Oh, but you do." Melita narrowed her eyes. "We want our money back."

Patrov laughed and his goons joined in. "Right you are, little missy. Right you are." He turned to his men. "Have you heard this? She wants her money back. She wants a refund like I'm running some upscale haberdashery." He smirked. "Do I look like a haberdasher to you?"

"What's he on about?" Lev asked.

Patrov grinned. "Ah, you remember how to speak, then?"

"I'm serious, Pat." Melita cut them off and edged forward. "You owe us."

"I owe you?" Patrov shook his head. "You see, talk like that's just not going to work for me." He pointed his pipe at her. "And if we really think about it properly, it's you who'll soon be owing me."

"Owe you?" Melita frowned. "How do you weigh that up?"

"I'm back in business. What can I say?" He set his pipe down and smiled. "And I seem to recall you and your little friends being under my protection."

Lev stepped forward. "It's you who needs protection, mate."

Melita raised a hand, silencing Lev, and drew her blade.

Both crossbows pointed at her.

Patrov studied the blade for several seconds before speaking. "And what are you planning on doing with that?"

"Maybe I'll finish the job we were paid to do in the first place."

"Oh, yes, your little assassin con, or whatever it was you had going on." He sighed and squeezed the bridge of his nose. "You should have listened to me. Didn't I tell you your little plan was bad business? Didn't I say that?"

Melita kept still.

"Let's be honest, little missy. You don't have the balls to back up your threats, so if you'll kindly toddle off back to your little tunnel with your little friends, that would be most appreciated."

Melita glared at him.

"And I'll be round this time next week to get my payment."

Melita took a step back and pointed her blade at him. "I gave you a chance."

"Right you are."

"Myker wants you dead."

"Yes. I know. That's why we're in this situation, isn't it?" He gave a half-shrug and picked up his pipe. "The thing you have to realise about Myker is that he's too greedy. And that's why I'm in a better position."

A crease set on Melita's brow. "What's that got to do with anything?"

"He's offering a fifty cut for protection. I'm offering twenty. And now people know I'm back, it won't be long before he crawls back into whatever place he came from."

"You're just lucky you've got your goons around," Melita said. "Otherwise, you'd be eating the tip of my dagger."

"Oh, please." Patrov waved a hand. "What do you want me to say? That I'll tell my men to stand down so we can deal with this one-on-one?" He sniffed. "Why would I do that? I'm running a business here. The exact reason I have bodyguards is to protect me from idiots like you who think they can wave funny-looking daggers near my face and get away with it."

"We want our money."

"Is that so?" He examined his fingernails. "Well, if you put it like that, who am I to argue?" He chuckled to himself. "Or, how about I don't give you anything and we end this conversation because as far as I'm concerned, we've got nothing more to talk about, and there's nothing I hate more than going around in circles."

Melita raised her chin. "You know what we're capable of."

Patrov laughed. "What are you going to do, eh? Set your plez-head friend here on me?" He shook his head. "You're desperate. I get it." He looked between Lev and Fedor, then back to Melita. "And based on the way you're behaving right now, I'm going to assume Myker's had some words with you."

Melita clenched her jaw.

"See?" He tapped the side of his head. "This is why I run this town, and you're in the tunnels begging for scraps."

"Myker wants you dead. And he wants us to do it."

"And that's between you and him. Leave me out of it."

Lev stepped forward and raised a finger. "I thought we were supposed to be under your protection."

"Interesting perspective, I'll grant you. But I'm not the one whose boss just came here pointing a dagger around. I'd say that puts us in a bit of an awkward position, wouldn't you agree?"

Lev's finger dropped to his side.

"Unless there's anything else," Patrov said, "I'm going to have to ask you all to kindly piss off."

Onwyth gazed across the library desk, trying to focus on the stolen ravenglass shield. Every time she moved her head, every time her eyes shifted, the form seemed to twist and warp, the library shelves behind it seeming to bend towards it, as if the shield itself possessed the ability to melt the world around it.

She drew her gaze away when Fedor arrived and squinted up at him, wondering whether it was her own eyes causing the illusion, or something in the ravenglass itself. "How did the forging work? There's no way we can afford to get these done at Gottsisle. At least, not yet."

Fedor drew his dagger and turned it in his hands, his ravenglass having the same effect on the bookshelves as the shield. "Soren got us to fill a small bottle with blood." He reached into an inside pocket and held up a pair of vials. "And another with tears."

"You actually cried?"

He gave a quick nod.

"Real tears?"

The corners of Fedor's mouth twitched and he placed the vials down on the desk. "I don't know how it works. I feel like there's...I don't know. If, like, it's connected to something."

Onwyth cocked an eyebrow. "What do you mean by something? Connected to what?"

Fedor shrugged. "I don't really know what it is."

"It's ravenglass."

"I know. But what's ravenglass? We don't even know where it's from."

"Didn't you get yours from a weathervane?"

"Yes. I mean before that. Where was it from originally? We know where iron and coal come from. We know where wood and bricks come from. But you ever hear about where ravenglass is from?"

"I don't know where iron comes from."

"Mines. Same with coal. You ever seen a ravenglass mine?"

Onwyth frowned. "I don't think I've seen any mines. And why are they called mines? Why not call them yours? Or his? Why's it a mine?"

"I don't know why things are called what they're called."

"We should find out."

Fedor shook his head. "Or we could try to find out where ravenglass comes from. If we knew where it was from, we might be able to get more."

"That would be more useful than knowing why a mine's called a mine."

"Is there anything about it in your books?"

"My books?"

"Our books." He shrugged a shoulder. "Whatever."

Onwyth sat up and looked around the shelves. "My books." She smiled to herself. "I never thought of them as my books. But I think they are, aren't they? It's not like anyone else is reading them. And I can't see Soren coming and demanding them back." She scanned the shelves again. "My books."

Fedor raked a hand over his hair. "But did you find anything? Surely there must be something in those books?"

"Only old stories." She sighed. "Nothing useful."

"So what are you going to do?" He gestured to the shield. "I bet there's enough there to make a dagger or two."

"I don't know. Maybe we could find some kind of smith. Get them to forge it. I mean, it might be weird trying to do it with ravenglass instead of metal, but we could tell them what to do and throw in the tears and blood and stuff."

"I'm not sure that will work."

"But it might."

"It seems a bit more specialised. I bet it's old knowledge that's passed down from master to apprentice, maybe."

"It can't be that difficult. We just melt it down, throw in the blood and tears, and then we shape it into the weapon. Easy."

"Right...if it was that easy, why don't you see loads of people going around with ravenglass weapons?"

"A few of my friends have got them."

"We've got two weapons. How many more do you think there are?"

"I don't know. A hundred? A thousand?"

Fedor held up his hands. "Could be. Could be more. Could be less." He held out his dagger. "But this one and Soren's are the only ones I've seen."

Onwyth nodded. "Maybe people are hiding them. Maybe you've just never been looking."

"Maybe, but we still don't know how this stuff works. We don't know whether it needs rituals and spells or whatever. We don't even know how hot it needs to be before the ravenglass melts. And when's the point where we start hammering it into shape?"

"I don't know. But a smith will."

"A smith will know about iron and steel. They're not going to know about this stuff, are they?"

"The one at Gottsisle did."

Fedor remained silent for several seconds. "Maybe he's the only one."

"You don't know that."

"I don't. But I know he does it. And I don't see any smiths advertising the fact they forge ravenglass around here."

Onwyth frowned. "I've never looked at a smith's billboard. Maybe they all do it. Maybe we just need to ask."

"I go back to my point. If smiths did it, you'd see more people with ravenglass weapons. I don't think this is something just anyone can do."

"You don't know that."

"I don't. But do you really think Soren would have taken a balloon to Gottsisle and paid however much he paid if it was something your average smith could do?"

Onwyth looked down at her hands and nodded—Fedor had a point. "I suppose."

Fedor moved towards the window and stared outside. "Ah, shit."

"What's wrong?"

He gestured down across Kathryn Square. "The Crows."

She joined his side as a couple of lads from the Crows circled the building. "What are they sniffing around here for?"

"I don't know." He met her gaze with purple-rimmed eyes. "I don't like it, though."

"I thought Myker gave you three days."

"He did."

One of the lads pointed up to Onwyth and Fedor. He leant back and hurled something towards the window.

Onwyth ducked and covered her face as the window shattered.

Glass shards spread across the floor and taunts joined the breeze blowing in through the broken window.

Onwyth pulled the curtains shut, her heart racing. "Bastards."

"Looks like they sent us a gift." Fedor gestured to a dead crow tied to a brick on the floor.

Onwyth knelt down and picked up the brick, turning it in her hand, her nose wrinkling at the faint stench of death.

Fedor set his hand on her shoulder. "You alright?"

She gave a quick nod and turned her attention back to the brick. She poked the dead crow, her lip curling. "What's it for?"

Fedor took in a breath. "It's a message."

"A message? What kind of—"

"What happened here?"

Onwyth turned to see Melita in the doorway and held up the brick. "The Crows sent us a message."

"Shit," Melita said. "Get this place cleaned up." She turned on her heels and left.

"Where are you going?" Fedor called after her.

She gave no response.

Melita hammered her fist against the door, the banging echoing around her.

A guard dressed in black with slicked-back hair emerged from inside, a zigzag scar set along his right cheek. He folded his arms, a scowl on his face. "What?"

She gestured up at the windows. "Is Brak in?"

The guard picked something from his teeth and looked Melita up and down. "Brak who?"

"Brak. Myker's second. You know who I'm talking about. Where is he?"

"You're after Brak?"

"Yes."

"As in Myker's second?"

"Yes."

The guard grinned. "And you want to know where he is?"

"Yes. For fuck's sake."

"No need to swear, love."

"I'm not your love."

"Just being nice, love. You don't have to be a bitch about it."

"Can't you just tell him I'm here?"

The guard gestured to the coin around her neck. "Brak get you that, did he?"

She slipped the coin back into her shirt and shot him a glare. "Where is he?"

"None of your fucking business, that's where."

She placed a hand on her hip and lowered her voice, her little finger pointing to her dagger's handle. "I need to see him."

"So? Let me tell you something, love. My job's to keep people like you out of here. That's it."

She frowned. "People like me?"

"You ain't with the Crows. And he don't like being bothered."

"Tell him it's Melita. Tell him it's important."

The guard tilted his head and smirked. "Does he know you're coming?"

She narrowed her eyes. "What do you think?"

"I'm just here to stop him being bothered. It's not really my business to think."

"Clearly." Melita pursed her lips. "Please. Tell him Melita wants to see him. And tell him if he doesn't see me now, he won't get to see me again."

"Oh, no. I'm sure he'll be devastated."

She stepped towards him and jabbed his chest. "Either you tell him I'm here, or the next time I see him, I'll mention that one of his lads with a jagged scar across his cheek kept me from him." She smiled and stepped back. "How does that sound?"

The lad gave a quick nod and went back inside, leaving Melita waiting.

Why did it have to be Brak? How could a relationship work with something like this hanging between them?

She began to pace and wondered whether the guard had gone to find Brak, or whether he'd simply left her waiting with the hope she'd get the message and leave.

She went to knock again, but the door creaked open and Brak stepped outside. "You need to stop doing this." He gestured behind him. "You can't keep coming here—"

She silenced him with a glare. "You need to get your lads to lay off my crew. We just had a brick through a window."

"That doesn't come from me."

"So what? Are you telling me that Myker's second doesn't have any pull around here?" She sniffed. "Come on."

He opened his hands and shook his head. "What do you want me to do, Mel? This is business. Your boys thought they could rip us off. This is coming from Myker himself. Nothing I can say will do shit."

"Well, you need to tell your boss to back off. We're dealing with it and having your lads interfering with our business is only making things worse." She clenched her fists. "We'll get Myker's money and we'll deal with Pat. We don't need bricks through our window to know the pressure's on."

"And what makes you think you can come round here telling us how to run our business?"

"I'm asking for a favour...as a friend. Please, Brak. Just get them to lay off."

Brak opened his hands and shrugged. "Nothing I can do."

"Fine." Melita turned and marched away.

"It doesn't have to be like this," he called after her. "Mel?"

She stopped and turned back to him. "What?"

"You have choices, you know? You don't have to run things like this."

She moved back towards him. "What are you saying?"

"It's Fedor and Lev who ripped us off." He gestured past her. "Them two and the wyvern. They're the ones behind this."

"That wyvern has nothing to do with me."

"I know. You did nothing. Your hands can be clean of all this." He pushed out his bottom lip. "You could walk away right now. No one would blame you. They're the problem—not you. You don't need to get roped into it. You aren't the one who ripped us off. Why should you be paying for their fuck-up?"

"You know I can't do that."

He laughed. "What? Because of your oath?"

She pursed her lips. "Exactly. It might not mean anything to you, but it means everything to me."

"Alright." He raised his hands and took a step back. "If they don't deliver, you're going to be caught up in this. And that ain't right."

"I'm already caught up in this. Maybe you need to think about your priorities."

"I've always said I keep business and personal stuff separate. It seems to me you can't do that."

"Your lads are attacking my home."

"Then walk away. It's that simple."

"From you, you mean?"

He shook his head. "I like you, Melita. I really do. I want to be with you, but this..." He curled his upper lip. "It's no good."

She cocked an eyebrow. "Why don't you walk away, then? Leave the Crows."

He laughed. "And become dead meat?"

"Don't you fucking laugh at me."

"I'm not laughing at you. I'm laughing at the idea I could leave, even if I wanted to...which I don't."

Melita's nostrils flared. "It's so easy for you, isn't it? You think you can make demands of me. Ask me to leave my crew. But Creation forbid the idea you'd consider doing the same."

"It's completely different."

"Yeah, right. What, because you're a bloke and I'm just—what is it your gang members call me—your bird?"

"Tell me this, then. What happens if you walk away?" He pointed past her. "What would happen to you if you packed up your things right now and left?"

She did not answer.

"Put it like this: if you leave, that's it. I bet your crew would send you on your way, maybe help you with your bags, and thank you for everything you've done. If I leave, I'm dead. That's it. No one leaves the Crows and survives."

"You make it sound so easy."

"I wish it was." His shoulders sagged. "I get that it's hard. But from where I'm standing, this isn't a difficult choice."

"So what's this, an ultimatum?"

He shook his head and sighed. "It's not an ultimatum. It's just reality. If you stick with your crew, and your boys don't deliver, Myker will send the lads after you...all of you."

"And if I leave, I'll be fine? I can just walk away from my crew and I'll be safe? Myker won't decide that I'm still dead meat?"

"If you're not in the crew, why would he?"

"And what about the others?"

"As I've already said, Fedor, Lev, and the wyvern are the ones who ripped us off. I don't know. Maybe if you give them up, I can make sure the rest of your crew are safe. Might not even have to leave."

"I'm not doing that."

"Why not? I would."

"I made an oath."

"Yeah. The oaths of thieves."

She gritted her teeth. "We might be thieves, but we've got one thing you lot haven't."

"And what's that then?"

She held his gaze. "Loyalty."

"Loyalty? We've got loyalty."

"No. You've got fear. We're loyal because we want to be, not because we're scared of becoming dead meat."

"That's a shame."

Melita frowned. "Why do you say that?"

"Loyalty's going to get you killed."

"You're wrong. Loyalty is everything."

Fedor sat up in bed and stared across at Lev and Vern, both barely visible in the darkness. How could they sleep with everything that was going on? They had only two days left—two days to kill Patrov. And two days to find fifty thousand krones.

He listened to their breaths, to Lev's occasional snoring, and wondered how he was ever going to sleep.

Cold sweat spread across his back and forehead, sending waves of ice down his spine. He hugged himself against the shivers washing over him and licked his cracked lips.

He punched his pillow and a barrage of curses cut through the silence.

Vern rolled over and mumbled something before turning back over to sleep.

Fedor did not want to wake the others. Why should they have to put up with his insomnia?

With a sigh, he dragged on his clothes and pulled on his coat. He crept over to Lev's dirty clothes piled in the corner, and rifled through their pockets.

He pulled out a fifty krone note and stuffed it into his jacket. The idea of stealing from Lev didn't feel right, but he swore to himself he'd pay Lev back when he eventually got his money from Melita. If she didn't want him stealing from the others, she shouldn't have stolen from him.

His breath caught when Lev stirred. Fedor remained still and silent until he was certain Lev and Vern were sound asleep.

He backed out of the bedroom, taking care not to make a sound. He made his way downstairs to the antique shop shrouded in darkness and stepped out into the night.

Cold wind slapped him as he half-jogged across Kathryn Square, his head buried in his hood. Moonlight shone down, bathing the square in a faint glow, highlighting the last Empress of Ostreich's blade.

He gritted his teeth and ducked into the wind, trying his best to ignore the sensation of ice enclosing his body.

He spun at the sound of movement behind him.

A tall lad dressed in black swaggered towards him holding a club in one hand, a knuckle duster on the other. "You ripped off our boss, you fucking Siesha prick."

Before Fedor had a chance to react, the lad landed a punch in his stomach and followed with a club strike to the chin.

Doubling over, Fedor cried out as his head struck the cobbles. The club came down on his back, sending shocks of pain up his neck.

A second lad emerged from the shadows, joined by a third.

Kicks rained down, heavy boots slamming against his arms and legs, while the club smashed on his back.

Something exploded in Fedor's nose, making it hard to breathe.

He rolled back and forth, covering his head and face, trying to block what he could, but the beating would not stop.

"Thirty-three! Thirty-three!"

The lads scattered at Dienerin's shrill cry. The wyvern swooped down from nowhere and clawed at the tallest lad's face. He flailed and swung at Dienerin with his club.

Before the lads had a chance to regroup, Fedor got up on unsteady feet and drew his dagger.

Blood dripped from his nose onto his blade, sending shimmers along its edge.

Fedor stepped forward as the dagger turned to flames, his mind filling with whispers calling for him to kill.

"He's a fucking warlock!"

The lads ran away at full speed, leaving Fedor and the wyvern alone in the darkness.

As the blade faded to its endless black, Dienerin landed in front of him and spread out her wings. "Fedor, Fedor, master. Are you hurt?"

He nodded and stood still for several seconds, staring up at the stars, his vision blurred by tears, his head throbbing with pain.

The blade slipped from his grasp and he dropped to the ground, his awareness fading to nothing.

Fedor groaned as he opened his eyes. He blinked up at two shadowy figures gazing down at him in the darkness.

"You alright, mate?"

"Lev..." Pain throbbed across his legs and back.

"Help him up," Melita said. "You think you can stand?"

"I...I think so."

"Dienerin told us what happened," she said, brushing him down.

Fedor winced as he put his weight down on his feet. He touched his split lip and tried to breathe through his blood-encrusted nostrils.

"Was it the Crows?"

"Yeah. Bunch of them ambushed me. I think it was a little reminder that time's running out."

Melita steered him back along the road towards Kathryn Square, her hand resting on the small of his back.

Lev joined Fedor's side and drew his club. "If those fuckers come back round here, I'll smash their teeth in." He turned to Fedor. "Your face looks pretty messed up, mate. How you feeling?"

"I'll be fine. Just bruising, I think."

"Your nose looks a mess."

Fedor reached up and cringed at the pain. "Shit."

"Did you get a good look at them?" Melita asked.

"It was a group of cocky lads wearing black feathers in their ears. Might be one with a few wyvern scratches, but it was dark."

"Dienerin said you scared the shit out of them," Lev said.

Fedor grinned then regretted the movement as pain shot across his lips and nose. "Blood dripped on my blade. They thought I was a warlock."

"That's good, mate."

"No, it's not good," Melita said. "I'm trying to keep us out of trouble and Fedor's showing off his magic tricks."

"I didn't do it on purpose. The blade reacts to my blood. They made me bleed. And anyway, if it means they'll think twice before attacking us, I'm glad."

Melita sniffed. "Maybe. We just need to be careful. We don't want anyone knowing about what you've got. What if it fell into the wrong hands?"

"It won't." He shuffled along Kathryn Square, each footstep bringing with it a bolt of pain along his back and legs.

As he reached the shop door, Melita ushered them inside and Fedor slumped against the wall, his head in his hands.

"So which colour did the blade go?" Lev asked. "Blue or orange?"

Fedor opened one eye and looked up at Lev and Melita. "Orange." He gestured to the blood around his nose. "Blue's the tears, remember?"

"And they think you're a warlock?"

"Yeah."

"Could work in our favour, mate."

"That's what I was thinking."

"Or they could report you," Melita said.

Fedor shook his head. "I can't see them doing that. Who would they tell?"

"Yeah," Lev said. "And who'd believe them?"

Melita pursed her lips. "The Magistrates. The Inquisitors." She looked through the shutters, her gaze fixed on Kathryn Square. Her jaw tightened and she turned to Fedor. "What exactly were you doing out? You know the Crows are after us. It's not safe."

Fedor closed his eyes. "I...erm."

"You fucking prick." She shot towards him, her eyes wild. "You were headed to the Sail, weren't you? You were going to get fucked up on that shit after everything we've talked about."

Fedor could not meet her gaze. "I'm sorry. You don't know how hard it is."

She shook her head. "This is what happens when you ignore the rest of the crew. It puts us all in danger."

"I was the only one in danger."

"No." She raised a finger. "You're injured. Luckily, it doesn't seem serious. But what if you'd been killed?"

Fedor sniffed. "Maybe I'd be less of a burden."

"Don't start your woe-is-me act again. We need you, Fedor. If our numbers are down, we'll all suffer."

"I was just lucky Dienerin was there."

Melita pursed her lips. "Maybe we can use that. Make sure she's around to protect us."

"I'm not sure how well a wyvern will do against a couple of crossbows," Lev said.

"True. I'm thinking of something else."

"What do you mean?" Fedor asked.

"I need you to order her to stop you if you're heading to the Sail."

"I'm not going to do that."

"Well, I'm saying you need to. You need to decide what's more important to you, the crew, or the drugs. It's that simple."

"She'll just stop when I order her to not do that."

"Can't you order her to do it, even if you say otherwise."

Fedor shook his head. "I don't think she works like that."

"For fuck's sake, you could at least try. You need to do something. I'm sticking my neck out for you with the Crows stuff, and I'm starting to wonder whether it's even worth the effort."

"How could you say that?"

"Do you know what Brak said to me earlier?"

Fedor looked at his hands. "Do I want to know?"

"He said I should leave. He said I should walk away from the crew. Keep me out of all this trouble. You two ripped off Myker and we're all paying for it."

"Nah, mate. That's out of order, that is." Lev stepped in between them. "I seem to recall you being on board with this. You can't suddenly turn round and tell us you're going to leave."

"I'm not. And that's not the point. I'm here, aren't I? I kept my oath."

"We appreciate that, but you can't go throwing it back in our faces when things don't work out. That's bad form, that is."

"Yeah," Fedor said. "It sounds to me like Brak's getting in your head."

Melita sighed. "You're missing my point. This stuff with the Crows is getting out of hand. We've got two days left and we're no closer to figuring a way out."

"We know what we need to do," Lev said. "It's just a case of doing it."

Fedor shrugged a shoulder and took in a sharp breath. "Maybe Onwyth and Vern can do it. At least they want to kill."

Melita and Lev exchanged a look, then Melita gave a slight nod. "Maybe." She gestured to the stairs. "Until then, we'll need to go to bed." She pointed at Fedor. "And you need to stay here. If you leave, I will consider you breaking your oath. Do that, and we're done."

VI. The Address

Fedor cradled his aching arm and stared out across Upper Nordturm, the morning sun shining across the rooftops into the distance. Lev and Melita spoke behind him, their words little more than a fuzz in his ears. His thoughts flipped between plez and revenge and running away, a whirligig of desires thrashing in his mind.

He needed to sneak out and get to the Sail, to get some plez to take the edge off and dull the pain. His grip tightened on the windowsill and he let out a shuddering breath, the window steaming up in front of him.

Clearing the condensation with his sleeve, he watched a balloon coming in from the north. How much would it cost him to hop on the next balloon out of the city and start a new life?

But then how could he leave his crew to face the Crows alone? And how could he stay?

He turned when Onwyth and Vern returned clutching bacon rolls.

"We have breakfast," Onwyth announced as she handed out the rolls to Lev and Melita. She stopped and did a double-take when she went to hand one to Fedor. "What happened to you?"

"Crows," he managed through swollen lips.

Onwyth sucked in a breath. "Ouch." She pointed to Fedor's nose. "That looks painful."

"It is."

She handed him the bacon roll. "At least the bruising around your eyes makes you look like less of a junkie."

"Thanks." Fedor bit into his roll, the salt from the bacon stinging his lips. He chewed through the pain, swallowed, and wiped his mouth. "Appreciate you getting these."

"You're welcome," Onwyth said. "I thought it might help heal your wounds."

"You know I like mine with egg," Lev said, studying his butty. "Bacon on its own's no good. You need the yolk to balance out the flavour."

Without a word, Onwyth plucked the roll from his grasp and stuffed it into her mouth. She chewed with bloated cheeks and mumbled something Fedor couldn't make out.

Lev looked on, his mouth gaping. "What did you do that for? I was only taking the piss." He removed his cap, looked around the common room, and breathed a long sigh. "What is it with everyone round here? You lot used to be able to take a joke."

Onwyth arched her head forward and regurgitated the half-chewed roll onto her open palm. She smiled up at Lev and offered it to him. "Here. You have it."

He scrunched his nose and recoiled. "No thanks. I'll get my bloody own, if it's all the same."

"That's gratitude for you," Onwyth said, seemingly to no one in particular. "First you complain how there wasn't any eggs and then you complain when I take it back." She raised a finger. "And then you have the gall to complain when I try to give you it back. I think Mister Complainy-Head needs to stop complaining and start being grateful when one of his crew goes out and buys everyone breakfast, with her own money, I might add."

"I'm not eating a roll after you've chewed it. That's disgusting, that is. Don't know what I'd catch."

Onwyth slapped his upper arm. "What you'd catch? What's that supposed to mean?"

Lev laughed and blocked her strikes. "It means I've seen some sailors with less diseases."

She glared at him. "I had one thing. One thing. And that cleared up...pretty much." She pointed at his face. "I bet you're the one riddled with diseases, the way you go around touring those brothels. We should start calling you Syphilitic Lev, or Mister Mouldy-Balls."

Lev laughed again. "I preferred Mister Complainy-Head, if I'm being honest."

"Or how about Mister Cock-Rot?" Vern asked.

Lev's smile dropped and he loomed over Vern. "What did you just say?"

Vern shrank in his seat and raised an arm as though expecting to be hit. "I didn't mean nothing by it."

"I asked you what you said."

"He said Mister Cock-Rot would be a better name," Onwyth said, grabbing Lev's shoulder. "Leave him alone. Or I'll...I'll push this bacon roll in your face."

Lev narrowed his eyes at Vern. "He's taking the piss."

"He's a kid," Melita said. "And I think Mister Cock-Rot quite suits you."

"Fuck you." He cast his gaze around the room and stopped on Fedor. "You got anything you want to add too? You got any dumb insults you want to hurl my direction?"

Fedor raised his hands. "Nope. Just enjoying the show." He nodded to Onwyth's hand. "You really should eat your butty before it gets cold. You'll only be complaining later if you don't."

Air whistled through Lev's nostrils. "This is just a bloody laugh to you lot, isn't it?"

Onwyth smirked. "What was it you were saying about not being able to take a joke?"

Lev raised his hands. "Alright. It's banter. You're taking the piss. I get it." His arms dropped to his sides and he began to pace. "I think this shit with the Crows must be getting to me. I'm always up for banter." He flopped down on the sofa and sighed. He turned to Vern. "Sorry, mate."

"It's alright."

"Nah. It's not. We've got enough shit to deal with without me being a dick. We should be pulling together."

"Lev's right," Melita said. "We can't keep taking jabs at each other."

Lev waved a hand. "It's just banter. It's all good. Ignore me. As I say, it's just this Crows shit getting to me."

Onwyth gestured to Fedor. "The thing I don't get about the Crows is why do they keep making it harder for us to do a job for them? You'd think they'd want us to do our best work."

"Who bloody knows?" Lev looked up at her and shook his head. "Can't believe you bloody stole my butty."

Melita cleared her throat. "Let's not get into that again. We've got two days. The Crows are escalating. We need to deal with this today."

"What about the money?" Lev asked. "It's not like we've got fifty grand knocking about, is it?"

"Perhaps we can find Pat's stash," Onwyth said. "I bet he's got loads of money."

"You reckon?" Lev asked.

"I don't know. Maybe."

"You really think he'd have fifty grand stashed around his house?"

Onwyth shrugged. "I bet he'd have some. And I bet he'd want to avoid working with the banks. Save paying tax."

Lev pushed out his bottom lip. "Maybe."

"Or we could just wait for this all to blow over," Fedor said. "Let them go to war."

"That's all well and good, mate. But if the Crows win, we're screwed."

Melita tapped her chin. "The Crows have the numbers. And Pat's still re-establishing himself. I hate to say it, but now's the perfect time to act and do what we should have done in the first place."

Fedor sighed and shook his head. "We should deal with the Crows. They want a half-cut from businesses and I'm sick of those little pricks running around thinking they run the place."

"I repeat, the Crows have the numbers."

"Can't you speak to your boyfriend again?"

"I've already told you Brak's position. He doesn't like to mix business with personal stuff."

"And yet he tells you to walk away."

"Fair point." She met his gaze. "But I'm still here."

"What's it to be, then?" Lev reached up and cracked his knuckles. "My belly's making weird noises, but I'm not budging until I know what we're doing."

"We need to find out where Patrov lives," Fedor said. "I think Onwyth's right. We get him at home. We take his cash. Maybe scare him enough to leave."

"I think we're past scaring him," Melita said. "It's time to act. Lev, Fedor, I need you to pull on a few contacts in the lower city, see what you can find out. Onwyth and Vern, you two can check the upper."

Fedor frowned. "So you want me on jobs now?"

She glared at him. "Yes. And don't fuck it up. I'm trusting you."

Fedor lowered his gaze. "I can do that."

"What about you, boss?" Lev asked.

"I'll speak to a few contacts, see what I can find out. Someone must know where he lives."

"We should take Dienerin," Fedor said. "I was thinking she could check-in on all of us, deliver messages, that kind of thing."

"Do what you need to." Melita clapped her hands together. "Right. Let's meet back here at the noon bell. Everyone happy with the arrangements?"

"If an opportunity to kill Pat happens to come, should we do it?" Onwyth asked.

"We're not killing anyone," Fedor said.

Onwyth sniffed. "I kill who I want, when I want. You can't tell me what to do."

"You've never killed anyone."

"So? I can if I want to. I just haven't yet." She looked him up and down and smiled. "You'd be surprised how easy you've made it for me to change my mind."

"Is that supposed to be a threat?"

Melita stepped between them and waved a hand. "Enough. For fuck's sake, you two. We've got our jobs to do. Let's focus on that. Any questions?"

"Yeah," Onwyth said. "If the opportunity arises with Pat, what should I do?"

Melita sighed. "Do what you need to. Just...just be careful."

After speaking to Dienerin about the plan, Fedor joined Lev outside and glanced up at the morning sun, the sky cold and clear. "So what are we doing, then?"

"We've already been through this, mate." Lev led the way across Kathryn Square and took the road leading towards the lower city. "Honestly, mate, weren't you listening to what was being said up there?"

"Of course. I mean, where are we going first?"

"Thought that'd be obvious. We check around his usual haunts, speak to a couple of people who're on the level. We'll have a look around the arena, the market. See if he's been around the Clam."

"What about the Sail?"

Lev sniffed. "Yeah. The Sail. I think it's probably best if I do that one alone."

"What happened to us sticking together? To having each other's backs?"

"And what happened to you not stepping foot in that place?"

"I'll be fine."

"Well, you don't look fine. You look pale. And if I'm being honest, those bruises aren't helping. You look like a proper junkie."

Fedor skipped past a puddle and followed the curve of buildings towards the Kusten Road. "You can be a right twat sometimes, you know?"

"What?" Lev held out his hands. "Just telling you how it looks."

"Onwyth said the bruises helped."

"Yeah? Since when do we listen to Onwyth?"

"She does loads for this crew and you never give her enough credit."

Lev stopped and inclined his head. "Did you have any when you sneaked out yesterday?"

Fedor shook his head.

"Good." He carried on walking. "Because with talk like that you'd forgive a bloke for suspecting." He grinned and patted Fedor's back. "But that's another clean day under your belt, mate. The more days you have, the easier it gets."

"And how would you know?"

"I just know." He tapped the side of his head. "You're not the first bloke I've known who's gone through this. It's going to be hard, but you'll get through it."

"Honest word?"

"Honest word."

"Who was it?"

"We had a lad who was with us for a few months. This was before your time. Back when Gavril was still in charge. He got into that shit, but Gavril got him clean. But then he had a run-in with the Erikson lot. Turned out he'd ripped them off for a couple of grand and they took him out."

"Shit."

"I know. It's why you don't fuck with the Eriksons. They're good when they're on your side, but they're a brutal bunch of bastards if things go south."

Fedor crossed the Kusten Road and followed the ramp down to the lower city, making his way into the tunnels and stopping at the edge of the arena.

The benches stood empty. The alchemical lights dimmed.

Lev rubbed his chin. "Well, it looks like we can rule this place out. Let's try the market."

Lev came to a halt at the top of the steps leading down to the market square and gestured to something going on below.

"What's up?" Fedor asked, joining Lev's side.

Lev nodded to the market's far end at three constables trying to break up a fight. "Looks like the Crows are causing shit again."

Fedor pointed to the men the Crows fought. "I think I recognise them."

"Yeah?" Lev squinted. "Hard to tell from here, mate."

"I think they're from Patrov's crew."

"Best stay clear." Lev tugged Fedor's arm. "Come on."

"Wait." Fedor shrugged him off. "If his crew are around, maybe Patrov's not too far away."

"Not necessarily. And if I'm being honest, I wouldn't mind keeping my distance as far as the Crows are concerned."

"What should we do?"

"We let them get on with it. Scum beating scum is a win–win for us. Maybe they'll kill each other and do us all a favour."

"We can only hope."

Lev turned to him and cocked an eyebrow. "So you're fine with that then? You're alright with killing?"

Fedor shrugged a shoulder. "If they want to kill each other, go ahead. Just keep us out of it."

Lev rubbed his chin. "Interesting."

"What is?"

"Doesn't matter, mate. Let's not hang around here and get noticed." Lev pulled down his cap and gestured to the Clam. "Come on, let's see if some of the girls can help us out."

"You sure you're going to be alright in there?" Fedor asked as they descended the steps. "You going to be able to keep yourself from hiring one of them?"

"Good one. I think you'll find I've got this little thing called self-control. I'll have to teach you how it works." Lev slipped a hand into his pocket and frowned. "Ah, shit." He checked his other pockets and scanned the ground behind him. "Bollocks."

"What's up?"

"Must have left my cash back at the den." He checked his pockets again. "I'm sure I had a fifty in here."

"And I thought you had self-control." Fedor grinned. "That didn't take long."

"And I thought you'd got your humour back, mate." Lev strode past the bouncers, who let him inside.

They blocked Fedor's way. "What's wrong? I'm supposed to—"

"You're barred."

"Barred?" Fedor's mouth dropped open. "What did I do?"

The bouncer looked down at him. "Step away from the door."

"You can't just go round banning people for no reason."

The bouncers exchanged looks and the taller one stepped forward, his arms folded, his expression blank. "You're barred because we say you're barred."

"Is this some Siesha thing?"

"No. You're barred because of the scene you made last time you were here."

"Fine, I'll wait."

"Well, make sure you keep away from the door. You get too close and I might have to smack you one."

Fedor walked back over to the steps and sat on a bench overlooking the marketplace, his attention split between the Clam and the far end of the market.

He watched as constables led away two of Patrov's men, their wrists bound with cuffs.

A third constable remained behind, talking to a pair of Crows.

One of the lads slipped something into the constable's hand. The constable looked around, adjusted his hat, and slipped the item into his coat, before giving the lads a nod and sending them away.

Lev emerged from inside and shook his head as he climbed the steps. "He's not been around today."

Fedor gestured past him. "Just saw the Crows paying off the watch. They had a couple of Pat's men arrested."

"And, don't tell me, the Crows walked away free?"

Fedor nodded.

"Well, can't say I'm surprised. The watch is as corrupt as the dodgiest fuckers around here." He turned to Fedor. "I think we should check the Sail."

Fedor stiffened.

"You think you're going to be alright?"

"Yeah. I can do it. Just need to keep focused on the job."

"You'll be right, mate." He got up and nodded to the tunnel leading to the docks. "Just stick close to me. Don't go wandering off."

Melita entered the lower city and strode across the market square. She pulled up her head when she spotted lads from the Crows milling around beyond the stalls.

She headed straight for an elderly woman sitting behind a stall, selling old pans, chipped ornaments, and broken toys.

The woman offered Melita a gap-toothed smile, her slack skin peppered with liver spots. "Ah, Melita, my dear. How goes it?"

"Same old. How about you? Business treating you well?"

The old woman's gaze shifted to the Crows at the other end of the market. She hesitated, her voice dropping to a whisper. "We are all feeling the pinch, dear. What with the gangs throwing their weight around..." She tutted. "Someone should do something about them. It's not right."

Melita nodded and slipped her a five-krone coin. "That's actually why I'm here."

The woman raised an eyebrow. "Oh?"

"I need his address."

"What kind of address?"

"Patrov's."

She chewed on her bottom lip. "Hmm. I'm not sure."

"He's causing trouble for all of us. It would mean a lot to me if you could help us out."

The woman rolled the coin in her hand and pushed it back to Melita. "I'd love to help you out. I really would. But if word gets out that I'm asking questions like that..." She shook her head. "It'll be my hide."

"I understand." Melita forced a smile and slipped the coin back into her pocket. "You don't happen to know where he is now?" She raised a finger before the woman protested. "I'm not talking about his address, just if you've heard word of him being around town?"

"Last I heard, he left. And then he came round only yesterday doing his rounds as if nothing's changed. So who knows what to believe."

Melita nodded. "But you haven't seen him today?"

"I'm sorry, dear." She took Melita's hand. "But if you do find him, make sure you do a good job. This city would be a better place without him." She glanced over to the Crows and curled her lip. "Of course, you didn't hear that from me."

"Hear what?" Melita smiled.

"That's my girl. You take care now."

Fedor followed Lev down the steps. He made a right through the tunnels and turned left onto the docks.

The great sea gate stood open. The morning sun shone through the cavern entrance, throwing golden light across the moored ships and glistening against the water's surface.

Sailors and dockers unloaded crates and barrels from ships, while men in white linen uniforms piled many-hued silks onto handcarts.

Fedor wended between women selling seafood from trays and a pair of young thieves trying to work the pockets.

He glared and pointed to his dagger when one of the pickpockets veered towards him.

The sunlight faded as he stepped into the commercial district, the golden glow making way for alchemical harshness. He weaved between shops and cafés.

Lev grabbed his arm and dragged him to join a queue.

"What are we doing now?"

"I'm hungry. You got any cash?"

Fedor nodded and reached into his pocket. His fingers brushed Lev's fifty and he shook his head. "Melita's got my cash, remember?"

"Ah, shit. I swear, mate. My belly's going to bring the watch out if it gets any louder."

"Have you not got cash at the den?"

"Yeah. But I don't like being out without any." He jerked a thumb back towards the docks. "Maybe we should shake those kids down. You see them trying to dip me?"

"One of them tried it on me too."

Lev shook his head. "Cheeky bastards."

Fedor sniffed. "I seem to recall that being us not too long ago."

"Yeah? Well, maybe it's time we showed them how things work around here."

"The way they're going about it, they'll be in a cell by lunchtime."

"Don't mention lunch, mate." Lev cradled his stomach and looked up at the cavern ceiling. "Creation, if you can hear me, send down some cash or a bacon and egg butty. Help your old mate Lev out just this once. I swear I'll try to get to church when I can."

Fedor laughed. "You're praying now?"

"At this point, I'll try anything."

"Is it working?"

Lev's nose wrinkled and pointed at something on the floor in a nearby alleyway. "And Creation delivers."

Fedor studied the rotten loaf and shook his head. "You need to pray harder."

"Nah, I need some cash." He looked behind him. "Might have to head back." He sniffed the air. "That bacon smell is too much. Can't bloody think."

"Let's just...let's just do what we came down here for."

"Yeah. You're right."

As the Rusty Sail came into view, something squeezed in Fedor's chest. Sweat blossomed along his flesh, a wave of cold washing over him. He rested a hand on a nearby wall for balance.

"You alright, mate?"

"Yeah. I'm fine. It's just..."

"Wait here. I'll go on, see what's what, and I'll be straight out."

Fedor licked his lips and nodded. "You go ahead."

Lev marched towards the Rusty Sail, stopped, and turned to Fedor. "Don't move."

"I won't."

Lev went inside, leaving Fedor alone.

The faint hint of plez sent his nerves roaring. It took everything he had not to move, not to rush inside, to take the pipe in his mouth and wash all the pain away.

He breathed deeply and tried to focus his mind, tried to stop his body from betraying him. His hand moved away from the wall as another hint of plez wafted by. The call was too much.

If he could sneak past Lev and get into the back room—

Lev stepped from the Rusty Sail and jogged back over to Fedor. "No such luck." He met Fedor's eyes. "What's wrong with you?"

"Nothing." He leant against the wall. "Can we just go?"

Lev gestured to the Rusty Sail's door. "It's this place, isn't it?"

"Yeah." He let out a shuddering breath. "But I'm still out here. I didn't go in. I wanted to...I really did. But I didn't."

"It's alright, mate." Lev put an arm around Fedor. "Come on."

Fedor glanced back over his shoulder as Lev led him away.

Onwyth kicked the tops off weeds poking through cracked paving stones and skipped over puddles and potholes. She covered her nose at the refuse stench wafting from alleyways as she trudged past tightly packed terraced houses.

Vern walked a few steps ahead, scanning the rooftops, and glancing down alleyways. He started when a pair of kids chased a cat down the street, the boys hurling roof tiles and stones at the creature.

"Stay cool," Onwyth said in a low whisper. "The kids round here smell fear."

"I don't like these parts. It's dodgy."

"We can work with dodgy."

Vern glanced back at the kids. "I don't think this is a good idea."

"It's just down here."

"But the Eriksons?"

Onwyth shrugged. "We go back years. Just don't do anything stupid and you'll be fine."

She made a right at the end of a row of houses and gestured to an old mill looming over the other buildings. "We're here."

Vern moved behind her as Onwyth approached a rangy lad lingering outside. He wore his blond hair in a ponytail, his skin almost translucent. He glowered at Onwyth. "What you want?"

Onwyth raised her hands, showing they were empty. She smiled. "Is Frank around."

"Who's asking?"

"Onwyth."

"Is he expecting you?"

"No. But he'll want to hear what I've got to say."

"Does he know you?"

"What do you think?"

He folded his arms. "I think you answer when I ask."

Onwyth looked around and gestured to the building. "You think I'd really come to this shit-hole if I didn't know him?"

"I don't know. Some people might."

"Just get him. He knows who I am."

"Alright." The lad disappeared inside.

"Why you getting him involved?" Vern asked.

"Because he might know where Mad Pat lives."

Vern shuddered. "I don't like it."

"He's an old friend." She nudged him. "Now, shut up. I think he's coming."

The lad with the ponytail came out with several others, led by a bulky man wearing an eyepatch.

"Frank," Onwyth said.

Frank tilted his head and grinned. "Onwyth, as I live and breathe. What you doing?"

She gestured to the door. "Can we have a chat...in private?"

"I've got no secrets from my boys. It's how the old man likes us to run things."

"And how is old Erikson doing? Not seen him around for ages."

Frank shook his head. "You know how it goes. The old have to make way for the young. But we know where we came from. We're building on what he started."

"That's good."

"So what's this about?"

"You seen what's been going down with the Crows and Patrov's lot?"

Frank leant forward, his voice dropping to a whisper. "I heard Myker tried to have him knocked off. Didn't have the bollocks to have his lads do it, though. Heard he hired some bloke to do it."

"That's what we heard too."

Frank gestured to Vern. "And who's this?"

"New kid. He's called Vern."

"He alright?"

Onwyth shrugged. "He's getting there. Bit green, but you know how it goes."

"You still knocking about with Yorik? Haven't seen the beardy fucker for a while."

Onwyth's chest tightened and she took in a breath.

Frank frowned when she didn't respond. "What's wrong? You need to sit down?"

"I'm fine. it's just..." Her words trailed off.

"He's dead," Vern said.

"Oh, shit." Frank rubbed the back of his neck. "Sorry to hear that. Always used to see him running games down by the docks." He placed a hand on Onwyth's shoulder and gave it a gentle squeeze. "Always seemed like a decent bloke. Respectful, you know?"

"He was...thanks."

"I take it you've not just come round here to exchange pleasantries. What can we do for you?"

"You get much hassle?"

"From the Crows?"

Onwyth nodded.

"Our boys can deal with the Crows."

"What about Pat's lot?"

Frank nodded. "Yeah. He's been round since he got back. We had a chat. He thinks we'll be paying him for protection. I said we'll see how this thing plays out with the Crows first."

"I take it he didn't like that?"

"He didn't. But he wasn't exactly in a position to throw threats around."

"You think he'll come back?"

"I'm banking on it." He shrugged a shoulder. "But as far as I can tell, best thing to do is stand back, let them fight it out. Someone will come out on top. And we can deal with them if we have to."

"What if it's the Crows?"

"We'll deal with them. They're asking for fifty." He spat on the ground. "Fuck that."

"Yeah. Fuck those feathery bastards."

"So what are you lot thinking?"

"Me, I'm just looking to find Pat. Twenty's better than fifty."

"True."

"Say, you don't happen to know where he lives? We're trying to get a sit-down, but he's keeping low."

Frank grinned. "You're kidding, right? Don't tell me you're going after him?"

"No. No. Nothing like that. We just need to see him. And soon."

"You tried that dive in the lower bit?"

"The Rusty Sail?"

"That's the one. You could try there."

"We've not really seen him since he came back. Not really."

"I guess if someone hired a hit on me, I'd keep a low profile too. My advice to you is wait until all this settles with the Crows. See where things fall." He raised a finger. "There's usually profit in the gaps."

"I think you're right." She gave Vern the signal to be quiet when he went to speak. "We'll keep our heads down too. See who comes out on top."

"Good call. Is there anything else?"

"No. That's fine. Let's hope this settles down sooner rather than later."

"I'm sure it will. You know we've got a card game coming up in a few days, if you're interested. Lots of players. Low stakes, big prizes. You in?"

Onwyth forced a smile. "Games were more Yorik's thing. I think I'll leave it. Too many bad memories."

"You still running with Gavril's old lot?"

"Yeah."

"Still doing sneak stuff?"

"Let's just say we're moving into a more lucrative venture."

Frank nodded. "And I take it that's why you're after Pat?"

"Something like that."

"So what is it you're doing?"

Onwyth leant forward and lowered her voice. "If you need an assassin, you know where I am."

"You still at Gavril's old place?"

"No. We're on Kathryn Square now."

Frank whistled. "Nice. You must be doing well. Have to say, I never had you down as a killer."

Onwyth swallowed. "Neither did I. But here we are."

"How much?"

"Ten."

"Grand?"

She nodded.

"That's pretty steep."

"Not if you want it doing right."

Frank shrugged. "If it's working, it's working, I guess. More power to you."

"Thanks. And feel free to spread the word. Might be able to give you a cut of any referrals."

"What we talking?"

"Let's say five hundred for a good referral."

"And for a bad one?"

Onwyth held out her hands. "We don't pay for bad ones."

"I'll let a few contacts know."

"Thanks. Always a pleasure."

He waved her away. "And let me know if you change your mind about that game."

"Will do." She grabbed Vern's arm and made her way back the way they had come.

"He was no use," Vern muttered.

"No use? If Frank gets some jobs our way, we'll be in the money."

"But it's going to cost us five hundred,"

Onwyth rolled her eyes. "It's the price of doing business. Come on. This address isn't going to find itself."

A bell tinkled above the door when Melita stepped into Walter's shop. She breathed in the silence and was surprise to see the shop empty.

"Won't be a moment," a voice called from a back room.

Melita studied the shelves of pottery, old books, and knick-knacks. She took in the smells of dust and candle smoke and turned when Walter entered through a bead curtain.

"Melita. What can I do for you?"

"I need your help."

"If it's about the ravenglass..." He opened his palms and shrugged. "I'm sorry. There's really nothing I can do."

She shook her head. "No. I don't care about that." She checked through the window to the street and locked the door.

A line set on Walter's brow. "What is it?"

"How's business?"

"Not the best." He shrugged a shoulder. "You know how things are right now. The Magistrates have been cracking down on some of the smuggling and this thing with the Crows isn't helping."

"Have you heard from Patrov?"

"We all have." His fists clenched. "Something has got to give. I'm on the verge of closing shop for good."

"That's why I'm here. I'm trying to find out where he lives."

He waved a hand. "If you're planning on going after Patrov, I want nothing to do with it."

"I'm just looking for an address. No one has to know it came from you. Please."

He took in a breath. "I wish I could help. I really do." He opened his palms again. "Have you tried the Rusty Sail? I understand he conducts much of his business in there when he isn't shaking down good honest folk like us."

"That's no good. I need to know where he crawls back to at night. I want to get him alone, without his gang around."

"Good luck with that." He glanced at the door and lowered his voice. "He is a dangerous man."

"I know. Do you know anyone else I could ask?"

"I don't know. I wish I could be more helpful."

"It's fine. I'm sure we'll figure something." She made her way back to the door and turned the key. "Thanks, anyway."

"If you do get him alone, give him a slap from me."

She smiled. "Will do."

Onwyth skirted past the balloon port with Vern following behind.

"Got any spare hack?" a half-familiar voice asked.

Onwyth almost tripped over a pair of legs and glared at a beggar leaning against the wall.

"You should watch where you're going."

"I thought you wanted hack?"

The beggar looked up from his bowl and smiled. "Onwyth? That you?"

Her shoulders relaxed. "Yeah. You alright, Jez?"

"You alright, flower?"

"I'm alright. You alright?"

"Yeah. I'm alright." He nodded at Vern. "Who's this?"

"This is Vern. I'm taking him under my wing."

"That's good. That's good." He turned to Vern. "You listen to Onwyth. She's the smartest girl I know."

Vern gave a slight nod.

"He's a talkative one. I bet you two have some right laughs." He grinned at Vern and waved a hand. "I'm just messing with you, kid. Me and Onwyth go back a long way."

"We need some info," Onwyth said.

Jez picked up his bowl and wobbled to his feet. "I thought you were looking for something."

"On second thoughts, I don't think you can help me."

"Ah, you'd be surprised." Jez tapped his earlobe. "Old Jez hears things."

"We're after an address."

"And whose address might that be?"

"Pat."

"Mad Pat or Axe Pat?"

"Mad Pat."

Jez smirked. "You messing with me?" He turned to Vern. "Tell me she's messing with me."

"I'm serious," Onwyth said. "Do you know where he lives, or not?"

Jez looked over his shoulder and lowered his voice. "You think I'm that stupid?"

"I can pay." She reached into her pocket. "Probably got some cash around here. Not just hack." She pulled out a ten-krone note and waved it just out of his reach. "I can give you this, if you tell me where he lives."

"I'm sure you can. But I'm not getting involved in any of that." He held up his hands. "I'm quite attached to my fingers, I'll have you know. Been out here this long and they're all still there. And I'd like to keep it that way."

Onwyth pouted. "I knew you wouldn't be able to help."

"What can I say?" Jez placed his bowl back on the ground. "You need anything else, flower?"

"No. It's fine. We'll give the cash to someone else."

"You look after yourself, Onwyth. Send my best to Yorik."

Onwyth sighed. "Yorik's dead."

"Oh, flower. I had no idea. Really sorry to hear that."

"It is what it is."

"Yeah. What can you do?"

Onwyth shrugged. "Take care of yourself, Jez. Been nice seeing you." She carried on and hopped onto the Kusten Road.

"Do you think he knows?" Vern asked when they were out of earshot.

"Probably. Probably not. I don't know. Doesn't matter if he does. He's not giving it up." She glanced back at Jez to see him talking to another man. He gestured towards Onwyth and Vern.

"Come on. I've got a few other places to try." She picked up the pace.

After a minute or so, a man stood in her path and drew a pistol.

Onwyth stopped and raised her hands. "We haven't got anything. Go mug someone else."

"Why you looking for Pat?"

Onwyth stepped forward and smiled. "Do you know where I can find him?"

"For what?"

"I was thinking about what he was talking about. I think he's right about the pattern. I see it now. You have to go there for a while. It's really obvious once you get going. But I think he's missed something."

The man frowned and lowered his pistol. "You talking about the fights?"

Onwyth gave a quick nod. "Yeah. But he's missing something vital. I knew when he was telling me about it something was off. But I've worked it all out." She raised a finger. "It's the big key to unlocking it all."

The man gave a shrug. "That stuff's on the money, then?"

"Yes! Well, no. Not quite. He's so close, but he's missing one important thing."

"And what would that be?"

"You wouldn't get it." She tapped the side of her head. "You need to understand the pattern before it can make sense. Do you understand the pattern?"

"They just look like scribblings to me."

"Exactly. So where is he? With his pattern and my key, we can make a fortune."

"Erm..." He slipped his pistol back into his coat. "Wait here. I'll go get him."

"Thank you. This is going to be so good."

She stood grinning as the man walked away. When he turned a corner, her grin dropped and she leant towards Vern. "Thirty-three."

Vern stood stock-still. "How did you do that?"

"I said, thirty-three." She yanked his sleeve. "Let's go. Before he comes back."

Melita approached the Crows' headquarters and took in a breath. She didn't want to keep annoying Brak, but this was too important to worry about niceties. She knocked at the door and waited. A few moments later, the guard stuck his head out and squinted. "You're back."

"Yes."

"You're Brak's bird, ain't you?"

"I need to speak to him. And don't give me any shit. This is important."

He closed the door without giving a response, and Melita waited for over a minute before Brak came down.

He stepped outside and made a loud sigh. "You need to stop. Honestly, Mel. You can't—"

"This is strictly business," she said, cutting him off. "I thought we were supposed to be under your protection? Or is that a convenient lie?"

He eyed her coldly and gave a slight nod. "What is it?"

"It's Patrov."

Brak laughed. "Patrov? Maybe if your lads had done their job, that wouldn't be a problem."

"Forget it." She turned and strode away with her chin raised. If he was going to be a dick about it, screw him. She didn't have the time to waste.

Brak caught up to her and grabbed her shoulder. "Wait. Wait. Come on."

"What, so you can laugh? So you can dismiss me without even hearing what I have to say?"

"I'm sorry." He smiled and glanced behind him. "Maybe...maybe I can help. It is putting me in a bit of an awkward position, though."

"As I've already said, forget it. Don't give yourself the trouble. I'm sure I can find someone else who can help me."

"Mel, please. You don't need to be like this. What is it? If I can help, I'll help."

She fixed his gaze for a long moment before speaking. "I need his address."

"You tried the Rusty Sail? He's—"

"His home address."

Brak nodded. "Just a second." He reached into his pocket and pulled out a slip of paper and a pencil. Melita watched him scribble something down. He handed it over to her.

Melita raised her eyebrows. "He lives up there?"

"Number thirty-three. Big place. You can't miss it."

"Thank you." With shaking hands, she stuffed the slip of paper into her pocket. She went to kiss him on the cheek then stopped herself. "You've been very helpful."

"My pleasure."

She turned and walked away. She had to let the others know.

"Wait. When can I see you again?"

Melita shook her head. "This is business, Brak. You said yourself not to mix things up."

"I know, it's just—"

"No, Brak. Just...no."

The closer Fedor came to the docks, the less his mind seemed drawn to the Rusty Sail. Perhaps if he kept his distance from that place, he might get through this. "Where should we go now?"

Lev removed his cap and scratched his stubble. "Who bloody knows, mate? Maybe we should take a look around the docks again, or come back later. Do another loop, or something." He flipped his cap back on and sighed. "It seems to me that when we don't want to see him, he's all over our business, and when we actually want to find him, he's a shadow."

Fedor nodded. "Maybe."

Lev looked around. "I mean, we might be in luck. Maybe Melita's had some luck with her contacts. Or Onwyth's managed to get something with Vern. You'd think someone would know where the prick lives. I bet people are just protecting him. I bet they're scared."

"Maybe."

"Is that all you've got to say, mate?"

Fedor shrugged.

"And maybe I know you're trying to get under my skin." He turned to Fedor and jabbed a finger towards him. "But I'm onto you. I'm not going to fall for it." He shook his head. "And after everything I've done for you."

"I'm not trying to get under anyone's skin, for fuck's sake. I'm keeping an eye out for Patrov. It's hard to concentrate, that's all."

"That'll be the plez, that will."

"I know. But I'm trying. It's hard. I just want to lie down in a dark room and sweat it out, but we've got this crap to deal with."

"I'm sick of this shit too, you know? All I want is a quiet life, maybe earn a bit of cash from blackmails on the side. But, no. Myker has to send us to find Pat."

Fedor's eyes narrowed at shifting shadows. He gestured towards an alleyway and drew his dagger. "There."

"What are you doing?"

"I saw him. I saw him again."

"There's nothing there."

Fedor signalled for quiet and crept forward, his heart racing, his hands shaking. He rounded the corner between two buildings and squinted into the darkness.

Lev joined his side, wielding his club. "There's nothing there." He placed a hand on Fedor's shoulder. "Come on. Let's keep focused on what we're doing."

A figure dressed in grey leapt across the rooftops ahead of them and disappeared from view. "You saw that, didn't you? Please tell me you saw that."

"Shit." Lev nodded. "I saw it, mate."

Fedor spun at the sound of flapping leather. His blade stopped a few inches from Dienerin's face.

"Fedor, Fedor, master. I've been asked to summon you."

Fedor glanced back along the commercial district and slipped his dagger back into its sheath. "What is it?"

"Melita says she has found the address. You should return to the den immediately."

"She's got it?"

"That is correct."

Fedor scoured the rooftops for signs of the assassin.

"Come on, mate. Let's do what the scaly bitch says. And then I'm going to get me some grub."

"What about the assassin?"

"What about him? Nothing we can do until he tries something. And there's two of us, remember?"

Fedor looked down at Dienerin. "Actually, there's three of us."

Lev wrinkled his nose. "Nah. It's you and me, mate. You and me. Screw that scaly bitch."

Fedor followed Lev up to the common room, the noon bells chiming across the city.

Melita stood gazing from the window. "I take it Dienerin found you?" she asked, without looking back.

"Yeah," Fedor said, joining her side. He scanned Kathryn Square, making sure they hadn't been followed. "The others not back?"

"Dienerin should be getting them...that's if she listens."

"I told her she needed to find everyone once she got the signal from you."

"Hmm."

"And she did come and find us."

"She found the master. We'll see whether she'll bother to find the others."

"I take it you got it then?" Lev asked from the nearest sofa.

"I have the address."

Fedor joined Lev on the sofa as Melita turned from the window and handed Lev a slip of paper.

Lev unfolded the address and looked up at her. "You sure this is the right place?"

She snatched the paper back and nodded. "I'm as sure as I can be. My contact has no reason to lie."

Lev whistled. "I suppose doing what he's done for years has to be a nice little earner. Fair play to the bloke."

"Fair play?" Fedor asked.

Lev shrugged. "All I'm saying is that he's done well for himself."

"This is Patrov we're talking about."

"Exactly. That's what makes it so surprising."

"Maybe his fight system works."

"Yeah, right." Lev grinned. "Nah, this is what happens when part of your business involves hacking off some poor sucker's fingers."

Fedor started when the door swung open.

Vern and Onwyth entered.

"Dienerin found us," Onwyth said. "Please tell me one of you has the address. We've been out looking for ages. No luck. Seems like no one knows where he lives, or at least they're not telling us." She raised a finger. "I bet it's that. I bet people are scared." Her finger dropped and she frowned. "But that doesn't explain why Frank didn't know. Can't see him being scared of Mad Pat."

"He lives on North End Road," Melita said. "Big house, opposite the park."

"Really?"

"Really."

Onwyth shook her head and sat down next to Vern. "I think we are in the wrong game."

"We need to visit him tonight," Melita said.

"That's if he's even there," Lev said. "He's usually knocking around the arena, chatting shit to anyone who'll listen."

"Or anyone who'll not complain," Onwyth said.

Melita nodded. "I'm talking late. Very late. Or very early. Either way, we need to get him when he's sleeping. We need to scare him and we need him gone."

"That's stupid," Onwyth said.

"Excuse me?"

"What makes you think scaring him will work? I'll kill him myself if I have to."

Fedor glared at her. "No."

Onwyth rolled her eyes. "I don't know if you've noticed, but this is serious. It's kill or be killed out there."

"She's right," Vern said. "I think—"

"No one asked you," Fedor snapped.

"It's just like with that Soren guy," Onwyth said. "He was going to kill us. He...he killed Yorik." She slapped a hand down on the sofa's arm. "And I'm not letting that happen again...to any of us."

"We should bag him," Lev said.

"We should what?" Fedor asked.

"Bag him." Lev rose to his feet and began to pace. "We get a sack. A big one. We break into his house, bundle him in the sack, smack him around a bit, then stick him onto a ship to the Northern Reaches, or wherever."

Fedor sniffed. "And you really think that will work?"

"What can I say, mate? It's better than we've got."

"What makes you think he's not going to hop on the next boat back and come round to smash some skulls?"

"If he comes back, we'll bag him again...and again. He'll soon get the message, mate. Trust me."

"And then Myker will know we didn't do what we were supposed to."

"Difference being we'll have bought us some time. And that's something we're running pretty short of right now."

"No," Melita said. "We can't keep putting this off. We need him gone."

"Alright," Lev said. "How about this? We swing by his place late tonight. We bag him. We beat him good and proper. Maybe smash his legs, or something. And then we deliver him to Myker."

"That's stupid," Onwyth said.

"How's it stupid?"

"Myker paid to have him killed, not delivered. He'll probably think you're trying to pull a fast one if he opens up the bag expecting a corpse and finds Pat grinning up at him."

"Be hard to grin without any teeth," Lev muttered.

"You can grin without teeth." Onwyth frowned. "At least, I think you can."

"You're missing the bigger picture," Lev said. "Myker wants Pat's territory. I think we're past the point where keeping the fact Myker wants him dead is anything resembling a secret. Trust me, this is the best way. We bag him. We break a few bones. We deliver him and work on getting the rest of Myker's cash."

Fedor's lip curled. "Is there any way we can do this without killing or maiming anyone?"

"We've been forced into a corner, mate. What else can we do?"

Fedor let out a heavy sigh. "We can run. We can hide. We can do whatever we want. I'm sick of feeling like a fucking puppet." He got to his feet and marched to the door. "You lot can drown in this shit if you want, but I'm not sticking around here anymore. I've had enough."

Fedor entered his bedroom, opened his drawers, and hurled clothes onto his bed in a haphazard pile. He dragged a backpack from under his bed and tossed clothes inside with gritted teeth, trying to ignore Lev eyeing him from the doorway.

"Mate, you don't need to do this."

Fedor pursed his lips and stuffed a scarf into his pack. "Yes, I do."

"If we need to run, we'll run. But not yet. Trust me, mate. Let's just see how this thing with Pat plays out and get a plan together."

Fedor turned to him, his nostrils flaring, heat rising up his neck. "Even if Pat is gone, we've still got to find fifty grand. Fifty fucking grand, Lev. I don't think we've earned that much in our entire lives." He held up a pair of woollen leggings and tossed them back onto the pile. "Myker wants payment overmorrow, one way or another."

Lev smirked. "Ooh, listen to you with your fancy words."

"What?"

"Overmorrow? Who are you, a bloody priest, or something? Listen to yourself."

"Better than saying the day after tomorrow."

"Is it?"

"It's quicker."

"Not if you have to explain it." Lev sighed and sat on the edge of his bed. "Listen, mate. We've got Pat's address. That's more than we had earlier."

"So?"

"So we go to his house. If he's not there, we'll ransack the place. I bet that arsehole's got loads of cash stuffed around. Who knows? Maybe our luck's come in. Maybe we'll get all the cash we need and Pat'll throw himself off a balloon, or something."

Fedor sniffed. "Yeah, right. And how are we going to get in?"

Lev licked his lips. "We use your blade. Go in...go in through that place."

"You want to go through the shadow realm?"

"Yeah. If that's what it takes. Desperate times and all that." Lev raised a finger. "But it needs to be quick and we need to do it right."

"And you're not afraid of getting stuck? You're not afraid of those things Dienerin mentioned that, what was it she said, feed on the lost?"

"Of course I'm bloody afraid, mate. That place scares the shit out of me. But do you know what else scares the shit out of me?"

"What?"

"How about what the Crows will do to us if we don't pay? How about what happens if we get caught breaking into Pat's place? That's not to mention that assassin bloke poking around." He looked down at his hands. "But if we can use that place to make things easier, that's what we'll have to do." He nodded slightly. "You're right about using it."

Fedor stuck his finger in his ear and twisted. "Sorry, say that again. Did you just admit that I was right about something?"

"Maybe a bit. But only about using the blade if we need to."

"What made you change your mind?"

"Erm...how about everything else we're having to deal with? It's a tool, plain and simple. It's dumb of us not to use it."

"You're a tool."

"No, mate. You're a tool."

Fedor grinned and grabbed his pillow. He flung it at Lev who batted it away with a forearm.

"Oh, mate. You've picked the wrong fight." He snatched up Fedor's pillow and threw it back. "Take that, you prick."

Fedor ducked and his grin dropped at the sight of Melita in the doorway.

"Is everything alright, lads?"

Fedor and Lev exchanged looks and both threw their heads back with laughter.

"What did I say?"

Fedor waved a hand. "It doesn't matter."

"Yeah," Lev said. "It's one of those you-had-to-be-there things."

She gestured to his backpack and narrowed her eyes. "Are you planning on going somewhere?"

Fedor shook his head. "I was just...I was getting a few things together in case we need to leave in a hurry. You know, if things don't work out with Patrov and Myker."

"So you're not planning on running out on us, then?"

"No." He sighed and looked at Lev and Melita. "We need to do this together. Better that than die alone."

"Good," Melita said. "We should scout his place before it gets dark. See what we're dealing with and draw up a plan."

Lev nodded. "Good idea. We should all go. Get a feel for the place."

"Sounds good to me," Fedor said. "When were you thinking?"

"Now." Melita gestured behind her. "I'll get the others."

Melita followed the gravel pavement north through the park, passing bare oaks and sycamores and empty flowerbeds that would no doubt bloom come spring.

Lev and Fedor spoke to each other in hushed voices, just out of earshot, while Vern and Onwyth trailed behind, laughing at something Melita could not fathom.

She gestured to a set of black iron gates looming ahead, their spiked tops daubed with gold paint. "It's just through there."

Reaching the gates, she came to a stop and pulled the address from her pocket. She scanned the houses, detached and tall and built from the same red brick. All had bay windows looking out onto the street. Some sported turrets and ornamental gutters.

Fedor gazed along the street next to her and whistled. "He lives around here?"

"Apparently so," Melita said.

"Wow," Vern said. "I wonder who lives in these? They must be well rich."

Melita nodded. "Probably Magistrates and bankers."

"Wankers, more like," Lev muttered.

"So which one's Patrov's?" Fedor asked.

Melita checked the address again. "Number thirty-three."

"You've got to be kidding me."

"What?"

Fedor laughed. "Thirty-three?"

"No." She glared at him before he had a chance to call the job off. "We're doing this."

"Let's just hope it's not a sign."

Onwyth stuck her head between Melita and Fedor and slapped a hand on each of their shoulders. "What's a sign?"

"Thirty-three," Fedor said.

Onwyth checked up and down the street. "We're not—"

"It's his house number," Melita said. "We're not doing a thirty-three."

"This is going to make things confusing."

Melita rolled her shoulder, freeing herself from Onwyth's grip. "No. It won't. We're going to check the house. It's number thirty-three." She let out a sigh. "Surely you can tell the difference?"

"Of course I can tell the difference." She jerked a thumb towards Lev. "But some people don't understand context."

"Screw you, Onwyth," Lev said. "I know the bloody difference between the number thirty-three and an actual thirty-three." He nodded towards Fedor. "I'm not the one who's confused by simple shit."

Fedor raised his hands. "I'm not confused. I just thought it was a sign, that's all."

Onwyth shook her head.

"You'll start seeing Creation in the clouds next," Vern said.

"No one asked you," Fedor snapped.

Vern met his words with a glare.

"Enough." Melita raked a hand over her hair. "It's just a number. Nothing more. Nothing less. Can we please just focus on the job?"

"No problem here, boss," Lev said.

Melita looked across the others' faces. "Anyone?"

No one moved.

"Good." She stepped through the gate and squinted along the quiet avenue. Lampposts stood at regular intervals, their stems glinting with a deep black gloss. She pointed to the house across the street. "That's fifteen." She took a left and began to walk, signalling to the houses as she passed. "Seventeen. Nineteen."

"Keep your voice down," Lev said. "Don't want people knowing we're not from around here."

Fedor chuckled. "Because we all look perfectly at home up this end of the city?"

Lev raised a finger and went to speak. His finger dropped. "Good point. Doesn't hurt to keep our heads down, though."

"Twenty-five. Twenty-seven." Melita pointed to a house further along the street. "It'll be that one there."

"Shit me." Lev's mouth dropped open. "Look at the size of that bloody place."

Melita stopped across the street from Patrov's house and frowned at the steel shutters barricading the windows. Spikes ran across the sills and gutters. "Place is like a fortress." She bit down on her bottom lip. "There's no way we're getting in there."

"What do you reckon, boss?" Lev asked. "Maybe we should have a look around, see what we're dealing with."

Melita glanced back down the street and sighed. "I don't know. It's—"

"I can get us inside," Fedor said, drawing his blade.

"What are you doing? This is supposed to be about checking out the place."

Fedor frowned at her. "I figured we could at least get into the house."

"There's no way we can break in there."

He splashed tears onto the blade and grinned. "We don't need to break in." He jogged across the road and drove his dagger into the door, tearing open a gaping portal.

"Are you sure it's safe?" Melita asked, chasing after him.

"If we're quick."

She nodded. "Right. Lev and Fedor, we'll go in. Onwyth and Vern can keep lookout."

"Nah," Lev said. "We should all go."

"But we need a lookout."

"Not round here, we don't. It's going to look dodgier if a couple of us are hanging round outside."

"Alright." Melita took in a deep breath. She stared at the portal and sucked in her bottom lip.

"I don't like it either," Fedor said. "But it's the best we've got."

"Come on, then." Melita glanced back at the others. "We'll all go in."

She followed Fedor inside and grabbed his shoulder as the world vanished. Colours disappeared. Sounds evaporated. She smelt nothing.

Lev signalled to the rift and Fedor sealed it shut.

Melita's eyes adjusted to the dizzying array of monochrome, the city like a net of chalk lines extending into the distance. She hooked arms with Lev and Fedor. Onwyth and Vern did the same, latching onto Lev's free arm.

She could tell they were inside Pat's house, or at least its simulacrum in this world, whatever this world was.

Fedor pointed to something glowing on what Melita took to be the floor above. Silent communication took place between Fedor and Lev, and Fedor cut a rift back through to the normal world.

Melita covered her ears when she stepped through. Colours glared, stinging her eyes. The smells of floor polish and lemon struck her. The city roared in her skull.

She rested her head back against the wall as her senses came back.

The others were half-dazed.

Fedor sealed the rift.

"What was that thing?" she asked him in a low whisper.

"What thing?"

She pointed up to the ceiling. "Glowing."

Fedor shrugged. "A mind."

"Do you think it could be Pat?"

"Who could say?"

She tapped her blade's hilt and gestured to the stairs. She led the way, testing each step before committing her weight.

The others followed.

She froze when the steps groaned beneath their weight and signalled for them to take it slowly. It had been too long since she had done a sneak job. But she refused to let the others know it filled her with dread.

When she reached the landing, she waited for the others to join her and signalled towards the only room with a closed door. "Was it definitely just him?"

Fedor nodded. "One mind. No more."

"And you can't tell whether it's him or not?"

"No."

"Right." She drew her blade. "Let's do this." She turned the handle and kicked open the door.

Patrov sat up in his bed, his eyes wide. "What are—"

"We warned you." Melita pointed her dagger at him, her eyes narrowing. "We had a deal."

Patrov pulled his blankets towards him and gritted his teeth. "How did you lot get in here?"

Melita took a step forward, her gaze burrowing into his, her fingers flexing around the blade's icy handle. "You crossed the wrong people, Pat."

"What do you want from me?"

"You know what we want."

His hand shifted.

A shot went off.

For a moment, Melita froze.

The light flashed.

A bang.

The hint of gun smoke.

Vern's scream.

She swung at the pistol, sending it smashing against the wall. "Thirty-three!"

Vern sank to the ground, blood oozing from his chest.

"You stupid fucking bitch!" Patrov lurched towards Melita, his hands clasping around her ankles.

She kicked free and leapt backwards. "Shit!"

Onwyth dived towards Vern and dragged him out of the room.

The others ran as Patrov scrambled to reload his pistol. "You're fucking dead. You stupid pricks. Who do you think you are?"

Fedor splashed tears onto his blade and drove it into the nearest door. He grabbed the others and tumbled inside.

Melita met Patrov's gaze through the portal. She saw his mouth gape and his hands shook as Fedor sealed the rift.

Fedor and Lev helped Onwyth carry Vern as he bled out.

Melita stopped as a white shape in the distance caught her eye. She pointed it out to Fedor.

A giant wormlike creature appeared to swim towards them.

Shifting frantically, Fedor drove his dagger into the door and returned them all to the real world.

He sealed the rift, his eyes darting, his breaths coming thick and fast.

Melita regained her centre and leant against Patrov's front door. "We need to go."

The four of them picked up Vern by his arms and legs and raced into the park.

They dipped into a copse of evergreens and set him down onto a carpet of pine needles.

"What the fuck was that thing?" Melita asked.

"I don't know," Fedor said. "But we're safe here."

Melita stared down at Vern as he lay bleeding, his breaths shallow and laboured.

"We need to find a doctor," Onwyth said, shaking Lev. "Get a fucking doctor. Now!"

Melita rubbed her brow and looked around. "Make him as comfortable as you can. Try to stop the bleeding. I'll see what I can do." She backed away and Lev knelt next to Vern.

"Where are you going?" Fedor asked.

"To get help."

Onwyth shook her head. "He's dead." She crawled over to him, weeping.

"He's not dead," Lev said.

"He is dead."

"He's not bloody dead." Lev gestured to his chest. "He still breathing." He looked up at Melita. "You don't have to get help. We need to get him to the infirmary."

She nodded. "Do you think you can carry him?"

Lev shrugged. "We're going to have to."

She glanced towards the gates. "What about Patrov?"

Onwyth glared at her. "Who cares?" She picked Vern up in her arms. "Which way is it?"

"This way," Lev said. "Come on."

VII. Vern

Fedor and Lev helped the infirmary's orderlies lift Vern onto the trolley. Vern stared glassy-eyed, his senses dulled by poppy milk, his shirt caked in half-dried blood. The stench of infection hung in the air, turning Fedor's stomach. He tried to block out the sounds of groans and cries and the occasional scream echoing along the tiled corridors.

He took a step back as the orderlies wheeled Vern through a set of double doors, revealing before the doors swung shut a leather-clad surgeon waiting next to a bench, with an assortment of tools and liquids.

He placed a hand on Onwyth's shoulder and forced what he hoped would be a reassuring smile. "You alright?"

She gave a slight nod, her gaze fixed on the double doors. "Do you think he'll make it?"

"I don't know."

Lev shook his head. "Mate, he'll be fine. Trust me. He's young. He's strong. You've got nothing to worry about."

"What is it about me?" Onwyth asked.

"Where to bloody start." Lev's grin dropped when Onwyth's eyes welled with tears.

"Everyone I get close to..."

Fedor turned to her. "Don't be ridiculous. This wasn't you. Patrov did this."

Onwyth held her eyes shut, her shoulders convulsing. "First it was Yorik. Now it's Vern."

Lev inclined his head. "Don't tell me you and him are a thing? Shit me, Onwyth, he's only been with us a few weeks."

Onwyth dragged a sleeve across her nose. "No. He's a friend. I've been teaching him. I'm like a mentor to him, or a big sister."

"Yeah, right. A big sister who teaches you about killing."

Fedor turned at the sound of footsteps and smiled at Melita's approach.

She came to a stop next to Lev and frowned. "Five grand."

"What is?" Lev asked.

"This operation. That's how much it's costing us."

"Shit."

"Don't worry." Melita raised her chin. "It's getting paid. We'll figure something out."

Onwyth closed her eyes again. "Thank you."

Melita began to pace.

Onwyth marched over to the doors and knocked. "You'd better be getting him fixed up in there."

"They will," Fedor said, steering her away from the doors.

Onwyth's fists clenched. "I should have killed him. We were there. I should have jumped on him and jammed my knife in his throat."

Lev clapped a hand on her shoulder and shook his head. "Come on. Let's get something to eat. There's nothing we can do here. And the last thing we want is everyone in this place hearing our business."

She sank her head into his shoulder and started to cry again. "I'm staying here."

"No, mate. Come on. You need to keep your strength up."

She shook her head and gestured towards the double doors. "No. I want to be here when he wakes up."

Lev and Melita exchanged a look and Melita gave a slight nod.

"Alright. Do what you need to." Lev squeezed Onwyth's shoulder. "We'll bring you something to eat."

"Don't forget about Pat. We can't let him get away with this."

"Don't worry, mate. We'll get it sorted."

Onwyth stuck out her chin. "And if you don't, I will."

Fedor stepped outside and breathed in the fresh air blowing in from the Braun Sea, grateful he was away from the stench of death and infection.

He squinted up at the midday sun as Lev and Melita joined his side.

"Bloody stinks in there," Lev said, gesturing behind him.

Fedor wrinkled his nose. "Makes you appreciate being outside. You think he'll be alright?"

"Who knows?" Lev removed his cap and squatted with his back against the wall. "He's in a pretty bad way."

"What happened to him being young and strong?"

"I was saying that shit for Onwyth. We need to face facts that we'll probably end up one down."

Dryness coated Fedor's lips and all he managed was a nod.

"We can't think like that," Melita said. "I've paid five grand to those doctors. They'd better do their jobs."

"They will," Fedor said. "But what now? We can't just wait around here when we've still got this Myker stuff hanging over our heads."

Melita sighed. "I don't know. I can't think. Not with him in there."

"Well, we need to start thinking."

"Fedor's right," Lev said. "You really think Myker's going to give half a shit whether one of our people is out of action?"

Melita dipped her head. "I know."

"But, first," Lev said, raising a finger, "if I don't bloody eat soon, I'm going to do something we'll all regret."

Fedor nodded. "Pasty?"

Lev smiled. "Sounds good to me, mate."

Onwyth rose slowly to her feet when the double doors opened. She stood back as a pair of orderlies pushed Vern along on the trolley, trailed by a doctor wearing a leather apron and blight mask.

She tapped the doctor's shoulder. "Is he alright?"

"And who are you?" The doctor kept walking.

"I'm Onwyth." She held out her hand, which the doctor ignored.

"And what is your relationship to the patient?"

"He's my, erm, brother." She matched the doctor's pace, almost jogging along the corridor at his side. "Is he going to be alright?"

"The wound was clean. The shot missed the heart and other organs." He stopped and met her gaze through the mask. "He was very lucky."

Onwyth clapped her hands together. "Thank you."

The doctor raised a gloved finger and carried on walking. "Just be careful of infection. I have sutured the wound. Now he needs to rest."

"How do I stop the infection?"

"Alcohol."

She frowned. "What, like beer? Rum? I know he's partial to a cup of cider."

"Use clear white spirit to clean around the wound. Keep a lookout for swelling or discolouration."

"Thank you, doctor."

"If you don't mind." He turned into a side-room and locked the door behind him.

Onwyth chased after the trolley and entered a ward filled with rows of beds. Men lay in various states of illness and injury, some wearing bandages, others wheezing and coughing.

She covered her mouth at the acrid stench of disease and stood back as the orderlies lifted Vern onto an empty bed.

When the orderlies left, Onwyth dragged a chair from the corridor and sat next to Vern. "Hey." She shook his shoulder. "Vern."

He opened one eye, his face creasing. "Onwyth..."

"You're alright." She squeezed his hands. "You're going to be alright."

"How...how long have I been here?"

"Not long. They rushed you in and out. There's nothing to worry about. Everything's alright. Everything's fine. Doctor said you just need to rest. You've got nothing to worry about."

"What about...what about paying?"

"It's sorted. Melita's got you covered. It's all paid for. You just need to get better."

"What happened?"

Onwyth leant forward, her voice dropping to a whisper. "Mad Pat shot you."

"Shot me?"

"Yeah. We thought you were a goner. We thought you were dead."

"Shit." He let out a shuddering breath. "It doesn't hurt, though. It just feels...odd. Like everything's...everything's soft...mushy..."

"That's just the poppy milk." She stroked his forehead. "Don't worry. We'll get him."

He closed his eyes and lay back. His hand drifted up to the wound on his upper chest. "I can't do this."

"What do you mean? Do what?"

He opened his eyes slowly. "Can't do this anymore. I'm done." He closed his eyes again. "The gang...all of it..."

"That's just the injury talking. It's the poppy milk. You'll be fine. You'll get better."

"No...I'm done...I can't...be bothered...anymore..."

"Damn it, Vern. You'll get through this. I swear it in the eyes of Creation. She'll protect you. The doctor said it was clean. You're going to be alright."

"No..."

"You need to do this. If we're going to be the best assassins this side of Hafendorf, you need to get better."

Vern turned to her. "No, Onwyth. I said...I said I'm done."

Fedor brought up his hood against the chill and trudged across the beach, damp sand making way for streaks of seaweed as loose shells cracked and clattered beneath his boots. He breathed in the air, fresh and salty, and welcomed the smells from the sea.

He followed Lev and Melita to an outcrop of rocks dappled with barnacles and sat with his back to the waves, his eyes fixed on the sea gate into the lower city docks.

Lev handed him a pasty. "Here you go, mate."

Fedor nodded his thanks to Lev and took the pasty in both hands. He took a bite, ignoring the flaky pastry cascading to the ground, latching onto his trousers and jacket.

He chewed on the gristly meat and allowed the tide's ebb and flow to wash over his thoughts.

"I think we need to go back to Patrov," Melita said between mouthfuls.

Lev snorted. "Are you kidding me? You want us to go back there?"

"We need to."

"What, so we can end up like Vern? Or worse..."

"Of course not. But we've still got a job to do. And we're not exactly flush for time here."

Fedor wiped gravy from his lips and cleared his throat. "I hate to admit it, but Lev's right. We can't go in there with daggers when Patrov's got guns and crossbows." He let out a sigh. "We're lucky only one of us got hurt."

"But things have changed."

Fedor turned to her and inclined his head. "What do you mean?"

She took in a breath. "He saw us. He saw us going into the shadow realm. I'd say that changes things, wouldn't you?"

"He saw the portal?"

She gave a nod.

"Oh."

Lev grinned. "This might work in our favour for once. If he's seen we're capable of magic and shit, that we're capable of getting into that fortress of his whenever we want"—he tossed the crust from his pasty onto the sand and a seagull swooped down to catch it—"yeah, I'd say that does change things. But it's how we use it that's important. We need to keep him on his toes, keep him guessing."

Fedor licked his lips and placed his hand on his dagger. "I think you might be right." He got to his feet. "Let's get back to the den and come up with a plan." He tried not to glare at Melita. "A better one, this time."

Melita pursed her lips and got to her feet. "Agreed."

Onwyth gazed across the bed at Vern, her nose wrinkling at the groans and laboured breaths of the dorm. An orderly lumbered past her with a sloshing bucket, the stench of shit and piss forcing her to gag. "No way anyone can get better in here."

Vern shifted on the bed, his eyelids fluttering. "Onwyth? That you?"

She set her hand on his. "How are you feeling?"

"I'm alright...I think. Can hardly feel much." He forced himself to sit and winced. "Can we go?"

"Go where?"

He gestured vaguely around him, his lip curling. "I hate it here. I just want to leave."

"What about getting better?"

"You think anyone's getting better in here?"

"That's what I said."

"Doctor's sewn me up. Nothing else to do here except catch some disease."

"I spoke to the doctor about your wound."

"Yeah?"

"Doctor said we just need to keep it clean with alcohol."

"Like cider and stuff?"

"That's what I said. But he reckons it needs to be clear spirits."

Vern rubbed his chest. "Be alright, I guess. And if it hurts too much, I'll knock some back too."

Onwyth nodded. "Are you sure you want to go?"

"Yeah." He slid his legs from the bed and wobbled to his feet.

"Take it steady, Vern. Here, grab my arm."

He gave a weak nod. "Thanks. Sorry."

"You didn't shoot anyone. You've got nothing to be sorry for." She took his weight as he made his first tentative step. "I've got you. Don't worry."

"Thanks, Onwyth," he said between breaths as they inched forward.

An orderly blocked the doorway as Onwyth tried to leave. "You can't take him. He's not well. You need clearance from the doctor."

"How's this for clearance?" Onwyth pulled her jacket aside, revealing her blade. "Are you planning on trying to stop me?"

The orderly's eyes widened and he took a step back. "You really shouldn't take him like this."

She helped Vern move past the orderly. "Why don't you tell that to my arse?"

"You'll at least need to bring him back so we can take his stitches out."

Onwyth stopped and turned to him. "When?"

"Four weeks." The orderly shook his head. "But you—"

"Yeah, yeah." Onwyth waved him away. "We're going."

"If it goes bad, bring him back," the orderly called after her.

Onwyth nodded. "Will do. Now, if you'll grab the door for us, I'm taking my friend home."

"I thought he was your brother?"

She shrugged. "Brother. Friend. What's the difference?"

He held the door open. "The difference is, you shouldn't be in here."

"Well, it's a good job we're leaving then, isn't it?"

"I hope Vern's alright." Fedor gazed towards the common room door, the bruises across his arms and chest aching. It was in those moments of stillness that the pain pressed down on him—the pain from his beating, the pain from his withdrawal.

Lev lay on the sofa across from him, his hands behind his head. How could someone look so relaxed with everything that was going on?

Melita paced the common room, wringing her wrists, her eyes darting between the window, the door, Fedor, and Lev. "We should go back. And sooner rather than later."

"That's what I was thinking," Fedor said. "Weren't we supposed to take her some food?"

"Huh?" Melita stopped and stared at him. "What are you talking about?"

"Going back to the infirmary."

She shook her head. "I'm talking about going back to Pat's place."

"Shouldn't we at least wait for Onwyth?"

"Who knows how long she'll be?" She gestured vaguely to the window. "We really don't have time to wait."

"Don't you think Patrov will be expecting us now? He knows we're out to get him. He's going to be ready. He's going to have his goons around."

"And he'll make sure they're armed," Lev said.

"Maybe," Melita said. "Maybe not." She pursed her lips and muttered something to herself. "But we need a plan." She turned to Lev. "Any ideas?"

"Nah."

"Fedor?"

Fedor shrugged. "I don't know."

She stopped and tapped her chin. "We need to get back in there. Send a message. Make him afraid of being at home. If he's out and about, it might make him an easier target for the Crows."

"He's already seen the portal," Fedor said. "He knows we can get in and out."

"That's true. Anything to make him know that he's not safe. People under pressure make stupid mistakes."

"Is that why we keep fucking up?" Lev asked.

Melita glared at him and took in a breath. "We just need something more, something that will leave him without a doubt that he's in danger."

"I like that," Fedor said. "We can scare him enough so he leaves for good. Make him stick to our agreement."

"I don't think so, " Melita said. "I think we need to accept we have to do what Myker paid us to do originally."

Fedor held his eyes shut. "Or we could leave."

"I've got an idea." Lev rose to his feet.

"Where are you going?" Melita asked.

Lev ran out of the room, leaving Fedor and Melita alone. She turned to him, her eyes narrowing. "Are you going to be a problem?"

He raised his hands. "What have I done?"

She sniffed. "What about that...that thing?"

Fedor shook his head. "In the other place?"

"That worm thing."

"I don't know."

"Have you seen them before?"

"No."

"Do you think it's dangerous?"

"Dienerin warned me about them. I bet it was attracted to the blood."

"What makes you say that?"

Fedor looked down at his hands. "I don't know. I figured I'd not seen one before. Then, as soon as someone is bleeding, it shows up."

"We don't know that for certain."

He shook his head and looked up as Lev stood in the doorway, holding up a tattered dead crow between a thumb and forefinger. "This is why we should never throw shit away."

Melita wrinkled her nose. "What in the void is that? It stinks."

Lev looked at the crow and tilted his head. "Looks like a dead crow to me."

"That's not what I mean."

"It was from that brick some lads from the Crows chucked up here. Fished it out of the bin." He let the dead bird twist in his grip. "Figured we could use it to send a message to Pat."

A crease set on Melita's brow. "But we need him to be scared of us."

"Honestly, boss. This should be bloody obvious." He turned to Fedor. "You get what I'm doing, surely?"

Fedor shifted in his seat. "Erm...I'm with Melita."

"You wish, mate." Lev grinned.

"Piss off."

"Enough," Melita said. "What are you getting at, Lev? We don't have time for your stupid comments."

Lev brought the bird close to his chest. "You think this is a game?" He tapped the side of his head with his free hand. "This is bloody genius."

"As genius as all your other plans?" Melita asked.

"You want to hear it or not?"

"Fine. Go ahead."

"Here's what I'm thinking. Pat's already seen the portal. We broke into his place without actually breaking in."

"So?"

"Unless he thinks he's seeing things, he'd be right to be shit scared of us." He puffed out his chest. "And who wouldn't be?"

"That still doesn't explain the dead bird."

"It's a crow...it's a message from the Crows. Keep up."

"What's that go to do with us?"

Lev groaned and rolled his eyes. "I can't fucking work with this. It should be obvious. We're putting pressure on from this angle. And if we leave Mister Pecky in Pat's house, that's pressure from another. Especially if he has reason to suspect we're not the only ones who can slip in and out of his place without breaking in."

Melita frowned. "You named it?"

"You're missing the point."

Fedor started at the sound of movement from downstairs.

Lev and Melita fell silent and drew their weapons.

Voices filtered up the stairs.

"Sounds like Onwyth and Vern are back," Melita said, her shoulders relaxing.

Lev slipped his club back onto his belt. "I'm looking forward to the day when we're not shitting ourselves at every bloody noise."

"We should go and see them," Melita said.

Fedor followed the other two downstairs and met Onwyth and Vern in the antique shop.

Vern clung on to Onwyth's shoulder, his eyes unfocused and watery.

"Come on, mate." Lev took Vern's weight on his shoulder and gestured for Fedor to join him. "Let's take you upstairs."

Fedor took hold of Vern and helped him up the stairs.

"How are you feeling?" Fedor asked.

Vern mumbled something.

"They pumped him up with poppy milk," Onwyth said from behind them. "He just needs to rest."

"You sure he's ready to come home?" Fedor stumbled with Vern's weight as he reached the top of the stairs. "He seems like he's in a bad way. I can't believe they sent him away like this."

"They said we just need to keep that wound clean," Onwyth said, holding the door open. "Have to use clean white spirit, apparently."

"So they're just done with him?"

"He needs to go back in a few weeks to get the stitches out."

Fedor steered Vern towards the bedroom. "What did the doctor say about his wound?"

"The shot passed through without hitting any organs. He's lucky to be alive. I think Creation was looking out for him."

"Shit."

Fedor helped Vern onto the bed and brought the covers up to his chest.

"I'll get him some water, mate," Lev said, patting Fedor's shoulder.

Onwyth remained in the doorway, her expression turning to a frown. "Why was Lev carrying a dead bird?"

"Oh, that." Fedor waved a hand. "We're going back to Patrov's with it. Send him a message."

Onwyth narrowed her eyes. "Good. I'm coming with you."

Fedor huddled with Melita, Lev, and Onwyth near the park gates as the last sliver of sunlight dipped beyond the horizon and the gas lamps along Patrov's street flashed to life.

"We all ready?" Melita asked, her breaths coming out in fine white clouds.

Fedor and the others nodded and checked their weapons.

Lev held up the dead crow. "Mister Pecky's ready too."

"We should keep an eye out for Pat's goons along the street. If he's smart, he'll have at least a couple of his men on guard outside."

Lev leant from the park gates and looked back to Melita. "His place looks pretty quiet. No lights." He turned his attention back to Patrov's house. "All looks clear."

"You know what we need to do," Melita said. "Remember, we need to make it look like the Crows."

"You sure we need to go back into that magic place?" Onwyth asked. "I didn't like it in there. Made me feel funny." She shuddered. "And I didn't like that weird worm–monster thing."

"It's the best thing we've got," Melita said. "And that place is like a fortress."

Lev gave the signal and Fedor stepped through the park gates. He followed the pavement along the opposite side to Patrov's house.

Fedor kept to the shadows and tried to ignore his aches and pains.

Lev signalled for them to cross the street.

Reaching into his coat, Fedor strode towards Patrov's front door. He took out his vial of tears and splashed some onto his blade, averting his gaze when it glowed bright blue.

When the others joined his side, he pressed his dagger into the front door, tearing a hole between realms. What would happen if he left a gate open, or if one of those things made it out?

He pushed the thoughts aside, gave the others a nod, and stepped through the portal.

The silence hit him. The stillness. The lack of smells and colours. Onwyth held onto his arm as the others looked around in all directions.

Fedor glanced up and scanned the other floors, searching for signs of a mind, but the house stood empty.

Lev jabbed his shoulder and gestured to the rift.

Fedor sealed the portal and gazed across the city for signs of that thing. Perhaps Vern had attracted the creature after all.

He stepped over to a nearby door and opened another portal. He ushered the others out before stepping through and sealed it behind him.

He stood with the others, all of them appearing shaken, Onwyth cringing and covering her ears.

Fedor closed his eyes and tried not to wince at the sounds and smells.

When his body adjusted, Fedor took in a breath. "The house is empty."

"And that worm–monster thing wasn't there," Onwyth said.

"Fedor thinks it might have been attracted by blood," Melita said. "So let's try our best not to get shot."

"It wasn't Vern's fault."

"No one said it was. We just need to focus on what we're doing."

Onwyth looked around the dining room and frowned. "And what are we doing?"

Lev pulled the festering crow from his pocket and plucked one of the feathers. "We make a right mess. Smash up a few things. Leave a message that he won't forget in a hurry."

"Smash things up?" Onwyth asked.

"Yep."

"I can do that." Onwyth drew her knife, stepped over to a leather-backed dining chair and slashed into its back. "That's for Vern, you fucker."

Melita yanked an oil painting from the wall, hurled it to the floor, and stamped down on its frame, sending splinters across the carpet.

Fedor backed out of the dining room and made his way upstairs. Lev followed behind, tossing feathers here and there.

Fedor checked his blade and gestured to the bedroom.

"Mate, I thought you said this place was empty?"

"It is."

"Good." Lev barged past him and shoved Patrov's bedroom door open.

The bed stood empty, its sheets ruffled.

Lev tore more feathers free and threw them onto the bed. He placed the crow on the pillow and gave Fedor a half-smile. "Mister Pecky's going to sleep now."

Fedor shook his head. "There's something wrong with you, Lev."

"Nah, mate." Lev straightened up and drew his club. "Let's make a mess." He swung the club at a cup on the nightstand, shattering it against the wall.

Fedor rooted through drawers and tore into clothes with his dagger, slicing them to ribbons and tossing them around the room.

He stopped when he touched something cold, something metal. He pulled the drawer out further and dragged out a steel box. "I've got something, Lev."

"What is it?" Lev rubbed his hands together.

"I think it's a lockbox." He placed the box on the bed and it formed a dip in the mattress.

"Looks heavy."

"It is. Might be too heavy to take with us."

"Nice." Lev gestured for Fedor to stand back. He cracked his knuckles and ran a forefinger around the rim. "It's a good one this is, mate. Proper craftsmanship. Must have cost a fair penny."

"Looks like a sturdy lock. You think you can do it?"

"That's not the real lock." He flicked a hidden switch, revealing a second keyhole, and grinned. "That's your lock."

Fedor whistled. "Nice."

Lev took out his tools and worked on the tumbler.

Fedor cringed at the sound of banging from downstairs and wondered how long it would be before Patrov returned, or a neighbour summoned the watch.

The lockbox clicked and Lev flipped open the lid.

"Fuck, yeah!" He pulled out a roll of cash and waved it in front of Fedor's face.

"Whoa!" Fedor snatched the cash, his eyes widening. "There's got to be at least ten grand here." For a moment, he considered pocketing some for himself, taking what was rightfully his.

"Mate?" Lev held out his hand. "You alright?"

"Yeah. I'm fine." He handed the cash back to Lev. "Seems our luck's finally turning around." He started at the sound of movement behind him and spun with his blade outstretched.

Onwyth stood in the doorway and folded her arms. "You should be careful waving that thing around."

Fedor placed a hand on his chest, his heart racing. "You really shouldn't sneak up on people like that."

Onwyth pointed at the lockbox. "What you got?"

"Cash," Lev said. "Fedor reckons there must be at least ten grand here."

Onwyth smiled. "Teach that no-good bastard for shooting Vern." She ran a finger along a bullet hole in the wall. "I think we should go. I don't like leaving Vern alone at the den. He might need something."

"Good point," Lev said. "I just want to pick his front door before we go. Maybe wreck the lock." Lev pushed past them and headed downstairs.

Onwyth looked around the room and scrunched up her nose. "That bird stinks."

"I know."

She shook her head and marched towards the bed, drawing her knife. She dragged the blade down a pillow, tearing a hole, and emptied hundreds of white feathers out onto the bed. She wiped her hands together and smiled. "Much better."

"You coming?" Melita shouted up the stairs.

Fedor took in a breath and followed Onwyth back to the hallway.

"You think this will get him to leave?"

"I hope so." He gave a helpless shrug. "Probably not."

When he reached the bottom of the stairs, Fedor dripped tears onto his dagger and gestured for the others to follow.

Moonlight shone over Kathryn Square by the time Fedor and the others reached the shop.

He pulled his hood down and waited as Melita fished inside her pockets and pulled out a key.

She wiggled the key in the lock and frowned. "I'm sure I locked this."

"Maybe you forgot," Onwyth said. "Wouldn't be the first time you messed up."

Melita sighed and entered the shop. She turned on the lights, filling the room with a soft alchemical glow.

Vases and bowls lay scattered across the floor, pottery fragments lying between fallen plinths and splintered wood.

Fedor shook his head. "Shit."

"Vern!" Onwyth shoved past him and raced upstairs.

Fedor gripped his dagger, his hands trembling, his pulse racing.

Lev stood at his side, his club drawn. "Shit me, mate. I bet the Crows did this."

"We don't know that for sure," Melita said. "We should look around. Keep your eyes and ears open."

"I've got an idea." Fedor splashed tears onto his blade and drove it into the door.

Lev grabbed his shoulder. "What are you doing?"

"I'll be two seconds."

"I'm not going back in there if I don't need to."

Fedor sighed and stepped through the portal. He stood for a moment, allowing his body to adjust, and gazed up through the building.

He caught sight of what he presumed was Onwyth following the stairs spiralling up the building.

Apart from Onwyth's, Lev's, and Melita's, there were no other minds.

Certain they were alone, he stepped back through the portal and sealed it behind him.

He cringed when Lev spoke to him, the words slamming against his ears.

When he finally regained his centre, he turned to Melita. "There's no one else here."

"No one else?" She frowned at him.

"I checked to see if there were any other minds. There weren't."

"I wondered what you were doing," Lev said. "Was worried for a moment you'd completely lost it."

Onwyth rumbled back downstairs and stopped in the doorway. "He's gone."

"Alright," Lev said. "I've changed my mind. This is Pat's doing, this is."

"You reckon?" Onwyth asked.

"Yeah. And I was just about to say how nice it is to have a successful job under our belts for once."

Melita gestured to the stairs. "We should split up. Look around." She checked through the windows before pulling down the shutters. "Maybe Vern's hiding." She turned to Fedor. "You said yourself there's some secret passages in this place."

Fedor shook his head. "I didn't see any sign of him in the shadow realm. Either he's not here...or he's dead."

Onwyth gasped. "You think someone killed him?"

"That's not what I'm saying at all."

"But you did. You said he was dead." Onwyth moved towards him and jabbed his chest. "He's not dead. He can't be dead. He wasn't there. He's gone and someone's kidnapped him."

"Did you see any notes or anything?" Lev asked. "Could be one of those ransom things."

"I wasn't looking for a fucking note," Onwyth snapped. "I was looking for Vern."

"We should look around," Melita said. "See what we're dealing with. See if we can find some clues as to where he might have gone."

"Gone?" Onwyth said. "He hasn't gone anywhere. Someone snatched him and we need to get him back."

"We don't know that for sure. Let's look around." She pointed to Lev and Fedor. "You two, check downstairs. Onwyth, you check the bedrooms and the common room."

Fedor made his way down to the training room to find weapons tipped from their racks and the dummies toppled.

"This has got to be the Crows," Lev said, righting one of the dummies.

"I thought you said it was Patrov's lot?"

Lev shrugged. "Either way, it's not good. Crows are more into smashing shit up for the sake of it."

"Maybe. But then didn't we just go to Patrov's pretending to be the Crows. Maybe they had the same idea."

"Ah, shit. Maybe."

Fedor checked the storerooms, found them untouched, and returned to the shop.

He kicked a path through the pottery shards and looked up when Melita came downstairs, her eyes darting this way and that.

"What's wrong?"

"The cash. It's gone."

"What cash?" Lev asked.

"All of it. The coffers. Gone."

"Shit." Fedor dropped to the floor and put his head in his hands. "This is fucking hopeless."

Melita raised her chin. "We've still got the money from Pat's place. That puts us at around ten grand."

"Shit." Fedor's flesh prickled. All he wanted to do in that moment was run to the Rusty Sail and forget about all of this. "What are we going to do?"

Onwyth joined them, her lips trembling. "He's gone...and he's taken his clothes."

Fedor looked around. "You think Vern did this?"

"No. He wouldn't."

Lev removed his cap and turned to Onwyth. "He might have done. I reckon getting shot might give you a different view on things. Maybe he thought 'Fuck it' and left."

Onwyth swept her gaze around the room, her hands flapping at her sides. "But why would he smash the place up?" She spun and turned to Lev, her eyes welling up. "It doesn't make sense."

Lev shrugged a shoulder and looked down at his fingernails. "Maybe he wanted to make it look like we'd been burgled."

"He wouldn't do that. Pat's goons must have come in here, smashed things up, and taken him hostage."

"With his clothes?" Fedor shook his head. "I think we need to accept he might be the one who did this."

"Where's that stinking wyvern?" Onwyth asked. "Maybe she's done something. Maybe she's the one who...who...I don't know. Maybe she smashed stuff up and scared Vern off."

Fedor shook his head. "That doesn't make sense. I haven't seen her. Not since she told us about—" He stopped and bit down on his bottom lip.

"About what?"

"Maybe it's the guild."

Onwyth frowned. "What guild?"

"The assassins' guild. Maybe one of them came here looking for us."

"What? Here?" She glanced around. "You think he's here now?"

"Maybe Vern ran away, scared. Or maybe he's had to pack a few things while the guild holds him...I don't know."

"Settle down," Melita said. "This is all speculation. We don't know anything yet."

"What's the plan, boss?" Lev asked.

"I don't know."

"We need to find him," Onwyth said. "We need to get him back."

Melita began to pace. "And what if he has betrayed us?"

"What if he hasn't?"

"This is ridiculous," Melita said. "This has got to be to do with Patrov. It's the only thing that makes sense." She stopped and turned to the others. "If we find Pat, we'll find Vern. I'm sure of it."

"Hmm." Lev rubbed his chin. "Still doesn't help with the cash though, does it?"

"We've got the cash from Patrov's. That's just shy of eleven grand."

"That leaves us with quite the shortfall," Fedor said.

"There's gotta be a way through this," Melita said.

Fedor turned to Onwyth. "Can we sell that ravenglass you and Vern got?"

"it's gone. I think whoever took Vern must have taken it."

Lev let out a sigh. "We need to face facts here, mate."

"What do you mean?"

"It was Vern. He did a runner. When we were out on the Pat job, he took our shit and did one."

"What if it wasn't? What if someone has taken him?"

"Nah. He did this himself. He packed up, knew what to grab, and left us in the lurch. When you think about it, it's the only thing that makes sense."

"But it's not," Onwyth said. "Why would he smash the place up?"

"Because he's a twat," Lev said. "He nicked our stuff and did a runner, end of story."

"It could be Pat's lot," Fedor said.

"Or the Crows," Onwyth said. "Or the assassins' guild." She sniffed. "It'd probably be easier to work out who you haven't pissed off around here lately."

Lev raised a finger. "I don't have to listen to this shit. You're just sticking up for Vern because you two were close. Doesn't mean he didn't rip us off."

"Onwyth's right," Melita said.

Lev's eyes widened. "I think the name you're looking for is 'Lev.'"

"No. I think between us"—she looked between Lev and Fedor—"well, between you two, we've pissed a lot of people off. Until we know for sure, we can't make assumptions."

"Now you're sticking up for him?" Lev asked.

She fixed him with a glare. "I'm sticking up for us. That's why"—her shoulders sagged—"that's why I think we should go back to the old den."

"The old den?" Onwyth asked. "We're not—"

Melita raised a hand, silencing her. "Just for a while. We keep our heads low. And we keep away from the Crows." She gestured to the pile of broken pottery. "We can't stay here."

"We'll be fine." Onwyth waved a hand. "We just need to know for certain what happened to Vern."

Lev snorted. "Find Vern? Don't you think we've got other more pressing matters to deal with? We can deal with Vern when we've got Myker and the rest of those feathery fuckers off our backs."

Onwyth pouted. "Maybe."

"Trust me, mate. All I know is someone's taken our stuff, smashed shit up, and Vern's gone. He's either with us or he's screwed us. Either way, that still leaves us having to deal with Pat and the Crows."

"I agree," Melita said. "The Crows stuff needs to be our priority. And who knows? We might get lucky and get Vern back in the process."

"Or we might not," Lev said. "Maybe whoever Vern's run off to, he's told them everything."

"Shit," Fedor said.

"Shit, indeed, mate. This whole thing's a complete pile of shit."

"But we can't stay here," Melita said. "Whether it was Vern, Patrov, or the Crows, this place is compromised."

"Or that assassin," Fedor said.

"Do you think Dienerin might be working against us?" Melita asked.

"I haven't seen her." He rubbed the back of his neck. "She does seem to know a lot about the guild stuff."

"It all goes back to Patrov."

"What does?"

"Think about it. If Pat's out of the picture, the guild has nothing to investigate."

"True," Lev said. "And at least we got most of the cash back from Pat after he ripped us off." He cracked his knuckles over his head. "At least that's a bonus."

Melita nodded. "It's settled, then. We'll go back to the old place and figure out our next steps. Anyone have a problem with that?"

The others exchanged looks and shrugged.

"Good."

VIII. The Hunt

Fedor approached the old den, making his way behind the others along the canal towpath. He glanced at the water's black surface, knowing what lurked beneath, and wondered for a brief moment what remained of Soren and Gavril, whether their bones lay at the bottom collecting silt, or whether the water had eroded them to nothing.

He may not have killed Gavril, but the disposal of his body still weighed heavy on his shoulders. He'd protected Melita—for what? So she could take over? So she could keep his money from him? Had his attraction to her clouded his reason and shattered his moral compass?

With a shuddering breath, he turned his attention to the others studying the door. He inclined his head. "What's wrong?"

Lev gestured for silence.

Fedor joined them and found the door hanging off its hinges, the wood around its lock and handle shattered.

Melita freed her dagger from its sheath.

The others drew their weapons.

She signalled to enter and remain silent.

Fedor followed the others inside and pushed the door back into place as best he could.

He stood by the door and listened as the others fanned out into the vestibule, the smells of stone and dust mingling with the canal's musty stench.

Alchemical light flooded the tunnels, forcing Fedor to avert his gaze as his eyes adjusted.

Lev gestured for him to follow and they made their way to the old common room.

It stood empty and silent, little more than a cavern without the furniture.

"I bet Pat has been here," Fedor said.

Lev shrugged. "I don't know, mate. Could be anyone."

They followed a downward tunnel to the training room, the familiar smells of stale sweat and damp lingering in the air. The old punchbag hung in silence from a chain.

Lev shook his head and sighed. "We can't stay here, mate. This place is done."

Fedor turned to him. "Maybe."

"There's no maybe about it. I can't believe we used to live in this shithole."

"We might not have much of a choice."

"There's always choices, mate." He clapped a hand on Fedor's shoulder. "There's always bloody choices." He jerked a thumb back towards the tunnel. "Come on. There's nothing down here."

Fedor trudged back up to the vestibule to find Melita and Onwyth waiting for them.

Melita slid her dagger back into its sheath and scanned the walls. "This was a bad idea coming here. Pat thinks this is where we live. We're safe from him in the other place."

"But what about the Crows?" Fedor asked.

"We can deal with the Crows."

Fedor smirked. "Oh, yeah. You and Brak. I forgot."

Melita glared at him and lifted her chin. "This place has been compromised. Whether it's Pat's lot, or the Crows, it's clear we can't stay here."

"So where does that leave us?" Onwyth asked.

Melita ran a hand back through her hair and sighed. "We go back to the new den. We prepare for a raid. We barricade the place if we need to."

Fedor folded his arms. "You do remember there's an assassin after us as well, don't you?"

Melita tilted her head slightly. "Do we know that for sure? As far as I can tell, you're just jumping at shadows."

"I saw him myself," Lev said. "Fedor's right about this one."

Fedor sneered at him. "This one? I'm right about—"

"Enough," Melita snapped. "You're both assuming the worst. Didn't Dienerin say something about an investigation?"

Fedor frowned. "Yeah, so?"

"Maybe, whoever's been following you is just trying to find information. I'm sure if he wanted you dead, he would have done it by now."

Fedor rubbed the back of his neck. "Maybe. I don't know."

Onwyth gestured to the door. "Lita's right, though. We can't stay here. And we need to be around at the new place in case Vern turns up."

Lev sniffed. "Vern?"

Onwyth glowered at him, her lips pursed.

Lev raised his hands and took a step backwards. "What? The fucker ran out on us. He raided the coffers and did a runner." He held up a finger. "And if I'm being perfectly honest, I'm not sure I can blame him. I reckon if I'd been the one getting shot, I'd be rethinking a thing or two."

"You wouldn't," Onwyth said.

"Wouldn't I?" Lev shrugged. He rocked his head from side to side and pushed out his bottom lip. "You know what, Onwyth? You're right. I wouldn't do that. I wouldn't rip off my crew and bloody scarper like some...like some ungrateful little arsehole."

"What if he didn't?" She pointed at the door. "What if Pat's lot grabbed him, or the Crows, or that assassin? Vern wouldn't do that. I know he wouldn't."

Lev shook his head. "No, mate. I can't see it. There's nothing in it for Pat. And have you seen how the Crows treat their young ones?"

"What about the assassin?"

"What about him? Maybe Vern's been stabbed up somewhere. And I can't see an assassin taking a hostage..." Lev raised a finger. "And that still doesn't explain the coffers. Nah, he's done a runner. Simple as."

Onwyth licked her lips. "It's got to be Pat's lot. That's the only explanation."

"Why?" A deep line set on Lev's brow and he removed his cap. "Vern ripped us off. You know it's true. I don't like it either, but we have to accept he screwed us. Maybe that was his plan all along. Run the long-con, get us to trust him, and then as soon as we left him alone, he took the opportunity."

"No." Onwyth held her eyes shut. "He wouldn't do that to me."

Melita seemed to force a smile. She placed a hand on Onwyth's shoulder. "I think we need to accept the possibility Lev might be right."

Onwyth looked between them. "How can you say that? He's one of us. We're supposed to have each other's backs, not...not accuse each other when things go wrong."

Fedor held open his hand and pointed to the fine scar on his palm. "He's not one of us. He might have been. But he never made the oath."

"You're wrong." Onwyth's nostrils flared. "You're all wrong."

"I'm sorry to say it," Fedor said. "But I'm with Lev. It's the only thing that makes sense. He got shot, it scared him, and he left...taking our cash in the process."

"Yeah," Lev said. "And if he's really smart, he'd have gone straight to the Crows and given them everything he knows."

"He wouldn't," Onwyth said.

"Like he wouldn't run off with our cash?"

"There's a big difference between running away and being a grass."

"Yeah? Maybe he thought he'd be covering his arse and in the clear if he did."

"Enough," Melita said. "We don't know anything, really. This is all speculation. And until we do know for sure what's happened, it's a waste of time. We need to come up with an arrangement."

Onwyth frowned. "What kind of arrangement? We need to find Vern."

"The kind of arrangement where we have a sit-down with Myker and get him to be more reasonable. It's clear we can't get him what he wants in time." She shook her head. "We need to accept that we can't do this in time...and so does Myker. We need to figure out another way."

"So what do we do?" Fedor asked.

"We'll put the feelers out about Vern. See if anyone's seen or heard anything. We need to get Pat on his own. And I'll see if I can arrange a sit-down with Myker."

Fedor nodded. "Right. And what about the assassin?"

Melita shook her head. "Figure it out. I've got enough to deal with."

"Can you get your boyfriend to help?" Fedor asked.

Melita narrowed her eyes. "Don't fucking push me, Fedor. Just don't."

"I'm not. You've got an in with the Crows. You should use it."

Melita remained still for a long moment before giving a quick nod. "Alright. I'll see what I can do."

Fedor entered the antique shop behind Lev and Onwyth and locked the door behind them, his head spinning, his body aching. Every nerve in his body cried out for plez. He placed his hand on the window and closed his eyes. Cold sweat prickled along his skin, chasing away waves of heat. If he could focus on something, anything...

"Mate? You with us?"

He blinked down at Lev's hand shaking his shoulder and tried to focus on his face.

Lev clicked his fingers. "You going to be alright?"

Onwyth ran behind the counter, grabbed a chair, and dragged it across the shop floor.

Fedor slumped down with a heavy sigh onto the seat and hugged himself.

"It's the plez," Lev said.

"Should I get him something?"

"He'll be alright. Maybe get him a drink."

Fedor waved a hand. "I'll...I'll be fine." He rocked back and forth, his teeth chattering. "Honestly."

Onwyth squeezed his arm. "Wait there. I'll get something."

When she climbed the stairs, Lev began to pace.

"Please," Fedor said. "I'll be fine. I just need to get my breath."

"She's getting you a drink, mate."

"I'm alright." Fedor forced himself to meet Lev's gaze. "Honest word."

"Still. Just stay there until you've had a drink."

Fedor nodded and immediately regretted the movement. He slumped forward with his head in his hands and cringed at the stabbing pain in his skull.

"You're alright, mate. You're alright."

Fedor glared up at him. "What would you know?"

Lev smiled. "Just have this." He gestured to the cup Onwyth held out.

Fedor hadn't noticed her return.

He took the cup with shaking hands and sniffed the water, scentless and clean.

He raised the cup to his mouth and sipped, the water icy against his lips. With each sip, the pain withdrew.

"There," Lev said. "You're already looking better. How're you feeling?"

Fedor swallowed the last of the water. "A bit better."

"Good."

"You think Lita will have any luck with Myker, or Brak, or whoever?" Onwyth asked.

Lev shrugged and began to pace. "I don't bloody know." He stopped. "I've got an idea."

Fedor looked up at him. "What is it?"

Lev continued his pacing and tapped his chin. "Mate, this is genius."

"Just tell us what it is," Onwyth said.

"We work with Pat. Team up with him."

Onwyth snorted. "Team up with Pat?"

"Yeah."

"Us? With Pat?"

"Why not?"

Onwyth shook her head. "You can't be serious. This is Mad Pat we're talking about. Pat the Rat. Pat the Plan. Fucking Mad Pat."

"Yeah. And it's bloody genius."

"It's not bloody genius. It's bloody stupid." Her fists clenched tight. "If Yorik were here now, he'd slap you sharp across the back of the head, you know that?"

Lev raised a hand. "Hear me out. It doesn't have to be for long. Just until the Crows are out of the way."

Fedor frowned. "Patrov won't go for this."

"Mate, people around here have said he's the lesser of two evils. Think about it. We work out an arrangement with Pat. We help each other out and use his crew to go after the Crows. We might even be able to keep our hands clean in the process, if you catch my meaning."

"I don't know about this," Fedor said. "Why would he suddenly go along with us after everything that's happened?"

"The difference is, he didn't know about the magic before. I bet we can use it to our advantage. Give him a taste of the other place. Get him on our side. Who knows? Maybe he'll start working for us."

Fedor let out a sigh. "You can't be serious."

"You got any better suggestions?" Lev loomed over him. "It seems I'm the only one coming up with ideas here."

"I have, as a matter of fact." Fedor wobbled to his feet. "I'm done with all this shit." He staggered towards the door. "I'm going out."

"Where are you going?"

"This is too much. I'm going to the Sail."

"You're fucking not. We've got shit to do."

"I'm just going to have a bit. Take the edge off. Then I'll be back."

"I'm not letting you do that." Lev barred the door with his arm.

Fedor drew his blade and pointed it at Lev. "You going to stop me?"

Lev's eyes widened and he took a step back. "This is bad form, this is, mate."

Fedor stepped outside and looked back. "And don't either of you think about following me."

Fedor flapped up his hood and kept hold of his blade, hiding it inside his coat. If anyone tried to stop him, he'd take them down. If Creation existed, she had turned her back on him. He didn't care anymore.

He checked his pocket for the cash he'd stolen from Lev, pleased it was still there. Maybe he should spend all of it and lose himself in the bliss forever. It was better than whatever this shit was.

He marched through the upper city, his head dipped, his jaw set tight. His body screamed at him to hurry, to rush into the Sail, to drift away from this nightmare.

Beggars called to him. Constables eyed him. But he kept his head down, kept moving. If someone stopped him, if someone tried to turn him away from his path, he didn't want to think what he might do.

All he wanted was plez. Nothing more. Nothing less.

He crossed the Kusten Road and ignored the curses of a driver whose cart swerved to avoid him, the horses' cries a distant echo in his ears.

Reaching the lower city, he passed through the arena and marketplace, and skirted along the tunnels towards the docks.

The Rusty Sail's siren call grew louder in his mind. The temptation of the void. The endless yellow nothing.

His hands tingled and his chest burnt as he jogged through the commercial district, lights and sounds washing over him.

Movement caught his eye. A figure in mottled greys hugged the shadows.

His jog turned to a sprint, his legs and arms pushing through the pain, his blade flashing for all to see.

He glanced back as the figure gave chase.

He whirled and scanned the alleyways. "I told you not to follow me."

The man stepped from the shadows and drew his own ravenglass blade.

"You're not—" Fedor blinked at the unfamiliar face. "What do you want?"

The man stood on bent knees and narrowed his eyes.

The assassin lunged towards him, his blade twisting in the air.

Fedor slapped the dagger out of the way and kicked him. "Why have you been following me?"

Heart racing, he fumbled in his coat and took out his vial of tears. He pulled out the stopper with his teeth and splashed the blade.

He stuck the dagger into the nearest door, tearing a rift to the shadow realm.

The assassin's expression did not change. He leapt again, his dagger slashing down.

Fedor stepped aside and shoved the man through the portal, sealing it shut behind him

He dropped to his knees, breathless and trembling, and spat on the ground, his vision blurring with tears.

He wiped his eyes and forced himself to stand. How much fight did he have left in him?

The door stood still and silent, with no signs of the rift, no signs of the assassin.

Had it really been that easy?

Not wanting to wait around for the answer, he turned and ran.

Melita returned to the den with Onwyth to find Lev pacing back and forth, his brow etched with a deep line.

"What's wrong?"

He stopped and blinked. "It's Fedor." He gestured to the door. "He's gone."

"Gone?" Melita let out a long sigh. "Gone where?"

Lev's nostrils flared. "Where do you think he's bloody gone?"

"Bastard." She glared towards the door and turned back to Lev. "Did you not think to stop him?"

"Yeah, I did as a matter of fact." He removed his cap and scratched his head.

"What is it?"

"The fucker pulled that dagger of his on me."

Onwyth's mouth dropped open. "He did what?"

"You heard."

"Shit." She looked down at the floor. "Are you sure?"

"I can't believe this," Melita said. "Please tell me you're lying."

Lev held his palms open and shrugged. "Honest word, boss."

"What did you do to him?" Onwyth asked. "You must have done something...that doesn't sound like the Fedor I know."

"It's that plez shit." Lev tapped his temple. "It's fucking with his head."

"What happened?" Melita raised a finger. "And don't lie to me, Lev. This is serious."

Lev shook his head. "When would I ever lie?"

"Just tell me."

"Fine. I said he shouldn't do it and tried to block his way. He pulled his dagger, shoved me back, and ran off." Lev licked his lips and held Melita's gaze. "Honestly, I thought he was going to do me."

"Shit."

"That's bad," Onwyth said. "You can't go round threatening people like that unless you're going to follow through with it."

Lev glowered at her. "Mate, I think you're missing the point. I don't think any of us want him to follow through with any threats like that."

Onwyth smirked. "Speak for yourself."

"Screw you, Onwyth."

"Screw me? How about—"

"Enough!" Melita snapped. "This is all so messed up."

"I know," Lev said. "Any luck with Myker?"

Melita sniffed. "What do you think?"

"Prick." He flipped his hat back on. "I was thinking, though, there might actually be a way around this. But we need to find Pat. And soon."

Fedor rushed into the den, breathing heavily, and slammed the door shut behind him. With trembling hands, he brought the shutters down and sank to the ground, his chest burning, his legs aching. Every part of him seemed to prickle.

Voices entered his mind. He looked up at the other three glaring down at him, his awareness shifting, his focus smashing into the present.

"You're back then?" Lev stared down his nose, his lip curled. "That was quick." He took a step forward. "I take it you didn't make it to the Sail, then?"

Fedor let out a shuddering breath. "Sorry...I had to...I dealt with the assassin."

Lev's frowned deepened. "What the fuck are you on about?"

"The assassin. The one that was following me. I dealt with it. We're safe."

Onwyth laughed. "You expect us to believe you dispatched a trained assassin?"

"It's true. I shut him in the shadow realm. It's over."

"You're alright with that now, then?" Lev asked. "You're happy shutting people in that place, like it's nothing?"

"It's not nothing." Fedor blinked away a tear. "But what choice did I have? He came after me from nowhere. I did what I had to do. I acted in the moment." He took in a breath. "I'm here, and he's not."

"Are you hurt?" Melita asked.

Fedor tried not to think about the pain gripping his entire body. "It doesn't matter. It's over. I've dealt with him. That thing in the shadow realm will get him. It'll teach those bastards to come after me...to come after us." He rose slowly to his feet and met Lev's gaze. "Look, I said some things I shouldn't have said."

"Damn right, you did." Lev shook his head. "Bad form, that was, mate."

"I know. I shouldn't have done what I did." He opened his hands. "I'm scared, Lev...I'm so fucking scared it hurts."

Lev squeezed his shoulder. "I know. But you threatened me. You've never done that before. I need to trust you, mate." He gestured to the others. "We all do."

"I'm trying to get clean. Honest word. But it's hard. I messed up." His hands balled into fists, his fingernails digging into his palms. "I'm messed up...and I'm sorry." He looked at Onwyth and Melita. "To all of you. I'm sorry."

Lev gave a slight nod and stepped back.

"Sorry's not going to cut it this time," Melita said, placing a hand on her hip. "Lev's right. How can we trust you?"

"I said I'm sorry. Please. You don't know what it's like."

She moved towards him and jabbed his chest. "No. I don't. None of us do. But that's because none of us chose to get into that shit. You've let us down. We're supposed to have each other's backs." She shook her head. "How can you have our backs when you're like this?"

"I know..." Fedor's shoulders sagged and he stared at the floor. "I want to help though...I want to make it right."

Melita nodded and turned to Lev. "What do you think?"

"Maybe. I don't know."

"We need all the help we can to find Vern," Onwyth said.

"We've got more urgent things to deal with," Melita said. "None of us will survive if we don't get to Pat."

"Yeah," Lev said. "It's not like we're in with a chance of getting the cash in time for Myker."

"Weren't you going to speak to him?" Fedor asked.

"I tried," Melita said. "But unsurprisingly, he refused to see me."

"How about your boyfriend?"

"How about you shut the fuck up?"

Fedor raised his hands. "I was only asking."

"Well, don't." She breathed out a long sigh and turned to the others. "I think we need to make some decisions."

"About what?" Fedor asked.

"About you."

IX. The Deal

Fedor kicked off his boots and flopped onto his bed. He stared up at the ceiling, his vision blurred by tears. He hated what he'd become. Two killed. Two sentenced to a fate worse than death. And now his friends hated him too.

He'd become such a burden, such a liability. It wasn't just him he was putting at risk, it was his friends, his crew, the only people in this damn world he cared about.

He considered getting up and heading back to the Rusty Sail. He'd heard of people taking more plez than they should and never waking up. Death in bliss. There were worse ways to go than drifting endlessly in the yellow nothing. And, perhaps, that was the only choice left to him. But was that his own mind talking, or the plez?

Did he want to die? Did he really want to snuff out his life and become one with Creation?

More likely he'd find himself in the void, or worse, as part of that thing in the shadow realm, sentenced to an eternity of non-death and endless torment.

If he really wanted to die, why didn't he stand with his arms wide open when the assassin came for him? No, he wanted to live. He wanted to survive, no matter what his mind told him.

He sat up slowly when Lev entered. He wiped his eyes and dragged a sleeve across his nose. "Hey."

Lev lingered by the door and inclined his head. "You alright, mate?"

"Yeah...I'm sorry."

"I know. I get it. Really, I should beat the shit out of you, but I'm not going to do that." He patted his club. "Don't think I won't, though. If you pull any shit like that again..."

"You'd be within your rights to."

"I know." He sighed and sat at the end of Fedor's bed. "I'm here for you. That's what mates do."

"Thank you."

"Seriously, though. If you do anything like that again, we're done. You understand?"

"I do."

"And this isn't just coming from me, you know?" Lev shook his head. "I had to really talk Lita round. Honestly, mate. She was this close to kicking you out."

"Thank you."

Lev waved a hand. "I'm sure you'd do the same for me."

"I just keep fucking up. Melita hates me. Everything's turned to shit."

"We'll sort it."

Fedor drew his dagger from its sheath.

Lev shot to his feet. "What the fuck are you doing?"

"Here." Fedor tossed his dagger towards Lev. "Have this. It's brought me nothing but shit."

"I don't want it, mate." Lev held his hands up. "It's yours."

"It'll work with you." Fedor tossed his sheet aside and gestured to the blade. "You just need to get some blood and tears and put them in a vial until you need to use it. Please."

Lev began to laugh.

"What's so funny?"

"It won't work for me."

"We both forged it with our blood and tears. We did it together. That's what Soren wanted. It was meant for one of us. But either of us can make it work."

"No, mate. You don't understand. I didn't use my tears."

"I saw your vial."

"What? The one I filled with seawater?"

"You did what?" Fedor began to smile. "You sneaky twat."

"Yep. Conned that psycho bastard good and proper."

"So it won't work for you? You can't get into the shadow realm?"

"Nope."

"Sneaky fucker." Fedor shook his head. "I can't believe you're only telling me this now."

Lev tapped the side of his nose. "You never asked, mate."

Fedor looked at the blade and shook his head. "Just can't believe you conned him."

Lev cocked an eyebrow. "Can't you?"

"Well, when you put it like that."

Lev picked up the dagger, turned it in his hand, and placed it down on Fedor's lap. "We can get through this, mate. I swear it."

Fedor shrugged. "You think?"

"Yeah. Why not? You got rid of the assassin. We've got a plan to get Pat on our side." He gripped Fedor's shoulder and met his gaze. "We'll sort this."

Fedor slid his blade back into its sheath and nodded. "Alright."

"But we need you sharp. No matter what Lita says, you're an essential part of this crew. I know this. You know this. Who else are we going to find with access to the shadow realm?"

"I guess. We did alright without it before, though."

"Mate, I'm serious. This'll be alright. We've just got to keep focused. Fuck that plez shit. Fuck what anyone else thinks. We can do this. You know—" He spun at the sound of loud crashing from downstairs.

Fedor shot to his feet and dragged on his boots. "What's that?"

"I think someone's here."

"Shit. It sounds like more than just someone."

Five lads from the Crows stormed into the shop, letting out birdcalls and swinging clubs.

"Where's Myker's cash?" one of them asked, his eyes fixed on Melita.

"You're making a big mistake," Onwyth said. "When the rest of our crew get here—"

The lad narrowed his eyes at her. "Shut the fuck up."

"Thirty-three!" Melita toppled a plinth, hurling it full-force towards a couple of lads, sending them sprawling to the floor.

The tallest lad swaggered towards Melita, twirling a knife in his hand, his teeth bared. "You stupid bitch. If you ain't got his cash, I'm going to gut you."

"Come on!" Melita grabbed Onwyth's arm and charged upstairs.

Footfalls and taunts joined the noise of shattering glass behind her.

She gritted her teeth and raced into her bedroom, locking the door when Onwyth tumbled inside.

"Furniture." She gestured to a chest of drawers and shoved it against the door.

Bangs came from the other side.

"What are we going to do?" Onwyth asked as they moved the bed towards the barricade.

"I don't know." Melita unsheathed her dagger and Onwyth drew her knife.

"Myker wants his money," came a voice over the knocking. "You need to pay us."

"Fuck off," Onwyth said. "You've got the wrong people."

"Bullshit." The knocks kept coming. "He wants his fifty grand now. Or you're all dead meat."

Lev pressed his back against the wall ahead of Fedor and gestured for quiet. "Sounds like there's a lot of them."

"How many?"

"Can't tell. There's got to be at least three or four" He inclined his head. "It's hard to tell."

"You think it's the Crows?"

"Who bloody knows? Could be. Could be Pat's lot. Could be that assassins' guild out for revenge."

"Shit." Fedor nodded and splashed tears onto his dagger.

"Whoa, what are you doing?"

"I'm going to find out how many there are." He opened a rift in the nearest door and stepped into the shadow realm.

Sounds and smells vanished and the city spread out around him, white lines and shimmering minds.

His focus adjusted and all he could hear was the pulse banging in his skull and the whoosh of blood in his ears.

He scanned the shadow realm in all directions, checking for signs of that thing. If he saw it now, what would he do? What could he do? Could a human fight such a thing?

Turning his attention downwards, he tried to make sense of the web of lines making up the building below, and counted seven distinct minds, all of them glowing purplish-yellow.

He stepped back through the rift and placed a hand on the wall as the normal world assaulted his senses. His breaths came deep and slow and he tried with all his will to speed up the adjustment.

"How many?"

"Seven...five. I think two of them are Melita and Onwyth."

"Five?" Lev rubbed his chin. "We can deal with five."

"You reckon?"

Lev shrugged. "Was it the Crows?"

"I couldn't tell. Just saw the minds."

"Right. Yeah." Lev gestured to the open portal. "You should probably seal that thing."

"No." Fedor yanked Lev's sleeve. "We need to go in and get them. As far as I can tell, they're both in Melita's room."

"I bet you'd love to get a sneaky look in there, wouldn't you?"

Fedor glared at him. "This is serious, Lev."

"So what are we doing?" He cracked his knuckles. "You got a plan, or is it up to old Lev to come up with something genius as ever?"

"We're going in."

"In where?"

Fedor gestured to the portal. "You know where."

Lev took a step back. "I don't think so, mate."

"No arguments."

Before Lev could protest further, Fedor dragged him through the rift.

Fedor sealed the portal and followed the stairs down to Melita's bedroom and opened a rift through her door.

He leant through to find the way partially blocked by a chest of drawers and the bed.

The knocking hammered against his ears.

"Come through." He pulled his back into the shadow realm, relieved when the sound stopped.

Melita and Onwyth clambered through and Fedor sealed the rift.

They passed the minds hovering near the door and followed the stairs down to the ground floor.

He pushed through the front door and stepped out onto the echo of Kathryn Square.

More minds lingered around the den, no doubt more men waiting in ambush.

He followed a route back into the lower city, emerging through a portal in the warehouse district.

Fedor stood in a daze as the smells and sounds from the warehouses washed over him—grain, spices, chickens, goats. Every voice and every movement seemed to scrape along his nerves.

He sealed the portal and his senses finally dulled. "What happened?"

"The Crows," Melita said, almost breathless. "They came in, demanding their money. We barricaded ourselves in my room. We thought..." She threw her arms around Fedor and he patted her back. She looked up at him. "I thought we were dead. I really did."

"You know that's it, now, right?" Lev pointed in the vague direction of Kathryn Square. "They'll take that place. And I'm sure they'll search every nook and cranny for any bit of cash or anything they can sell."

"I'm sorry," Melita whispered.

"I don't know if you noticed, but we didn't exactly have time to think," Onwyth said.

Fedor placed a hand on Lev's shoulder. "Getting pissed off isn't going to do anything. Let's work this out."

Lev shook his head. "What's the point? I'm sick of all this shit. We've got nothing."

"We've still got the old den." Fedor shrugged a shoulder. "At least that's something."

"Yeah, right. Until Pat and his goons arrive. And then what?"

"We'll be ready," Melita said. "But I think Pat has got bigger things to worry about right now than coming after us."

Lev folded his arms. "I bloody hope so."

Fedor, Onwyth, and Melita gathered in the old den's common room, while Lev repaired the front door. Fedor sat with his back against the wall, his arms wrapped around his shins, his chin resting on his knees, the warm stone doing little to abate the chills raging across his body.

Melita and Onwyth sat on the floor across from him.

"Thank you, by the way," Melita said.

Fedor blinked. "Huh?"

"If you and Lev hadn't come in when you did..." She shook her head and stared down at her open hands. "I don't know what would have happened."

Fedor waved a hand. "We swore to have each other's backs, remember? You'd do the same if we'd been in the same position."

The corners of her mouth twitched.

"I still can't believe how lucky you are," Onwyth said. "If I could slip in and out of that place at will, I'd do it all the time. Think of all the places you could sneak in without anyone knowing. The fact we're not rolling in cash just shows what little imagination you and Lev have."

Fedor frowned. "We do alright."

"If I had that thing, I'd be richer than Mad Pat. I'd be doing sneak jobs all the time. Slip in a place, snatch some cash, add it to the pile. Mix it up with some assassin stuff and I'd be making more cash than I'd know what to do with...actually, that's a lie. I know exactly what I'd do with it."

"Right," Fedor said.

"It's true. The trouble is with you and Lev is you overcomplicate things. What's the point in doing blackmails and stuff like that when you could just sneak in there and stick them with your knife before they even know what's happened, and walk away with a shit-load of cash."

"You really think it's that easy?"

"I think it's easier than you've been making it."

Fedor puffed out a breath. "Maybe. But we know what's in there. Dienerin's said what that thing does. I'd say that puts a bit of spin on things, wouldn't you?"

"Where is that slimy bitch?"

Fedor shrugged. "Who knows? I haven't seen her around since this shit with Myker."

Melita looked around the walls and let out a long sigh. "I suppose we'll have to stay here for a while. Who knows what the Crows have done to the new place. I don't even know if we'll be able to go back. They might have burnt it down for all we know."

Onwyth sniffed. "Once we've dealt with them, we should be able to move back in. They're looking for us, not for a building."

"We don't know that for sure, though. In the meantime, I still think we need to go with Lev's plan."

"What plan?" Fedor asked.

"To try and work with Pat. We get him on our side. We work with him to take out the Crows."

Fedor laughed. "Work with Pat? Pat the Rat? Pat the Plan?"

Melita glared at him. "Do you have any better ideas?"

"No. But, working with Mad Pat..."

"Think about it." Melita raised a finger. "He's got the incentive and the motivation."

"And he's got the muscle," Onwyth said.

Fedor shook his head. "I can't see him going for it."

"Why not?"

"Because Myker hired us to kill him. Why would he assume things have changed? If someone who wanted to kill me suddenly suggested working together, I think I'd be suspicious."

"We can tell him we're even," Melita said.

Fedor pointed to the door. "He ripped us off. He agreed to a deal and he went back on it. What makes you think we can trust him?"

"As far as I can tell, we're even."

"Even?" A crease set on Fedor's brow. "How do you figure we're even?"

"We got the cash from his place...or at least most of it."

"It's not just about the cash. If he kept his end of the bargain, we wouldn't be in this mess."

"I'm sure Myker is thinking the same, if we'd have kept our end of the bargain."

Onwyth turned to Fedor. "See? I told you. I knew we should have killed him when we had the chance. But, oh no, you had to overcomplicate things."

"Whatever."

Melita rose to her feet. "I think this could work. We just need to play it right."

"I don't think it will," Fedor said. "They're already at war. We should leave them to fight it out. Keep our heads down and wait."

"This is the difference between using a hammer and a needle."

Fedor and Onwyth exchanged shrugs. "What do you mean?"

"What I mean is maybe we arrange a sit-down with Patrov to discuss Myker, I don't know."

"But then aren't we just helping Patrov?" Fedor asked.

"True. But Pat and his crew haven't been round our den trying to get us. He's not the immediate threat. The Crows are."

"That still doesn't explain why we need to get involved."

Melita glared at him. "The reason we need to get involved is because we are the Crows' number one target. And the longer we leave it, the worse it will get."

"Honestly, I think we should just leave."

"And go where, Fedor? You know it's not as easy as that. If we could just find a new den, we would. We've been down this road before. Everywhere is somebody's. It's not like we're popular with other crews. They're hardly going to want us on their turf."

"We can't stay here." Fedor gestured towards the door. "We know someone broke in here looking for us."

"And Lev is fixing the door," Melita said.

"But someone was looking for us. Who's to say they won't be back?"

"Maybe it was that assassin. And now he's dead...or whatever you call it in that place."

"You shut him in there?" Onwyth asked.

"Yeah," Fedor said.

"How do you know he's dead?"

"Because I shut him in the shadow realm. And we know what's in there."

"But if he's an assassin like Soren. Doesn't he have one of those ravenglass blades?"

Fedor's mouth dropped open. "I never thought about that." He pulled his coat around him. "I never saw one. Maybe he's just a regular assassin."

"It's possible," Onwyth said. "But you don't know for sure?"

"He has to be."

"But what if he's not? I bet you've just annoyed him more."

Fedor shook his head. "No. I trapped him in there. It's over. I'm sure if he was still after me, I would have seen him by now."

Onwyth pushed out her bottom lip. "Maybe. Maybe not."

"I'm sure of it."

"If you say so."

"I do."

"Good." Onwyth looked around. "Because he could be lurking just beyond us in that other place, waiting to pop out and strike."

"Enough, Onwyth," Melita said. She turned to Fedor. "Just keep your wits about you. We don't know for sure. There's nothing to say that another assassin would have the same type of weapon. But...there's a chance."

"So what do we do?" Fedor asked.

"We focus on finding Pat."

Fedor looked up as Lev arrived in the doorway. He gestured behind him. "All good." A frown etched his brow. "What you talking about?"

"She wants us to team up with Pat," Fedor said. "I think it might be a bad idea."

"Nah, mate. It's genius. Trust me. He knows what we can do. He's seen the magic. I'm sure he'd rather work with us than against us."

"Yeah," Onwyth said. "And if it means we can bring down the Crows, we should do it."

Fedor shrugged and got to his feet. "Alright. Let's do it."

Fedor shuffled from the den with his hands stuffed deep into his pockets and glanced down into the canal.

"Mate, I'll go with you," Lev said.

Fedor turned to him and nodded.

"Lita, you and—"

"No," Melita said, her voice firm. "We stick together." She raised a hand when Lev went to speak. "And before you say anything, I know it will take less time if we split up, but the Crows are looking for us. There's strength in numbers. We need to do this carefully. We need to stick together."

"Good thinking, boss," Lev said. "Where are you thinking?"

"We'll check his usual haunts. The Sail. The arena. If we can't find him in the lower city, we'll go back to his house."

"What if we can't find him at all?" Fedor asked.

"We keep looking. We need to find him. It's all we've got."

"Maybe we should try his house first," Onwyth said. "If I were him, that's where I'd be. That place is like a fortress."

Melita shook her head. "In fact, we should avoid trying his house at all."

Onwyth frowned. "That doesn't make sense. He might be there."

"He might be. But we want him on our side."

"Lita's right," Lev said. "He's bound to be twitchy with everything, and I don't know about you, but I'd like to avoid getting shot, if it's all the same."

"Fair point," Onwyth said. "So what? Sail?"

"Yeah." Melita led the way along the canal path and passed through the docks.

Fedor stood back with Lev and Onwyth as Melita spoke to an old woman at a market stall and slipped her a coin. He sighed and looked over the market square, his gaze landing on a shoeshine boy. He wondered for a moment where he would be now if he'd stayed away from the gang and remained with the priests. He shuddered at the thought.

"What's she say?" Lev asked when Melita re-joined the group.

"He's been around, apparently. She said she saw him head into the commercial district not too long ago."

"The Sail," Onwyth said.

"My thoughts exactly."

Lev turned to Fedor. "You think you can do this?"

Fedor nodded.

"You're not going to sneak off, are you?"

"No." He tried to not glare at Lev.

Melita blocked his view. "This is important, Fedor. We need to trust you. You need to swear you're not going to put us at risk."

"You can trust me."

She narrowed her eyes. "Can we?"

Fedor's fists tightened. "Yes."

"Swear it."

"Swear it?"

Melita nodded. "Swear it in the eyes of Creation. Swear it to your crew, whatever it takes."

Fedor licked his lips. "This is—"

"Just do it," Lev said.

"We need to get there before he moves on," Fedor said.

"Not before you swear to us," Melita said.

"I swear it." Fedor looked up. "In the eyes of Creation. I won't sneak off."

"Or put us at risk," Onwyth said.

"I can try...I can't swear that. I don't know what puts us at risk or not. Walking through the docks could put us at risk, I don't know."

"It's alright," Melita said. "He swore." She held his gaze. "And he's not going to let us down. Are you?"

"I'm not."

"Good. Let's go."

Fedor walked at Lev's side as they passed back through the docks and weaved through the shops and bars in the commercial district.

Something pulled at his chest, the fluttering of anticipation, the thrill of the Sail's back room. His breaths grew deep.

He started when Lev jabbed him with an elbow. "You sure you're up to this, mate? You don't have to come if you think it's going to make things worse."

"I'm fine. It's just...I'll be fine."

"Is that them?" An unfamiliar voice called from behind.

Fedor spun as a trio of lads from the Crows moved towards them.

"Oh, for fuck's sake," Lev said, rolling his eyes. "Not these pricks again."

The taller of the three squared up to Lev and flicked out a knife, its edge catching the alchemical light from a nearby junk shop. "The boss is looking for you lot. Why you ducking him?"

Lev held a hand up to cup his ear and leant forward. "Sorry, mate. You'll have to speak up. I'm a bit hard of hearing."

The lad leant in. Lev landed a quick headbutt, the lad's nose exploding with a sickening crunch.

As the other two jumped, Fedor drew his blade and smashed its handle down on the back of one of their heads.

The lad rolled over and groaned. The other flailed, his fists, his brass knuckles striking Onwyth's jaw, sending her spinning to the ground.

Melita stabbed the lad's thigh and kicked him.

He screamed and clutched his leg, blood oozing from the deep gash.

Fedor stood over the lad with the shattered nose and pointed his dagger at him. "You need to go. We will finish you off if you don't go now."

Lev got to his feet and joined his side as Melita crouched over Onwyth.

They scrambled to their feet, the tallest one cradling his nose, another holding his leg as they hobbled away.

"You alright?" Fedor asked when the last of them disappeared into a tunnel.

Onwyth got up and rubbed her jaw. "No...hurts."

"We can leave, if you want. Maybe try again later. See if we can get some ice from the docks."

"No." Onwyth winced. "Be fine."

"So long as you're sure."

She wiped blood from her mouth and grinned. "Let's keep going." She glanced towards the tunnels. "You know they'll just come back with more if we hang around."

Fedor slipped his blade back into its sheath and they carried on towards the Rusty Sail.

When the pub came into view, Fedor stopped and took in a sharp breath.

"You can do it, mate." Lev clapped a hand on Fedor's shoulder. "Don't let us down. You need to stick with us. Stay focused."

Fedor nodded and Melita entered first. He stepped through the door and the faint hint of plez sent his nerves on end. Sweat prickled across his body and his mouth turned dry.

The robed man who had first offered him the crystal recognised him across the bar and rose to greet him.

The man sat when Lev tapped his club and shook his head.

Melita pointed to a group of men huddled in a shadowy corner. "He's here."

Melita lifted her chin and approach Patrov's table wearing what she hoped would be a non-threatening smile. She signalled for Onwyth, Lev, and Fedor to keep back and be ready.

Deep in conversation and surrounded by pipe smoke and a trio of men, Patrov did not look up from a pile of notes.

Melita stood over the table and cleared her throat.

Patrov grinned and looked up at her, his pipe drooping from the corner of his mouth. "Ah, little missy." He scanned the bar area and nodded. "And you've brought your little friends." He leant back and cracked his knuckles. "What can I do you for?"

"We need a sit-down."

He arched an eyebrow. "A sit-down? When were you thinking?"

"Now."

Patrov pulled out his watch and tucked it back into his pocket. He whispered something to the man who stood up and gestured for Melita to sit.

The other two crew members vacated their seats and Patrov waved at Fedor and Lev. "You want to join us, lads?"

Fedor remained stock-still, his eyes jerking towards the back room.

Patrov shrugged when neither Lev nor Fedor answered. "Suit yourself, you little pricks." He gestured to the seat across from him.

Onwyth dragged a chair across the bar-room and sat across the table from him. Melita sat next to her.

Patrov eyed Onwyth and nodded to himself. "Olive, isn't it?"

"Onwyth."

"Onwyth. Right you are. That could be my nickname, you know? I'm always on with something."

"Ha." Onwyth's fake laugh came out flat.

Melita had to force herself not to nudge her. The last thing she needed was for this thing to fall apart because of Onwyth's sarcasm.

Patrov smiled at Melita. "Your friend's a laugh, isn't she?"

"Can we get down to business?"

"Ah, business." He took a puff from his pipe and let a stream of smoke erupt from his nostrils. "I like a woman who gets straight to the point. So what's this about?"

Onwyth snorted. "Like you really need to ask?"

He narrowed his eyes. "You're lucky you're alive."

"Yeah, well, we could say the same about you. How do you like that?"

Melita signalled for Onwyth to keep quiet. "We had a deal, Pat. I thought you were a man of your word. But here we are."

"Right you are." Patrov shrugged. "You see, the thing is, I've got a business to run and your little payment covered me for a week. What can I say?"

"You know Myker wants you dead, don't you?"

"Already dealing with it." He tucked his notes into his pocket and sighed. "Don't you worry about me." He glanced up at Fedor. "You know what I'm more interested in is how your friend here got into my house."

"We can talk about that later."

"And don't think I don't know it was you lot who came back and stole cash. Your little trick with the feathers isn't fooling anyone."

Melita frowned. "I've literally no idea what you're talking about."

"They were a nice touch, I'll give you that. But you can't shit a shitter." Patrov raised a finger. "Let me be clear, little missy, that cash you stole...keep it. I'd say it makes us even."

Melita smiled. "As I say, I've no idea what you're talking about."

Patrov drummed his fingers on the table and shook his head. "So what's the point in us having this sit-down if you're just going to lie?" He got to his feet and nodded towards the door. "I think we're done."

"No."

Patrov tilted his head and grinned. "For a woman, I have to say you've got some balls. But don't think—"

"Just stop." Melita folded her arms. "I haven't got to my point yet...our proposition."

"Alright." Patrov sank back into his seat. "I'm listening."

"I think we can work together. We have a common enemy and I believe we can help each other."

Patrov lounged in his seat and took a long puff from his pipe. "You really are full of surprises, aren't you?" He leant towards her. "But you see, I know this is a setup." He gestured to Fedor and Lev. "I'm onto your little games."

"I assure you, it's no such thing."

Patrov smirked. "Like you assured me you didn't come back to my house. Do you see why I have an issue with trust? It seems any time one of your lot's mouths move, a great fountain of bullshit sprays out."

"Look. Myker wants us dead. Myker wants you dead. The only reason we are in this mess is because you couldn't keep your side of a deal."

Patrov shook his head. "That's not how I see it. Let me paint you a little picture I hope you and your friends will understand. The only reason you're in this mess is because you lot thought you could pull a fast one on Myker." He leant back and grinned. "Tell me I'm wrong."

"I'm not here to debate who did what. We both made mistakes, let's be honest. Maybe we should have dealt with things in a different way, but that doesn't change the fact that Myker needs stopping. We can team up. We can work together. We can join forces."

"I'm sorry. I still don't buy it. Word is that you and Myker's second are an item."

"That's nothing to do with our business."

"Bullshit. You're compromised." He looked at Fedor and Lev. "I'm surprised the rest of you lot put up with it, if I'm being perfectly frank. Where's your loyalty? Where's your allegiance? You can talk all you want about business and private lives, but when they impact each other, something's got to give."

"No." Melita pursed her lips. "My priority is my crew. Yes, I've been seeing Brak. But that was before all this stuff with Myker." She gestured to Fedor. "Let me put it to you like this. You've seen what he can do. You know who he killed and you've seen his...his magic. I'm sure you can think of some imaginative ways to use it. Ways we can all benefit."

"Interesting." He appraised Fedor for several seconds before turning back to Melita. "So what is it exactly you're proposing?"

"We work together. We deal with the Crows. Nothing more. Nothing less." She shrugged a shoulder. "But if we find it's a beneficial arrangement, who knows what the future might hold?"

"You lot want to go after the Crows?"

She gave a slight nod.

"You might have fancy magic, or whatever it is." He pointed at Onwyth's face. "But look at the state of you." He gestured to Fedor. "And you, for that matter."

Lev stepped forward. "Mate, you should have seen the other blokes."

"No one was talking to you." Patrov frowned. "I get it now. You lot can't handle yourselves. That's all it is."

"You think you know all the stuff going on in this city," Melita said. "So you must know there's a lot of people out there getting pretty pissed off with you and the Crows eating into their businesses."

"I'm more than aware. Believe me."

"If we work together and get rid of the Crows, the city is yours."

Patrov held Melita's gaze for a long moment before getting up and holding out a hand. "Well, little missy, it looks like you've got yourself a deal."

"Excellent." She shook his hand and smiled.

Pat turned to Fedor. "How's it work, then?"

"How does what work?" Fedor asked.

"Your little gate thing."

Melita gave Fedor the nod and Fedor showed Patrov his dagger.

"That's very nice, but it doesn't explain shit."

"There's a shadow realm that exists all around us."

"A shadow realm?" Patrov smirked. "Really?"

"Honest word."

"Judging by those dark circles around your eyes and that nice washed-out tone you've got going on, I think it's fair to assume you've been on the plez." He removed his pipe from his mouth. "I don't know about you, but I don't trust the rambling of junkies."

"He's telling the truth," Lev said.

"So what? You expect me to believe he can slip between worlds?"

"Believe what you want, mate. How else do you think we got into your place so easy?"

"I wasn't sure I could believe what I saw." He shook his head. "If it really is what you say it is, I think we can use it. How does it work? You just, what? Stick it into a wall and rip open a gate?"

Fedor shrugged. "As far as I can tell, it needs to be something like a door or window."

"And you just cut into it?"

"Pretty much."

"It requires ancient magic, though," Lev cut in. "Spells and shit."

"Could I use it to get my men inside the Crows' building?"

"I don't see why not."

Patrov whistled. "I think I underestimated you lot." He looked Melita up and down. "We need to pay Myker a little visit."

"When?"

"I've got a few things I need to sort out. But let's say we all meet outside Myker's place at the first bell tomorrow." He rubbed his hands together. "With any luck, he'll still be asleep and we can finish this once and for all. How does that sound?"

Melita returned his smile. "Like a plan."

Fedor and the others returned to the old den and sat in the common room on the bare stone floor. His mind still reeled from being in the Rusty Sail.

"We should try to get to sleep," Melita said. "We need to be up early if we're going to go after Myker."

"Can't believe he went for it," Lev said. "Dodgy fuck like Pat's probably got some other plan in the works. I don't trust him."

"I do," Melita said. "It makes sense. We've got something he hasn't. And we both want the same thing."

Fedor took in a breath. "So we're getting in there to take out Myker?"

Melita nodded. "But I was thinking we stand back. We get Pat's crew inside and let them do the dirty work."

"Or," Lev said. "And I can't believe I'm saying this. What if we get Pat's lot into that place and then—"

"No." Fedor glared at him. "We're not doing that."

Lev held up his hands. "Why not? You did it to that merchant bloke. You did it to the assassin. How's this any different?"

"It's not." Fedor's head slumped forward and he toyed with his fingernails. "That's the problem."

"It's not the worst idea Lev's ever had," Melita said. "But Pat's lot aren't an immediate threat to us. The Crows are. That's our priority. That's our focus. We need to work with Pat on this." She turned to Onwyth. "You've been awfully quiet. What do you think?"

"I'm quiet because I got smacked in the jaw and it still hurts," Onwyth said. "If Pat and his crew aren't a problem, that's better for us."

Lev shrugged. "Fine. Stick with the original plan, then. See if I care."

Fedor got up. "I'm going to bed."

Lev laughed. "You think any of us are getting any sleep?"

Melita tossed and turned on her old bedroom floor, her blankets smelling of damp and stale sweat.

Onwyth lay on her back across the room, snoring.

Muttering curses to herself, Melita got up and pulled on her jacket and boots.

She crept around the den's tunnels, listening to see if anyone else was awake. But the den remained still and silent.

Making her way out, she headed for the Crows' headquarters, its windows glowing with soft alchemical light.

She knocked at the door and waited.

A guard with spiked hair opened the door and studied her face for several seconds before speaking. "You're Brak's bird, ain't you?"

"Is he here?" She brought her jacket around her, hugging himself against the cold when the guard disappeared inside.

She waited for more than a minute before Brak slipped through the door and closed it behind him. "Bit late to be out, wouldn't you say?"

"I need to see you."

"Yeah, well. I'm busy."

"You're in trouble."

He narrowed his eyes. "What kind of trouble?"

"The kind of trouble where you keep away from this place tomorrow."

"What do you know?"

"Not much. Just heard a few things, that's all. Thought I'd give you the heads-up."

"What sort of things are we talking here?"

She took a deep breath. "I think Patrov is planning a raid here tomorrow. I might be wrong."

"He wouldn't do that."

"Just, please. Make yourself scarce."

Brak sniffed. "You think I can run off like that?"

"Say you've got something to do." She tried to keep the pleading tone from her voice, but it was no good. "Say you're going to do something important."

"You know this isn't going to help you."

She rolled her eyes. "This isn't about that. I'm here for you."

"Will you be bringing Myker's money tomorrow?"

She shook her head. "As I'm sure Myker is well aware, some of your lads smashed our place up. All the money's gone."

He opened his hands. "And there's nothing I can do about that."

"Right." Melita took a step away from him and folded her arms. "Where does that leave us?"

He shrugged. "That's up to you, isn't it? If your crew does what Myker asks, there won't be a problem. I guess we just need to see where everything falls."

"And you're going to stand back and let that happen?"

"What do you want from me, Mel? I'm just doing my job."

"You could stand up to your boss."

Brak laughed. "And become dead meat? I don't think so."

"So what am I supposed to do? There's no way we can get the money and we've had no luck finding Patrov."

"You could leave your crew."

"You know I can't do that."

The faint trace of a smile twitched the corner of his mouth.

"What is it?"

He shook his head. "Doesn't matter."

She lowered her voice. "Tell me."

"One of your people is with us now."

Her eyes widened. "Vern?"

He looked down at his nails. "He never really left. Once a Crow, always a Crow."

"I can't believe he'd do that."

"You can step away too. You could join us. That way, you know you'll live."

"You can't be serious."

"Can't I? You've done nothing wrong. It's that wyvern and those two lads who ripped Myker off. Why should you get caught up in this?"

"Because they're my crew."

He took out his pocket watch and tapped the glass. "You've not got long. Once Myker says you're dead meat..." He slipped the watch back into his pocket. "Make the right decision, Mel. If not for you, then for us."

"I'll think about it."

"Tick tick."

Daring not to meet his eyes, she turned and walked away.

Melita slammed the den door behind her and marched back and forth in the vestibule, her fists clenching and unclenching, her head throbbing.

The others were right. Patrov was right. It was a bad idea to try to make things work with Brak. But, then again, maybe he was right. Maybe she should leave, let the others deal with this. This wasn't her mess...but it was.

"What's going on?" Onwyth asked.

She stopped and met Onwyth's bleary eyes. "It's Vern."

"Have you seen him?"

"The Crows have him."

"Bastards."

"Apparently, he never left them."

Onwyth frowned. "Wait, wait, wait. Are you saying he's defected?"

"Or, at least, he's gone back to them."

"That can't be true. Vern wouldn't do that to us. There must be a mistake. There must be something else to it." She glared at Melita. "Did you see him?"

"No."

"Then how do you know for sure? They might be holding him prisoner. They might—"

"I swear it in the eyes of Creation. It's true. Vern's with the Crows now."

Onwyth stepped backwards and shook her head. "I don't believe it. This is bullshit. He wouldn't." She wagged a finger at Melita. "You'd better not be lying to me because I swear, I'll cut you if you are."

"I'm telling you the truth."

"But you didn't actually see him?"

"No. Brak told me."

Onwyth's jaw set.

"I'm sorry, Onwyth. He conned us all."

"I swear to Creation, I'll fucking kill him." Onwyth stopped and inclined her head. "When did you see Brak?"

Melita gestured behind her. "Just now. I went to see him."

"You did what?" She took a step towards Melita, her eyes wide, her nostrils flaring. "With everything we've got planned with Pat? Why?"

Melita dipped her head. "To warn him."

"To warn him? To fucking warn him? Have you lost your fucking mind?" Onwyth clawed at her hair. "This time tomorrow, we'll all have a price on our heads if this thing with Pat doesn't work out, and you're going out there to tip him off that we're coming?" Her mouth dropped open and she glowered at Melita. "Maybe it's not just Vern who's defected."

"It wasn't like that. This was personal. It's got nothing to do with business."

"I can't believe I'm hearing this." Onwyth wiggled a finger in her ear. "Tell me I'm not mad. Tell me you didn't go to the fucking Crows to fucking warn them about our fucking plan."

"You can swear all you want, but I made an oath to this crew." She showed the scar on her palm.

"Funny way of showing it."

Melita edged forward and raised her chin. "Do you know what Brak said to me? Do you know what he offered?"

"Let me guess. He said you should fucking join them. Betray us like Vern."

"He did. That's exactly what he said. And do you know what I did?"

"Who knows? You've already tipped him off about Pat."

"I didn't give him any specifics."

"They're going to be ready for us now. Brak's going to tell the rest of his gang of feathery pricks that we're coming and to sharpen their weapons. I can't believe you'd do this."

The truth of Onwyth's words came like a punch to the gut. "I screwed up. I'm sorry." She sighed. "I think we've all done our fair share of messing up lately."

"Speak for yourself, traitor. I can't believe—"

"Shut the fuck up, Onwyth. I haven't betrayed anyone. I'm here. I walked away." Her voice turned to a growl. "Don't you dare question my loyalty to this crew—"

"Everything alright, you two?"

Melita turned to see Lev and Fedor watching them.

"We're fine," Melita said.

"Yeah?" Lev asked. "You looked like you were about to chin Onwyth."

Melita met Onwyth's gaze. "Is there a problem?"

Onwyth shook her head. "No, boss."

Silence hung between them for several seconds before Fedor spoke.

"So what we doing, then?"

Melita squeezed the bridge of her nose and took in a deep breath. "We stick to the plan. We meet Pat on the first bell. We get inside. Let him take the lead."

"That's unless Brak has told everyone to expect us," Onwyth said.

"Even if they are expecting us," Fedor said, "we have an advantage they haven't got." He gestured to his blade.

Lev nodded. "Yeah. Let's get our shit together and do this."

X. The Plan

"I miss my bed," Fedor said between yawns as they stepped from the den.

"Me too, mate," Lev said, rubbing his hands together, his shoulders hunched.

It was too early to be up and about, and certainly too early for a job.

Melita locked the old den's door behind her, and without a word, she gestured for them to follow.

Fedor limped along the canal side, kicking tiny stones into the water as he went, his breaths coming out in fine clouds.

They headed through tunnels and as the first bell tolled across the city, they emerged opposite the Crows' headquarters.

Fedor pointed to a group of men huddled near a gas lamp, their forms hazy through a cloud of pipe smoke. "There's Patrov."

"Let's speak to him." Lev waved a greeting and strode towards the group. "Early start, eh?"

"Right you are," Patrov said. "Very early indeed. But you know what they say: the early bird catches the worm."

"Good one, mate. And we've got ourselves a worm to catch."

Fedor scanned the faces of Patrov's men and recognised one wearing a hood. He inclined his head, noticing the crow-feather earring. He turned to Melita, his eyes wide. "Thirty-three! It's a fucking trap."

The men fanned out in a semi-circle, some holding pistols, others holding crossbows. A few blades glinted against the gas lamps.

Lev shot past Fedor, racing with Onwyth into the shadows.

A pair of hands clamped down hard on Fedor's shoulders.

He ducked and rolled and leapt to his feet.

A club swept him back to the ground, the back of his head bouncing off the cobbles, filling his vision with a brilliant flash of white.

A boot pushed down on his chest.

His eyes focused on Patrov sneering down at him, a plume of smoke billowing from his nostrils.

Myker stood at Patrov's side, his lip curled. "Is this the one?"

"This is the one I told you about. He's not much to look at, but rest assured, this one's a warlock."

"Where is it?" Myker asked.

Fedor blinked up at him. "Where's what?"

"Your magic dagger. Where is it?"

Before Fedor could answer, Myker tore open Fedor's jacket, and dragged the dagger from its sheath.

He whistled and turned it in his hands. "Look at this thing. It's pure ravenglass."

A pair of lads hoisted Fedor to his feet and held his wrists behind his back.

Myker pointed the blade at Fedor's chest. "Looks like your crew's abandoned you. Luckily for you, we've got a lot to talk about."

Fedor tried to shift free, but the hands held him in place. He spat at Patrov. "We had a deal."

Patrov wiped the spittle from his cheek and grinned. "This is what's called best for business. Why be at war when we can work together, pool our resources?" His shoulders bobbed with his chuckle. "The best thing is, it was you lot who gave me the idea."

Myker prodded Fedor's chest. "You got my money?"

Fedor shook his head.

"Didn't think so." He swung an uppercut deep into Fedor's gut.

He fell to the ground before being yanked back up to standing.

Dozens of eyes watched him—lads from the Crows, men from Patrov's crew taunting him.

He spotted Vern near the back, a black feather earring hanging from his ear.

"Traitor," Fedor managed through gritted teeth as Myker ushered him inside.

Fedor did not resist as they steered him along a corridor and down a flight of stairs into the basement area.

Fingers pressed into his arms and twisted his elbows high up his back.

He wondered whether he could roll free and mount an escape. But there were too many men, too many weapons, and not enough room to get back through to the entrance.

Myker opened a door and shoved Fedor inside without another word. He slammed the door shut, enclosing Fedor in darkness.

He hoped the others had managed to escape.

The lock clicked and footsteps faded.

Lev raced down the stairs to the market square and ran over to the Clam.

"This isn't the time," Melita called after him. "Lev!"

"We can hide out. They know me in there. Come on."

"No." Melita grabbed his arm, forcing him to stop.

"I can't believe that's the first place you'd think to go," Onwyth said, gesturing to the red lantern.

Lev glared at them both. "You got any better ideas?"

Melita nodded. "We'll go back to the new place. Check the damage. See what's happened. Maybe it's not as bad as we assumed."

Lev removed his cap and scanned the market square, his chest rising and falling with each pained breath. "What are we going to do about Fedor?" He squeezed his eyes shut. "If they hurt him, I swear to Creation I'll fucking gut them all."

"I don't know yet," Melita said.

Onwyth rested a hand on Lev's upper arm. "We need to assume the worst."

Lev shook his head. "No. Lita's right. We should check what's left of the new place. We can check the weapons. A long shot, maybe, but we can see if they found the cash."

"Agreed," Melita said. "That would be a real help."

"That's good, mate. Then we need to figure a way to get Fedor back."

Onwyth smiled grimly. "We might not get that chance."

Fedor brought his coat around himself as he shivered uncontrollably, part cold, part withdrawal. Waves of nausea passed over him. The dark pressed down, thick and heavy.

How many hours had he been down here? Were the others working on getting him out? What in the void would happen if Patrov and the Crows had access to the shadow realm?

He pulled his knees up to his chin and began to rock back and forth. His mind drifted to thoughts of plez, thoughts of his crew. After everything he'd put them through, why would they bother trying to rescue him? They were better off without him.

Lev would be upset for a while, but Melita would most likely be glad to see the back of him. And Onwyth wouldn't care either way. He ran a finger along his palm, tracing the faint scar. But what did an oath really mean when everything else was stripped away?

Tears welled in his eyes. How could they have been so stupid? How could they have taken Patrov at his word when it was trusting his word in the first place that got them into this mess?

Occasionally he heard muffled voices and shuffling outside, but after a while, they would always fade...always fade.

The darkness was absolute. It magnified the depression, magnified the pain. It was only a matter of time before they came in and killed him, or worse, allowed him to starve to death.

Maybe that was their plan—leave him to the darkness until he expired. But, then again, he held knowledge they wanted. Perhaps he could use that as leverage, use it to escape.

He started when the lock shifted and the door swung open. A bright beam of alchemical light cut through the dark.

He covered his eyes with a forearm and cowered from the brightness burning his retinas.

Four lads entered and stood over him without speaking.

"What do you want?" Fedor managed, his voice like stone.

Kicks rained down on his back and side.

He covered his head with his arms as taunts followed punches followed kicks. The blows to the head filled his vision with white and purple flashes.

Motionless, he waited for death.

But the beating stopped and the door slammed shut, the darkness returning.

He lay on the floor, bruised and bloody, his breaths laboured, his right eye swelling shut.

He groaned when he tried to sit up and instead lay in a foetal position, awash with pain and withdrawal.

He couldn't bring himself to cry again. If death came, he would not resist.

Lev entered the antique shop behind Melita. He stopped and surveyed the shattered pots and wrecked plinths. The counter was little more than a pile of splintered wood. "Shit. Looks like they were thorough."

"That's one word for it," Melita muttered as she closed the shutters.

"You think anyone's here?" Onwyth asked.

"Sounds quiet enough," Lev said. "But who bloody knows? Just make sure you're ready if any of those feathery fuckers jump out on us."

Onwyth led the way upstairs. Lev and Melita followed.

She raced into the library first and skidded to a halt. "Bastards."

Lev entered and shook his head at the books strewn across the floor, their covers torn, their pages in tatters.

"I can't believe they did this," Onwyth said. "All that knowledge, lost." She sank her head into her hands. "I'll never learn how to be an assassin now."

Melita patted Onwyth's shoulder. "It's alright. Some of the books don't look too bad."

"Yeah," Lev said. "You might be able to stick them back together. It's not like they burnt the place down."

"Come on," Melita said. "Let's see what else we've got to deal with. On-wyth, you stay with me. Lev, you check the common room and your bed-room."

"You sure that's a good idea? Don't you think we should stick together?"

Melita nodded. "Good thinking. Come on."

They checked the kitchen and workshop to find them untouched.

The common room sofas lay as if deflated, their frames bent and cushions torn open.

Lev's bedroom was no better. White feathers covered the floor and the mattresses rested at awkward angles on twisted bedsteads.

"This is so fucked up," Lev said. "They wrecked the place."

"We can deal with it." Melita slapped her hand against the wall. "The structure's still intact."

Lev rubbed his chin. "Yeah, maybe."

"We should check whether they got to the weapons," Melita said as they headed back down the stairs.

Reaching the training room, Lev found the light on and the weapon racks empty.

A dummy lay on its side, its straw innards tumbling onto the floor.

"They really did a number on this place," Lev said.

He turned to find no signs of Melita and Onwyth.

"Lita? You about?" He drew his club and climbed the stairs slowly, his ears prickling. "Onwyth?"

He carried on up to the shop and pursed his lips. "There you are. What happened to us sticking together?"

Melita held up a wad of cash and smiled. "They didn't find this."

"We can take the next balloon out of here," Onwyth said.

"A balloon?" Lev asked. "What are you on about?"

"This place is done. Pat knows where the other den is. We can't stay here. We need to leave."

"Nah, mate. That cash we got from Pat's is only going to take us so far."

"Then we'll figure out a way to sell this place and start again somewhere else. If we stay in Nordturm, we're dead. It's that simple."

"But it's not that simple, is it? What about Fedor?"

"I think we need to assume Fedor is dead," Melita said. "There's no way they'll let him live."

Lev shook his head. "No fucking way. We're getting him back...whatever it takes."

Melita folded her arms. "There are three of us, Lev. And there are Creation knows how many of them."

"I don't give a shit. We'll figure a way."

"No." She shook her head. "We won't."

"Get up," said an unfamiliar voice.

Fedor squinted at the figure in the doorway.

"Get up."

Struggling to his feet, Fedor tried to ignore the pain in his ribs, the bruising he could feel around his eye, and his swollen bottom lip.

His stomach rumbled audibly and he pulled his coat around him as a chill pressed against his neck.

"Don't try anything funny now. Easy does it."

Fedor caught sight of a pistol held by a lad leaning against the corridor wall.

"Slowly now. This way."

Fedor followed the man up the stairs, each step a chore.

He breathed heavily and he worried his legs might buckle under him at any moment.

Reaching the top of the second flight of stairs, Fedor glanced behind him and considered allowing himself to fall backwards...but if he survived, it would only make matters worse.

His escort came to a stop outside a door and knocked.

After a few seconds, the door opened and the man gestured Fedor inside.

He stepped into a large office.

Patrov and Myker sat behind a desk, while members from both gangs sat on chairs along either side.

Fedor locked eyes with Brak, Melita's boyfriend, and wondered how much Melita knew about this, how much she was involved.

The door was locked behind him and Myker signalled for him to come forward.

He took a few tentative steps and a Crow lad placed a chair down behind him.

"Sit," Myker said.

Fedor remained standing and glared at Patrov, his jaw tightening, heat rising up his neck. "You betrayed us."

Patrov shrugged. "What can I say? It's your lot who planted the seed. I just took the idea in a different direction."

"We're not here to talk about that," Myker cut in. "We're here to talk about this." He slammed Fedor's dagger on the desk. "Now, take a fucking seat, or I'll get one of my lads to make you."

Fedor sat and the blade's whispers called out to him.

"Pat's told us some interesting things about this dagger of yours." He drummed his fingers on the desk. "I need to know whether it's true."

Patrov nodded. "Show him."

"Show him what?" Fedor asked.

"The magic." Patrov waved a hand. "Show him how you make the gates."

Fedor's brow creased and he shook his head. "You know they call him Mad Pat for a reason, don't you?"

Myker exchanged whispers with Brak.

Patrov raised a finger and chuckled. "You're a good one, you are, lad. I'll give you that. I know what I saw. And you're not fooling anyone."

Fedor opened his hands and tried to keep the pain from his face when his arms moved. "I don't know what to say. I think you can put this in the same—"

Patrov shot to his feet and reached across the desk, yanking Fedor down by the collar. "Don't you make me look like a wanker. Show me the fucking gate. Show all of us." He released Fedor and shoved him back, almost sending him toppling over the chair.

Fedor pulled his collar away from his neck. "I swear it. I honestly don't know what he's talking about. What is it he's told you?"

Myker picked up the dagger. "He said this blade's magic. He told us you can use it to open magic gates to another world."

Fedor smirked. "Really? A magic blade. And you believe him?"

Myker shrugged. "There's a lot of stories about ravenglass. Why not?"

"They're stories. Nothing more." Fedor sniffed. "And I had you down as the sane one."

Myker narrowed his eyes. "What's that supposed to mean?"

"Did he tell you he's also worked out the pattern for the fights in the arena?"

Myker turned to Patrov. "What's this?"

Patrov reached into his pocket and pulled out several papers. "It's just a theory. But there's definitely a pattern. I think an observant gambler could use this formula to predict the fights."

Myker squeezed the bridge of his nose and let out a long breath. "You're telling me you can work out who's going to win before the fight even takes place?"

"Exactly. But that's not how I'm going to make the money." He smiled. "You see, I can sell the formula. Then everyone's a winner."

Brak leant forward and examined the papers. With a sigh, he looked between Fedor and Patrov. "This is ridiculous."

"No. He's ridiculous." Patrov jabbed a finger at Fedor. "You listen here, you little prick. I know you're lying. And you know you're lying. Your little games aren't going to fly."

Fedor rolled his eyes. "I'm not lying. It's a blade. That's all."

"Really? And how much did a blade like this cost you? A fair penny, I'd wager."

"We stole the material. Someone else made it. It's just a dagger."

Patrov lit his pipe and leant back. "So tell me this. Why ravenglass? Why not steel?"

"It wasn't my choice. The bloke who trained me, Soren, he had it made when I became his apprentice."

"But why ravenglass?"

"I don't know. Tradition. Maybe it's because it doesn't need sharpening."

Myker cocked an eyebrow. "Really?"

"You could drop that thing from a balloon and it wouldn't leave a scratch."

Myker pushed out his bottom lip.

"And it's magic," Patrov said. "You know it's true."

"There's no magic. It's just a dagger."

"You did something to it. I remember. You splashed something on it and it changed colour. Water, maybe."

"I honestly don't know what you're talking about."

Myker rose to his feet. "I've heard enough. Take him away, while I think about what I want to do with him."

Brak moved over to the door and signalled for Fedor's escort to stand. "Take him back to his cell."

"Come on, this way." He led Fedor back to the stairs.

When they reached the basement, Fedor stepped into the cell and the door closed behind him.

He stood alone in the darkness and tried to keep himself from smiling.

Melita sat with her back against the common room wall. She glanced up at Lev and Onwyth and did her best not to flinch at their glares. "I've made my decision. There's nothing we can do."

"Bullshit," Lev said. "There's loads we can do."

"Yeah," Onwyth said. "He's one of us. We're not losing another member."

Melita's fists tightened and she held her eyes shut. "I think we need to accept that Fedor is gone. For all we know, he could already be dead."

Lev snorted. "You reckon?"

"Yeah," Onwyth said. "He might still be alive."

"Until we know for sure," Lev said, "we need to do what we can. You know he'd do the same for us."

Melita looked down at her hands and shrugged. "I'm out of ideas. I thought we had Pat on our side..."

"So? Pat swerved us," Lev said. "It's our stupid fault for trusting that dodgy fuck in the first place."

A deep frown shaded Onwyth's features.

"What's up?" Lev asked.

"If he's teamed up with the Crows, between them, they'll know where to find us, wherever we are."

Melita nodded. "I know. This is why I think we should leave. We can—"

"No." Onwyth gritted her teeth. "They've been terrorising this city for too long. Between them...I don't know. Someone needs to stop them."

Lev nodded. "Maybe we should."

"I repeat," Melita said. "There's three of us."

Onwyth smiled. "No. He's right. We get everyone together."

"Erm...mate, that's not what I'm saying."

"No. We call on every favour, pull every contact, get everyone we know—everyone who's been affected by either Pat or the Crows—to join up."

Lev pushed rubbed his chin and nodded. "If Pat and the Crows can join together, we can do the same."

"Exactly." Onwyth's smile widened. "We can take them down. We can get Fedor back. We can get Vern back. We can get everyone to turn the fight on them. We can't lose."

Melita shook her head. "I can't see it."

"I'm with Onwyth," Lev said. "Individually, there's not a lot we can do. There's three of us and dozens of them, if not more. But if we get the word out, get some of the other gangs, some of the fences, every dodgy fucker in the city together, we can do this."

"It's a lot to ask."

"It is. I'll grant you that. But fifty's a big cut for hardworking criminal folk. If we can get everyone working together, we'll be unstoppable."

"We're talking a lot of people here," Melita said. "I really can't see how we're going to get the numbers."

"The Crows only do well because they gang up on people," Onwyth said. "They surround them and intimidate them, but most of them are just kids. If we can get Erikson's lot and some others involved, I think we can do this."

"I wish I had your faith," Melita said. "But people don't do things like that. People look out for themselves. You're talking about getting them to stick their necks out and stand up. It's easier to pay up and keep your head down."

"We can convince them," Onwyth said. "We can talk to them, persuade them. When they see they have a choice, I know they'll go with the best option."

"This is it, boss. This is the moment. It's time to shit or get off the privy." Lev joined Onwyth's side and raised his chin. "You in, or are you done? Because if you're done, I think we're all done."

Melita got up and pulled on her coat. "Fuck it. I'm in."

The cell door opened.

A spark from a pipe illuminated Patrov's face in orange and shadow. He reached down and yanked Fedor to his feet. "You little prick."

"Get off me." He tried to free himself from Patrov's grip, but it was no good.

"You think you're so clever, don't you?" He shoved Fedor back against the wall. "You might have Myker fooled, but you can't fool me."

Fedor squirmed, but Patrov's hand remained firm.

"You're a liar. I don't like liars." Patrov's voice dropped to a whisper, his breath brushing against Fedor's ear. "Do you know what I do to liars?" He twisted harder, cutting off Fedor's breath for a long moment before relaxing slightly. "I asked you a question."

"No."

"It's the same as what I do to people who don't pay their debts." He grabbed Fedor's left hand. "Lads."

Four of Patrov's men entered and held Fedor by the arms and legs.

He tried to kick, he tried to flail, but each movement only brought more pain.

Patrov bit down on the little finger on Fedor's left hand.

Fedor screamed as teeth tore through his flesh just below the knuckle and ripped the finger away.

Patrov spat the finger into his hands and grinned a bloody smile.

Fedor cried out.

"I warned you," Patrov said, wiping his mouth. He turned the finger in his hand. "I warned you this would happen."

Fedor cradled his hand as blood oozed from the joint, his vision blurred by tears.

Patrov took out his pistol and pointed it at Fedor. "Now, I know that hurts. But that's what happens when you lie to me. I don't like hurting people. I really don't. But you made me look like a tit back there."

"You took my finger."

"And I'll take more if you keep lying. I'll take more. Then I'll move onto the rest of that little gang of yours. Though I might just forget about fingers and hang them up over the sea gate. What do you say to that?"

"You took my finger."

Patrov tilted his pistol and knocked some gunpowder onto his palm.

He grabbed Fedor's injured hand and rubbed the powder into the wound.

Fedor cried out again, the pain unbearable.

He thought he might faint, thought he might die.

Patrov lit a match, setting the gunpowder alight with a blinding, crackling flash.

Fedor screamed until his throat was raw. He sank to the floor, holding his hand, weeping.

"You'll thank me for that. You see, there's nothing worse than having someone useful bleeding out. That should seal the wound."

Fedor rubbed the cauterised stump.

Patrov squatted next to him and spoke in a soothing tone. "Let's start again, shall we? Are you going to show me how that blade of yours works? Or, are we going to go through this again?"

"I don't know what you're talking about."

Patrov tutted and stood over him. "You're a dickhead, you are." He kicked Fedor across the face.

Fedor's head bounced off the floor, but he didn't care.

Without another word, Patrov and his men left the cell, leaving Fedor alone.

He lay on his side, shaking and sobbing, the pain in his body absolute.

Melita jogged across the market square and stopped next to the old woman at the junk stall. "I need your help."

"Ah, Melita." The old woman smiled a gap-toothed grin. "How goes it, my dear?"

"Not good."

"Oh? What do you need?"

"I need help."

"Calm down, dear." She glanced across at the market square to a constable lingering near the steps to the arena. "Obviously, I'll need a few krones to grease the wheels, so to speak."

Melita shook her head. "This is bigger than that."

The woman inclined her head. "Come on, dear. You know how this thing works."

"This is about protecting your business...all our businesses."

The woman leant forward and rested her chin on her hands. "I'm listening."

"I need help to get the word out."

The woman cocked an eyebrow. "About what?"

"To everyone who's interested. Kathryn Square. Sunset. Tonight. We're going to take down the Crows and Patrov's gang, once and for all."

The woman threw her head back and laughed.

Melita folded her arms. "I'm serious."

"I'm sure you are, dear. But we're talking about the Crows and Pat's lot here."

"And you know this place would be better off without them."

"You do realise they're dangerous, don't you? No one will want to get involved in that."

"They intimidate us because they get us alone. But we have the numbers if we come together. We can take them out for the benefit of everyone."

The woman rubbed her chin and seemed to consider Melita's proposition for several seconds before nodding.

"You'll do it?"

"I'll do it. But I don't favour your odds."

Melita took in a breath. "It's about strength in numbers. We need to do this...for everyone."

"I think a few stallholders around here would like to give those Crows a good hiding. I'll get the word out."

"Thank you." She began to walk away. "Sunset. Tonight."

The opening cell door roused Fedor from a fitful sleep. His hand shot to the phantom pain where his little finger should be and he hoped it had all been a dream. He looked up as Brak stood in the doorway.

Fedor sneered up at him and held his injured hand close to his chest.

A couple of lads came in and one of them placed a cup on the floor next to Fedor.

"Drink."

Fedor licked his parched lips and reached for the cup, expecting it to be empty or for Brak to kick it over. But instead, Brak just watched.

"Thank you," Fedor managed.

Brak sent the other lads out and closed the door, bright light filling the room as he shook an alchemical orb to life.

The glow revealed the cell to Fedor for the first time. He held his hands to cover his eyes and curled his nose at the walls and floor encrusted with dry shit and blood.

"Pat went too far," Brak said.

"He's mad. He threatened to hurt Melita."

"This is business. I keep work and personal stuff separate."

"Please. You need to stop him. He's going to kill her."

"Give him what he's asking for."

"He wants magic. What am I supposed to do?"

Brak shrugged. "I don't know. Between you and me, I'm not happy with any of this myself."

Fedor cocked an eyebrow and cringed at the pain in his face.

"Don't look at me like that. Myker's the boss. This is his call. I'm just a soldier."

Fedor glanced down at his hand and shuddered at the mangled wound. "I can't believe he took my finger."

"You're lucky you're not dead. He was fuming after you were brought back here. But it's him who wants you alive. Myker wants you dead. And if what Mel says about you and your little habit is true, I bet she'd like to be rid of you too."

He opened the door and left, flooding the room with darkness.

Lev sidled up to the bar and waved at the woman serving drinks.

"What can I get you?"

"Nothing today." He forced a smile. "Is she around?"

The woman nodded and spoke to a girl at the end of the bar who went through a curtain to fetch Tara.

Lev perched on a stool and glanced over to the booths. The bar was quieter than usual.

"Back so soon?" Tara arrived wearing a bright red dress and her hair loose. She sat next to Lev. "Usual?"

"This is something different. This is business."

She inclined her head. "Business? You have a proposition for me?"

"Something like that." He gestured to the curtain. "Any chance we can talk somewhere quieter?"

She gave a quick nod. "Follow me." She took Lev up to their usual room and locked the door behind them. She sat on the rocking chair and gestured for Lev to sit on the bed. "So what is it? If you're proposing something where you get free—"

"It's nothing like that, honestly." He removed his cap and let out a sigh. "This is about the shit we've all been getting from Pat and the Crows."

She pursed her lips and raised her chin. "I'm listening."

"We're going to take them on. This needs to stop."

She laughed. "You? Take on the Crows?" She slapped her thighs. "And Pat?"

"Yeah."

"Remind me, Lev. How many are in your crew? Five? Six?"

"Four." He shrugged. "Maybe three."

"And you're going to take on two of Nordturm's most dangerous gangs?"

"Something like that." He raised a finger. "But it's not just going to be us. We want everyone to join us. It's about strength in numbers."

"Who's everyone?"

"I don't know. Anyone who wants to be free of them. Their shit works because they come to us in gangs. But there's way more of us than there is them, it's just they don't think honest folk like us will come together."

"I see..."

"Think about it. We're the ones with the numbers. Imagine if all the businesses around here stood up to them, there's no way Pat or the Crows could do shit. But we don't. And that's why it works. They scare us...but we don't have to be scared. We've got the numbers. There's way more of us than there is of them."

"And you really think people will be willing to help? You really think they'll take that risk?"

Lev gave a slight shrug. "Not everyone, granted. But we need to do something. They've joined forces. We should be doing the same."

Tara frowned. "Who's joined forces?"

"Pat and the Crows. They're working together."

"Shit. I had no idea."

"So what do you say? You think you can help? You think you can get the word out?"

"Leave it with me. I'll see what I can do."

"Please. If people don't turn up, it's not going to work."

"When?"

"Sunset. Tonight. Kathryn Square."

She frowned. "Why Kathryn Square?"

"That's where I live. It's a big open space. We can get people together and move in on the Crows' place."

"I had no idea you lived in the upper city. Good for you."

"Yeah, and we want to keep it that way."

Tara got to her feet and opened the door. "I guess I'll see you tonight, then."

"You're coming?"

She took in a breath. "If it ends their stranglehold, I'll be there."

"What about the others?"

"Some of the girls feel like they've got nothing left to lose. I'm sure they'll come along too."

"Grand. And if you can help spread the word."

Tara nodded. "Of course."

"Thanks, Tara. You're the best."

"So I'm told." She kissed his cheek. "You stay safe now, Lev."

Fedor sat alone in the darkness, wondering whether Pat had sent his men to kill his friends. He hated feeling so helpless, so alone. He had no idea he could live with so much pain—the finger, the beatings, the withdrawal, the hunger.

Death would be a blessing.

And maybe Brak was right. Melita had obviously talked about him, about what a burden he was, what a liability he had become.

If he got out of this, maybe he would leave and never look back. He didn't want to have to deal with Patrov or the Crows, or get into pointless debates about who they should or should not kill.

He craved a simple life, an easy life.

But the pull would always remain—the pull of the blade, the pull of the drugs, the pull of friendship.

What would he do if he left?

Where would he go? How would he survive?

He had no skills. And how could he work, lacking a finger?

He'd be better off dead.

The cell door creaked open.

Fedor remained perfectly still, his head pressed against the cold wall, and stared straight ahead.

"Come on," an unfamiliar voice said.

Fedor didn't move. He couldn't move. What was the point?

"Get up." The lad shook an alchemical orb to life, filling the room with light.

Fedor squinted and blocked the iridescent glow with a forearm.

"You're not dead, then?"

Fedor shrank back and covered his eyes.

The lad stepped forward and stood over him. "Get up. I won't ask you again."

Fedor let out a sigh and shook his head. "What's the point?"

The lad jerked Fedor to his feet. "Get up."

Without a word, Fedor's knees buckled—deadweight falling to the floor.

He lay motionless as the kicks came down, no longer caring whether he lived or died. He just wanted it all to end.

Onwyth arrived at the Erikson den and found Frank and some of his lads lingering outside.

"Twice in one week," Frank said. "This is becoming a habit."

"I need your help. The city needs your help."

"What about that other thing?"

She waved a hand. "Doesn't matter now. This is what's important. A bunch of us are going against the Crows and Pat's crew tonight. We're going to take them out for good."

Frank smirked. "Really?"

"Really. But we can't do it alone. There's already going to be loads of us. But the more we can get in on it the better. We're going to take them both out. This is good for everyone."

"Wait, wait, wait. You're going to fight the Crows and Pat's crew at the same time? Bad idea. You should target one at a time. You never want to split your—"

"They're together."

Frank tilted his head. "Who is?"

"Pat and the Crows." She laced her fingers together. "They're one big crew now."

"Shit." Frank rubbed his chin. "That does change things. Shit."

"Shit, indeed."

"Shit." Frank began to pace. "That's bad. That's really bad." He met Onwyth's gaze. "When did this happen?"

"Last few days. It doesn't matter when, it matters that they are." She grabbed his lapels and shook him. "Please. Frank, I need you."

He grinned. "Can you maybe say that in a more sultry voice?"

She shoved him back and glared at him. "Pig."

He raised his hands. "I'm joshing with you."

She pursed her lips. "You're still a pig."

"Oink."

Onwyth laughed. "Fine. You've got some of the toughest lads around, so I'll forgive you just this once."

"What's the plan?"

"We meet tonight. Just as the sun is going down, we'll get together on Kathryn Square. Once we're all together, we'll pay the Crows a visit."

"Alright. We can do that."

"And spread the word. Bring as many people as you can. Let's end this."

Frank nodded. "Right. I'll call in a few favours."

"Thanks, Frank."

"If this works, we'll be the ones thanking you."

"I've got more people to recruit. I'll see you tonight."

"Yep. Kathryn Square, right?"

Onwyth strode away. "At sunset. Don't be late."

XI. The Shadow Realm

The aroma of roasted chicken wafted into the cell. Fedor's nose twitched and his mouth filled with saliva. The smell was somehow worse than the pain—a different form of torture, worse than any beating.

The door opened.

"You hungry?" Brak asked from the doorway.

Fedor wobbled to his feet. "You brought food?"

Brak shook his head. "No. Come on. I'll take you to the mess hall."

He placed an arm around Fedor and led him up the stairs, the chicken smell growing stronger.

Brak led him into a room dominated by a long table lined with benches. Lads from the Crows ate from bowls, a few eyeing Fedor, most focusing on their meals and conversations.

Myker sat at the end of the central table on a high-backed chair, a plate of steaming chicken, turnips, and carrots set out before him. He looked up at Fedor and gestured to the bench to his right. "Sit."

Fedor looked around and saw only lads from the Crows. "Where's Patrov?"

"Don't worry about him. He went too far." He cut into a slice of chicken and popped it into his mouth. "Does this look good?"

Fedor nodded. "Yes."

"I bet you're hungry, aren't you?"

"Famished." Fedor sat on the bench next to Myker, his eyes fixed on the plate, his mouth watering, his stomach roaring.

Brak placed a plate of fresh chicken, turnips, and carrots in front of Fedor and handed him a fork.

"Go ahead," Myker said.

Fedor drove his fork into the chicken breast and shoved it into his mouth. He closed his eyes and chewed, grateful for the heat and flavour.

"Tell us about the blade."

"I told you everything I know."

Myker slapped the plate away from Fedor. Chicken and turnip dripped down the wall. The hall dropped silent, all eyes on Fedor. "You're lying."

"I'm not."

"I thought we could have a nice chat. Sit down and have a meal. Talk about how this thing works. But you had to go and ruin it, didn't you?" Myker gestured for one of the lads to clean up the mess on the floor. "I admire whatever this is. You've been locked up, beaten. You've lost a finger and now you've lost a meal." He drummed on the table. "Maybe I need to try something else. Maybe I'm going about this all wrong. There must be some other way I can tempt you."

Fedor shook his head.

Myker whispered something to Brak and Brak left the hall.

He returned with a decanter filled with clear liquid.

"How about some rum? It'll help to dull the pain. I bet your finger stump hurts. Nose broken. Those bruises look pretty nasty."

Fedor reached up to his jaw. "How many times? Pat's lying. He's mad. You know this. But I guess you must be mad to be working with him."

Myker narrowed his eyes. "Don't presume to tell me how to run my business. At least I hold up my end of a bargain."

Brak poured the rum into a cup and swirled it near Fedor's nose. "It will really help dull the pain."

"I can't give you what I don't have," Fedor said.

Myker nodded and Brak pulled a purple crystal and a thin copper pipe from his jacket.

"How about something stronger?" Myker asked. "Take all this away."

Brak placed the pipe and crystal in front of Fedor.

"Go on," Myker said. "You know you want to."

Fedor stared at the crystal, his heart racing, his skin prickling. A layer of sweat washed over him and a chill filled the air. He reached forward, his hand shaking.

Myker waved a finger. "Tell us what we need to know."

Fedor leant back and growled. "How many times? He's talking shit. There's no magic. It's just a blade made of ravenglass. Nothing more. I don't understand why you're doing this to me. You should be more worried about what Patrov's got in store for you. You can't trust him. He's insane."

Myker shook his head and gestured to Brak.

Brak snatched up the pipe and crystal and the pair exchanged words in a low whisper.

When Brak left, Myker stared at Fedor. "You're tough, I'll give you that. But I also think you're stupid."

Brak beckoned Patrov and four of his men strode over to Myker.

Hands clamped down on Fedor and Pat stared at him. "You're still sticking to your lies, eh?" He held up Fedor's little finger and turned it in his hand. "I bet one day doctors will work out how to reattach these things. Seems a shame, really." He pulled out a pair of cutters.

Fedor began to thrash. "No!"

"I'm done with fingers. Let's get that little cock of his."

Fedor cried out as a man yanked down his trousers.

Patrov laughed and pointed at Fedor's crotch. "Might need a smaller pair of cutters, eh lads?"

The others joined in with the laughter.

Patrov leant forward. The chill of the cutters pushed against Fedor's thigh. "Remember what I said about the early bird catching the worm? Well, it looks like I'm the early bird."

"I'll tell you! I'll tell you! Stop. Please. Please..." His pleading turned to whimpering sobs.

"Let him go," Patrov said. "Our worm's going to talk." He turned to Myker and grinned. "See? I told you he was full of it, didn't I?"

As the late afternoon sun began to dip, Melita gazed down from the library window overlooking Kathryn Square. "No one's turned up yet."

"It'll work," Lev said. "It's got to."

"Where do they lead?"

"The portals?"

Myker nodded.

Fedor took another sip of water and licked his lips. "It's like an echo of the city. I don't know how to explain it. It's like a shadow version of where we are. But there's only lines and darkness. No sounds. No smells. No nothing."

"And that's what your crew have been using to get around?"

"Sometimes. We don't really like going in there. It's...it's too strange."

"So you just cut into the wall and it opens a gate?"

Fedor shrugged. "As far as I can tell, it only works on doors and windows. It's like they already need to be portals in this world for the magic to work."

Myker nodded. "The mind boggles."

"You could get in and out of anywhere with that," Patrov said. "We could give up all this protection shit and go straight for the banks."

Fedor didn't correct him.

Myker got up with the blade and stabbed it towards the door, its point driving into the wood. "How's it work, then?"

"You need tears."

"That's what he must have splashed on it," Patrov said.

"Whose tears?" Myker asked.

Fedor swallowed. "Mine."

Patrov grinned and got to his feet. "I can help with that." He grabbed Fedor's hand and prodded the finger stump, digging into the half-healed flesh with his fingernails.

Fedor cried out, his eyes watering, but Patrov did not release his grip.

Tears began to flow.

Myker removed the blade's tip from the wood and handed Patrov the dagger. He held it out to catch the drips of Fedor's tears.

"This isn't doing anything—" Patrov's mouth dropped open. The blade glowed bright blue. He gestured to Fedor. "Now what?"

"Do what Myker did with the door again."

"I just stab through?"

Fedor nodded. "And pull down."

Patrov walked over to the door and the blade went in with ease. He looked around at the others, his eyebrows raised, and opened a rift to the shadow realm.

They gasped.

Patrov put his arm through and then his head, before stepping inside.

"Fuck me," Myker said. "It fucking worked."

Patrov returned a few seconds later, the blade clattering to the floor. He sank to the ground with his hands clasped against his ears, his head shaking.

"What's wrong with him?" Myker glared at Fedor. "What did you do?"

"There's no sound, or smells, or anything in there. When you come back, it's like everything hits you at once. He'll be fine. It just takes a few seconds to adjust."

After a long moment, Patrov shook his head, picked up the blade, and got to his feet. "That was interesting."

"What's it like?" Myker asked.

"He's right about it being like an echo. It's the city alright." He smiled. "We can use it. We can get into anything with that. It's amazing."

Myker snatch the blade from Patrov and grabbed Fedor's arm.

"You're coming with me." He yanked Fedor through the portal.

Sound and smells disappeared.

Myker said something to him, but his words did not come out.

He stood stock-still, his mouth gaping, his hands trembling.

Fedor followed his gaze as a shape moved in the distance towards them.

A wormlike creature approached. It glowed white and stretched at least forty feet in length, its torso as broad as Fedor was tall. It moved as if swimming through water, its sides rippling in slow undulations.

The dagger dropped from Myker's hand, its glow now faded to black, and he leapt back through the rift.

Fedor snatched up his dagger and fumbled in his pocket to retrieve his vial of tears. He popped the cork and splashed some on the blade.

With frantic movements, he raced towards the still-open rift.

He glanced over to the creature and froze. Should he return to Patrov and the Crows or give himself up to the worm–monster, allowing it to feed, allowing himself to become one with the creature in a permanent state of non-death? It couldn't be worse than what he'd already been through, could it?

He sealed the rift shut. They were alone. He turned and ran through the shadow version of the Crows' headquarters, slipping past glowing minds gathered around where the rift had been.

He pushed through a gel-like door and charged down the stairs.

The worm drew closer.

Fedor stared at its sides and found himself unable to move.

Thousands of twisted faces—human faces—contorted and warped along its side, caught in a perpetual silent scream.

The worm sped towards him, its maw opening wide, revealing a circle of jagged teeth around a pit of endless black, as dark as ravenglass.

Fumbling with his blade, Fedor drove it into what he hoped was the outside door and tore open a portal.

He slammed through into the real world.

Every pain in his body ignited. Every sound in the city pummelled his ears. But that thing was coming.

He spun on his heels and sealed the rift shut.

His breaths came out in ragged, staccato bursts, his pulse and heartbeat hammering through his body, blood thundering in his ears.

He glanced up at a pair of eyes watching him from an upstairs window.

Gritting his teeth through the pain, he ran to find the others.

Melita stepped outside with Lev and Onwyth as the sun set over Kathryn Square.

Men and women filed in from all directions.

"I think it worked," Lev said. "It bloody worked."

People came armed with sticks and swords and guns.

Melita shook her head at the sight. She recognised fences and gangsters, prostitutes, and strippers. She raised her chin and marched over to the statue of the last Empress. She heaved herself up onto its plinth. "Everyone." She waited for the gathered crowd's attention. "Enough is enough." Her words echoed across the square. "We come together today to fight. To fight for what is ours. To fight for a better life. We are done with the Crows. And we are done with Patrov terrorising our lives. It ends today!"

Cheers rose through the crowd and Melita frowned at the scores of constables marching towards her. "Shit."

The crowd parted, allowing the officers a path through.

"What should we do?" Onwyth asked.

Melita shrugged. "I don't know."

The watch sergeant stopped in front of Melita and gazed up at her. "We have it on good authority that you're planning to attack the Crows."

She shrank back for a moment then lifted her chin, her gaze set on the rest of the crowd. "We've been under their thumb for long enough. Perhaps if your men hadn't been so quick to accept bribes, we wouldn't be here." She held out her hands, awaiting the cuffs. "If you're here to arrest us, then arrest us. But we will not be stopped. More will come. More will fight. We refuse to be victims."

The crowd cheered around her.

The sergeant removed his cap and shook his head. "We don't want to arrest you." He glanced around at the gathered criminals. "We're here to join you."

Fedor ran as lads from the Crows piled out of the headquarters behind him and gave chase.

He pushed through the pain, through the burning in his chest and thighs. If they caught him, he would die.

He raced out into the upper city, surprised to find the sun setting. He'd lost track of time, lost track of days. How long had he been in that cell?

Lads called after him.

He dipped in and out of alleyways and scurried along rooftops. But no matter which way he went, he could not shake his pursuers.

Catching sight of Kathryn Square, his heart raced. If he could make it to the den, if he could make it to the others, maybe, just maybe, he could find a place to hide.

He ignored the stitch gripping his belly and frowned as he approached the crowds of people, beggars and gangsters mingling with men from the watch.

"What's going on?" he asked a man wielding a rusty pitchfork.

"We're going after the Crows."

"What? All of you?"

The man nodded.

"Mate!"

He turned at the sound of Lev's voice and spotted him with Melita and Onwyth near the central statue.

Barging through the crowds, he pushed his way towards the plinth.

"Fedor! Over here, mate."

"I'm coming."

When he reached his friends, it took all he had not to collapse.

"You're back." Lev grinned at him. "Honestly, mate, we thought—" His eyes widened at the sight of Fedor's missing finger. "Shit...what happened?"

Fedor held up his hand and shrugged. "Patrov."

Lev shook his head. "We're going after the Crows."

"I know." He glanced over the crowds. "You got all these people together?"

"Yeah. You alright going back there? We're going to take them on at their place. Strength in numbers and all that."

"No need." Fedor gestured behind him and shook his head. "They're already here."

When the Crows arrived, the crowd attacked.

The square filled with shouts and cries.

Melita scrambled up the statue and sat on its right shoulder to survey the scene. Men and women swarmed the Crows with clubs and axes. A butcher struggled to pull his cleaver free from a lad's neck.

More Crows arrived with members of Patrov's gang. Constables worked in groups of three, isolating individual gang members and beating them until they no longer moved.

Melita slipped down and the crowd surged around her. She joined Fedor, Lev, and Onwyth as they subdued one of Patrov's goons.

"Myker's not here," she said over the noise.

"He'll still be at the headquarters," Fedor said.

"We should go." Melita dropped down and weaved through the crowds, many of them breathless and bloody, and stepped over the bodies. "This way."

Fedor struggled to keep up as he jogged through the lower city and back to the Crows' headquarters.

He let out a shuddering breath, the sense of looming dread sweeping through him.

"You going to be alright?" Lev asked, placing a hand on Fedor's shoulder.

"Yeah. I'm alright." He let out a breath. "I can do this."

"Come on, mate. Before they regroup."

He jogged towards the building as a dozen or so Crow lads emerged from inside.

"Shit."

Melita slipped her dagger back into its sheath and stepped forward with raised hands. "We don't want any trouble. I'm just here to see Brak. Tell him Melita is here."

"Ain't gonna happen," one of them said.

She squeezed the bridge of her nose. "I'm his bird. Just, one of you, please, tell him I'm here."

"You're all dead meat."

Fedor spotted Vern standing with the Crows and nudged Onwyth.

"What?"

He gestured to him.

Onwyth stepped forward, her eyes meeting Vern's. "Traitor."

He shook his head and flashed his switchblade.

Onwyth drew her knife and the pair stared at each other, exchanging hand signals.

Taking a breath, Fedor reached into his jacket and retrieved his vial of blood. He uncorked the stopper and splashed his blade. He pointed the dagger over his head. "I am a great and powerful warlock. Surrender or die."

A few lads laughed.

But their laughter stopped when the blade began to glow and turned to molten fire in his hands.

Vern lunged forward, slicing across the nearest Crow's neck. He spun and slashed another. And another.

Three lads dropped to the ground before they had a chance to move.

Lev roared and swung his club.

Melita and Onwyth charged forward.

Fedor stood back and watched, his energy spent as the others made short work of the guards.

Onwyth grabbed Vern and shoved him against the wall. "What the fuck is going on?"

"Wanted to take them out from the inside."

"Bullshit."

"No."

She shook him, her eyes wild. "You betrayed us."

"No. It was a plan."

"Why didn't you tell us? You should have told us."

He rubbed the back of his neck and looked to his feet. "Only came up with it when they caught me."

"You left us."

He nodded and met Onwyth's gaze with teary eyes. "I was going to." He glanced down at his blade. "I'm sorry."

"Are you with the Crows?"

"No. I was. They think I am, but I'm not."

"Did you spy on us?" Melita asked.

"No. I told them some lies. I didn't betray you. Honest word."

"We'll deal with this later."

Lev checked through a few lads' pockets and held up a set of jangling keys. He unlocked the front door and gestured for the others to step inside behind him.

Fedor directed them to Myker's office and Melita entered first.

Brak's eyes widened. "What are you doing here?"

Patrov gestured to a few of his men. "Don't just stand there. Kill them."

"No," Melita said. "I was thinking about what you said. You're right, Brak. You're right."

Brak held out a hand to her and smiled.

She drove her dagger into his chest and twisted, pushing him back against Patrov's men.

Onwyth and Vern flew in, their blades flashing, and took out anyone that moved.

The pistol went off.

Plaster shards sprayed from the wall.

Melita turned and stabbed more men, as Onwyth and Vern continued slitting throats.

Lev swung his club, smacking men aside, pushing them into Onwyth and Vern's frenzied attacks.

He started when a pistol shot went off and swung his club towards Myker.

He shoved Myker to the ground and mounted him, his club coming down again and again and again. Myker's face turned to mush. His body no longer moved.

Fedor leapt at Patrov, clawing at his face. He smacked the pistol away and cried out when Patrov's hands clasped around his throat.

Flailing, he spat in Patrov's eyes and rolled free of his grip. "You took my finger." He pulled his blade as blood dripped from his nose onto its edge. "Now, I'm going to take yours." He grabbed Patrov's wrist and sliced through his little finger.

Patrov cried out and stared wide-eyed at his missing digit.

His eyes grew wider and something hissed.

Fedor staggered backwards as flames tore through Patrov's body, searing his flesh and burning his hair. Fire licked from his eyes and his flesh melted away from the bones.

Fedor turned away and vomit spewed from his mouth.

The blade slipped from his hand.

Melita took him in her arms. "It's over," she whispered through sobs. "They're all dead."

Fedor looked back at the corpses lying around him, his gaze fixing on Patrov's blackened skeleton.

"We should get back to Kathryn Square."

"You killed Brak," Fedor said.

She nodded. "I made an oath." She touched the coin around her neck. "I don't want to talk about it now."

Fedor supported Lev as they hobbled back to Kathryn Square.

When they arrived, they found men and women sitting around, groaning and crying. Others lay dead among the bodies of the Crows and Patrov's gang.

Men from the watch helped lads from Erikson's crew apply bandages and dressings to the injured.

Fedor stopped, ice seizing his chest at the sight of Soren's old building wrapped in flames and billowing smoke. "They burnt it."

They stood and watched as fire erupted from the windows.

"At least we've still got the old place," Lev said.

Fedor shook his head. "So many dead."

"But we're alive, mate. The Crows are gone."

"And Patrov."

Melita nodded. "It'll be better for everyone now."

"All in all, it's a good day," Onwyth said.

Fedor, Melita, and Lev turned to her.

"Good day? A bloody good day?" Lev gestured to the burning building. "Our home is gone, Fedor's lost a finger, and my leg's fucked."

Onwyth smiled. "We're alive. Vern's back. And our troubles are over."

Fedor flinched at the sound of flapping wings.

Dienerin landed in front of him and bowed her head, her wings spreading across the ground. "Fedor, Fedor, master. The den is on fire."

"Where the fuck have you been?"

She pointed a wing to the building. "Some men came in and lit fires."

"I can see that. Tell me something I don't know."

"The assassin has gone."

Fedor frowned. "Yeah. I know. I shoved him in the shadow realm."

The wyvern looked up. "You shouldn't have done that."

"It was either him or me. I did what I had to do."

"If he has tears, he will be able to escape."

"You sure?"

"I don't believe the assassin is dead. But I'm certain he's no longer in Nordturm."

Fedor took a breath. "Let's just get back to the old place."

Lev took over. "Yeah, mate. Let's go home. This place is done."

Fedor and Lev lifted the new sofa into place in the old den's common room. They sighed.

"At least we've got somewhere to sit now, mate."

"I still think we should have got beds first."

"One thing at a time."

Fedor sat down and tried to push images of Patrov's death from his mind. "What are we going to do now? The blackmail stuff's done. And I don't want to go back into that shadow place."

Lev shrugged. "There's room to start a new protection racket."

Fedor glared at him.

"Mate, I'm kidding."

"Good."

"We'll figure something. The main thing is, we're still alive and we're out of trouble."

Fedor started when Melita entered.

"Come," she said. "It's time."

Fedor nodded and followed her and Lev out of the front door to find Onwyth and Vern waiting on the canal side.

Melita took out her dagger and cut a nick into her palm. Lev did the same.

Fedor took Melita's blade, made his own cut, and handed it to Onwyth.

As she slashed across her hand, Vern squeezed his eyes shut. She elbowed him that it was his turn. He opened his eyes, grabbed the blade, and ran it across his hand. He held up his bloody palm to show the others.

Melita, followed by Lev and then Fedor rubbed their palms into Vern's.

Onwyth went last.

"I swear to have your backs," Vern said.

Epilogue

The journeyman placed the ravenglass shield and ledger in front of his master and dipped his head. "It's all here."

The master flipped the ledger's pages and slammed it shut, his nostrils flaring. "And you're sure they were using this to blackmail Soren's old contracts?"

"That's what it looks like."

"And there are five of them working beyond the guild?"

"As far as I can tell, there are five. Two have ravenglass blades and I believe they were looking to create more." He gestured to the shield.

The master steepled his fingers. "This is not good. And you are sure they can access the shadow realm?"

"That is correct. One of them sealed me in there."

"This is very troubling. Very troubling, indeed." The master rubbed his chin and got to his feet. "Where is Dienerin? This cannot stand."

THE END

Author's note

Well, that was intense! I don't know if you could tell, but I had an absolute blast writing this book.

It couldn't have been more different from my experience writing *Trial of Thieves*. I felt focused, like I was in the zone, like I was firing on all cylinders, and a bunch of other cliches that mean this project couldn't have been more fun for me to write.

So, what changed?

The simple answer is I went back to doing what worked for me in the past.

I wrote a 'shitty first draft'. This meant getting the story out of my head and onto the page as quickly as I could. Then I rewrote it, almost doubling the wordcount. And then I made the world feel lived in and made sure the words flowed in the right way and got rid of some annoying writing tics that you will never have to read.

This was the first book I wrote since experiencing burnout earlier in 2022. After taking a few months away from writing, I came back recharged, energised, and with my enthusiasm restored.

My hope is that you'll love this book as much as I enjoyed writing it.

If you did, could you please leave a rating or review and recommend the series to a friend.

You could talk about it on social media, recommend it on BookBub, post it on billboards, produce high-budget TV adverts, or employ one of those aeroplanes that writes stuff across the sky...whatever works for you.

Finally, I'd like to invite you to join the Ravenglass Universe Facebook group. Visit: facebook.com/groups/theravenglassuniverse[1]. I post there several times a week to geek out about all things fantasy. Hope to see you there!

Take care,

Jon

---

1.   https://facebook.com/groups/theravenglassuniverse

Want the Ravenglass Universe starter library?

Get your Ravenglass Universe starter library for free when you join Jon's VIP newsletter.

You will receive the exclusive novel *Birth of Assassins,* the *Ravenglass Legends* prequel novella *Blades of Wolfsbane*, plus more stories set in the Ravenglass Universe.

Visit: subscribepage.com/ravenglassuniverse[1] to join today.

---

1.   https://subscribepage.com/ravenglassuniverse

Where to find Jon online

Amazon. amazon.com/author/joncronshaw[1]

BookBub. bookbub.com/authors/jon-cronshaw[2]

Facebook. facebook.com/joncronshawauthor[3]

Instagram. instagram.com/joncronshawauthor[4]

TikTok. tiktok.com/@joncronshawauthor

Twitter. twitter.com/jon_cronshaw[5]

YouTube. youtube.com/c/joncronshawauthor[6]

Website. joncronshaw.com[7]

Email: jon@joncronshaw.com

Search for Jon Cronshaw's Author Diary podcast wherever you listen to your podcasts to follow the ups and downs of his writing journey, or download the episodes directly at anchor.fm/joncronshaw[8].

1. http://www.amazon.com/author/joncronshaw

2. https://www.bookbub.com/authors/jon-cronshaw

3. http://www.facebook.com/joncronshawauthor

4. https://www.instagram.com/joncronshawauthor/?hl=en

5. https://twitter.com/jon_cronshaw

6. https://www.youtube.com/c/joncronshawauthor

7. http://www.joncronshaw.com

8. https://anchor.fm/joncronshaw

Also available

The Ravenglass Chronicles
The Ravenglass Chronicles complete omnibus collection[1]
Dawn of Assassins series
Dawn of Assassins (Dawn of Assassins book 1)[2]
Trial of Thieves (Dawn of Assassins book 2)[3]
Crucible of Shadows (Dawn of Assassins book 3)[4]
The Gambit series
Blind Gambit (Gambit book 1)[5]
Blind Reset (Gambit book 2)[6]
The Wasteland series
Wizard of the Wasteland (Wasteland book 1)[7]
Knight of the Wasteland (Wasteland book 2)[8]
King of the Wasteland (Wasteland book 3)[9]
Cleric of the Wasteland (Wasteland book 4)[10]
Black Death: Survival[11]

---

1.   *https://geni.us/ravenglassbox*

2.   *https://geni.us/dawnofassassins*

3.   *https://geni.us/trialofthieves*

4.   *https://geni.us/crucibleofshadows*

5.   *https://geni.us/blindgambit*

6.   *https://geni.us/blindreset*

7.   *https://geni.us/wasteland1*

8.   *https://geni.us/wasteland2*

9.   *https://geni.us/wasteland3*

10.   *https://geni.us/wasteland4*

Acknowledgements

Thank you to everyone who made this work possible. Especially to my family and friends who've supported me in countless ways.

I've got a great team of people helping me get my books to the highest standard I can, so thank you to all my Beta readers and team, you guys rock!

I also want to thank the members of the Why Aren't You Writing, 20 Books, Authors of IFA, and Sci-fi Roundtable groups for their support. Sometimes writing books can be a lonely business, so having that kind of support means a great deal.

I need to give special thanks to Claire Cronshaw, Isaac Cronshaw, Diane Cronshaw, Colin Cox, Laura Marconi-Cox, Russell Evans, Alison Ingleby, Paul Teague, Geoff Ryman, Simon Ings, RJ Barker, Brandon Ellis, Emily Cronshaw, Samantha Sandal, Niall Cronshaw, Ben Hennessy-Garside, Freda Jones, Lynn Sheridan, Patrick McLaughlin, Shane Thomas, Adam Stump, Damon Ballard, and my guide dog, Digit.

Clarissa Yeo at Yocla Designs made the cover. I think it's great.

Thanks again to Claire at Cherry Edits for her great work turning my words into something coherent.

About the Author

Jon Cronshaw writes fantasy and speculative fiction brimming with adventure, escapism, and an exploration of life's big questions.

He lives with his wife and son in Morecambe, England.

Read more at https://joncronshaw.com.

Printed in Great Britain
by Amazon

17689201R00144